THE CHOOSING
ANNABELLE JACOBS

D1607845

Dreamspinner Press

Published by
Dreamspinner Press
5032 Capital Circle SW
Suite 2, PMB# 279
Tallahassee, FL 32305-7886
USA
http://www.dreamspinnerpress.com/

ISBN: 978-1-62798-190-3
Digital ISBN: 978-1-62798-191-0

Printed in the United States of America
First Edition
October 2013

The village of Eladir lies deep in the forest of Arradil.
The people of the forest villages follow the old ways,
and when a boy comes of age, he must go through the Choosing.

PROLOGUE

IT'S almost dusk. Jerath should be on his way home for supper, but the note he received earlier has him sneaking out behind the back of the barns. The three large wooden buildings sit at the edge of the village, and at this time of night there aren't many people around. Which is why Jerath is here.

"Jerath…." There's a hushed whisper from the dark shadows. "Over here."

Jerath squints in the dim light of the early evening, and can just about make out the figure leaning against the side of the barn. He smiles and feels the anticipation coil deep in his belly. "Hey, Balent." Jerath walks toward him, and strong hands reach out and grip Jerath's hips as he gets within touching distance.

"You're late," Balent whispers against the sensitive skin of Jerath's neck. "I thought you weren't coming." His breath is hot, and Jerath shudders as it washes over him. They've met here a couple of times already this month. Jerath was surprised when Balent first approached him—since Balent will be going through his Choosing this full moon—but he wasn't going to turn down the chance to fool around a little. His options are somewhat limited in Eladir.

"Caleb gave me extra chores to do, because Kyr went home sick," Jerath answers, and Balent grunts in acknowledgement. It's not the first time Kyr has claimed to be unwell to get out of doing his work. Jerath closes his eyes, refusing to let the anger get the better of him again.

Instead he focuses on the feel of Balent's tongue as it licks just behind his ear. "But I'm here now."

"Yeah, you are." Balent pulls Jerath closer still until they're flush against each other, their bodies touching from thigh to shoulder. Jerath feels the hard length of Balent's cock as it presses into his stomach, and he can't help but shift a little so his own hardness rubs alongside it.

"*Fuck*, Jerath." Balent draws back just a little and takes Jerath's face in both his hands. He gently tilts Jerath's head to the side and kisses him. It starts off soft and gentle. Jerath lets Balent explore his mouth, opening up to let him lick and nip his way inside until Jerath is moaning softly and clutching at Balent's shirt.

"I don't have long," Balent mutters, and he spins them around so that Jerath's back is up against the rough wood of the barn.

Jerath bites his lip, trying to keep quiet as Balent tugs on his breeches until they're halfway down his thighs. Then Balent shoves his own out of the way, and Jerath barely manages to stifle his gasp as they brush against each other—skin on skin. Balent reaches between them, fumbling a little until he gets his hand around both of them and starts to stroke up and down.

It's a little dry and neither of them is that experienced, but Balent's hand is warm and firm and it feels so good. Jerath grips Balent's shoulders and holds on tight as he feels the familiar tightening in his stomach. "Balent…." Jerath pushes into Balent's hand, arching away from the side of the barn as he stills and shudders his way through his release.

Balent buries his face in Jerath's shoulder and follows him a few seconds later.

Jerath takes a moment or two to catch his breath, glancing down at the sticky mess between them. He grins up at Balent, who just smirks and bends down to wipe his hands on the grass.

"Nice." Jerath blushes a little at the casual way Balent cleans himself up, and rushes to get his breeches back up so he's no longer exposed.

Jerath slides down the wood of the barn and sits on the ground, arms resting idly on his drawn-up knees. He looks over at Balent when he flops down beside him and notices the slightly sad look on his face.

"This is the last time, isn't it?" Jerath asks. He's not at all surprised when Balent nods.

"Yeah." Balent looks out into the fading light and sighs. "My Choosing is in two days, Jerath. After that, I'm going to look for my mate."

He doesn't say it, but Jerath knows he means his *female* mate. "I hope you find a match," Jerath answers, and he means it. He likes Balent well enough, but he knows that this was never serious. "Are you worried about the ritual?"

Balent cocks his head to the side and looks a little confused. "What do you mean?"

Jerath's cheeks heat up again and he mumbles out a "*You know….*" and gestures between them.

Balent laughs as he suddenly gets what Jerath means. "No. I like girls well enough, Jerath." He stands up and shakes the dirt out of his clothes. "I'm looking forward to it." He holds out a hand to help Jerath up from the ground.

"Well, good luck," Jerath says awkwardly. He doesn't really know how he's supposed to act now that they won't be doing this again.

"Thanks." Balent smiles and leans in and places a soft, chaste kiss on Jerath's lips. "Take care, Jerath." He smiles again, then turns and disappears around the side of the barn.

Jerath rests back against the wood, enjoying the silence for a few moments more before heading back home. He breathes in the cool night air and tries not to be too envious of Balent and his easy acceptance of the Choosing.

CHAPTER 1

FOUR months later….

"Serim!" Kinis chastises her daughter. "Are you even listening?"

Jerath nudges Serim hard in her ribs and forces her to look away from the window, where they've been watching the boys fighting over by the woods. Serim glares at Jerath before tossing her long, dark hair over her shoulder and turning to face her mother. "Yes, of course. It's just…."

"Just what?"

"You've told me all this before," Serim says, and rolls her eyes. "I don't see why I need to be told it again." She glances back out the window and watches the shirtless boys tear around and laugh as they wrestle each other to the ground. Jerath sniggers behind his hand as he notices Serim's eyes pick out a certain lithe body and familiar dark hair. She smiles as the boy in question slips in the mud and ends up flat on his back.

"He's a terrible fighter," Jerath whispers. They watch a little longer until a loud cough behind them makes them jump. They both turn around again to find Serim's mother staring at them with a slightly worried look on her face.

"I'm telling you again, Serim." Kinis walks toward her daughter and takes her hand. "Because you're eighteen now and this is the first time that you'll be eligible for the Choosing." She looks at Jerath as if to say, "Tell her, Jerath," but he ducks his head and keeps quiet. This particular ritual is a sore point for Jerath, and he tries to avoid talking about it at all costs.

Serim pulls her hand back, and Jerath sympathizes, he really does; it's not as if anyone will let her forget. He knows from painful experience that it's all the girls talk about when the full moon approaches. They watch and whisper to see which boys, if any, have come into their fangs. If there are no boys of age by the eve of the full moon, then there is no need to perform the ritual. This is the first Choosing to happen in over three months, so everyone is overly excited.

Jerath sighs and runs his tongue over his still-normal teeth and doesn't know whether to be upset or thankful that his have yet to appear. Serim catches his movement and reaches out to squeeze his fingers. She knows all his secrets, and Jerath thinks again how lucky he is to have her as a friend.

Serim's mother is still watching her expectantly. Jerath knows there's only one boy Serim's interested in, and as far as he's aware, this particular boy has yet to come of age. He squeezes her hand in return, giving her a subtle shake of his head when her eyes flicker toward the window again. It won't do any good to make her mother overly suspicious.

"Yes. I'm well aware of that, Mother," Serim replies, and Jerath hears the resignation in her voice.

"I want to make sure you know what's expected… just in case."

Jerath closes his eyes and waits for what he knows is coming. He listens to Serim sigh before she begins to recite the oldest of the forest laws. "When the moon is full, each and every boy who is of age shall choose a willing female. If the boy is deemed worthy, together they will consummate their union and invoke the spirits of the forest to bless the boy with their magic. Only then will his animal form be revealed."

The people of Eladir can shift their human form into that of one of the sacred beasts of legend: the lynx, tiger, black panther, and jaguar. These animals used to roam the forest when there were no villages here, so the village elders tell. It was by the Goddess's goodwill that people were allowed to settle in the forest, and in return the villagers accepted her magical gift—the power to shift—and helped protect her animals whenever they were in danger.

Jerath opens his eyes as Serim finishes speaking and smiles when she walks over and takes both her mother's hands. "I understand what happens at the Choosing, Mother. But since there's only Kyr who's of age this moon, I will not be taking part."

"So far," her mother answers, and Jerath doesn't miss the quick glance she casts his way. "There's only Kyr so far, but there's plenty of time left before the full moon. Kyr's very handsome," her mother adds, smirking in a way that has both Jerath and Serim blushing. "Most girls wo—"

"I am *not* most girls," Serim cuts in, dark eyes flashing and her hands now resting on her hips. Jerath coughs to cover his laughter.

Although undeniably handsome and strong, Kyr is arrogant and mean. Unlike the rest of the girls in their village—and many of the neighboring villages too—Jerath knows that Serim doesn't find Kyr appealing in the least, and he has to agree. There's no way she'll consent to being *Kyr's* Chosen.

"No," Kinis says with a laugh, but looks at her daughter with pride. "You certainly aren't."

Jerath hopes that Kyr will find another girl for the ritual, because one way or another, Kyr will need a female partner. It's very rare for a boy to go Unchosen, and it has only ever happened before when there were no unattached females. But if none should be forthcoming by the eve of the full moon, then the choice will be made by the village elders.

The ritual needs to be performed by the second full moon after the boys come of age. If it isn't, then the ability to shift will be lost, and no one in the village would wish that on Kyr. Not even Serim.

"I DON'T understand why you don't just say yes," Mahli mutters as she, Serim, and Jerath hide out by the small lake just outside their village. There are three more days until the eve of the full moon, and Kyr has been pestering Serim nonstop all morning. "He's not exactly unpleasant to look at," she adds, smirking.

Jerath grins as Serim ignores Mahli and stretches her legs out. She dips her toes in the cool water and splashes her feet, wetting Jerath in the process. He sighs, leaning back on his hands; the sun is high in the sky and feels like a warm blanket on his skin.

"He wouldn't be your first, so I don't see what the problem is," Mahli continues, batting her blonde hair out of her eyes and squinting in the glare of the sun.

"The problem is that I just don't like him," Serim whines, lying flat on the grass and closing her eyes. "He's so full of himself and mean and just expects everyone to do as he says. Do you want to help him through his Choosing?"

"Well…," Mahli starts, and Serim turns to glare up at her. Jerath watches them both with amusement. "Okay, okay," Mahli laughs and holds up her hands. "No, I really don't."

"What about you, Jerath?" Serim asks, and Jerath's face heats up. "Would you do it if you could?"

Only Serim, Mahli, and a few others are aware Jerath prefers the boys in their village to the girls. It's not exactly frowned upon, but it's not encouraged either because it can complicate things when it comes to the Choosing. As Jerath is well aware. There are others who Jerath knows like to go with both boys and girls—like Balent—but in the end they always end up with a female mate. Jerath isn't attracted to any of the girls in their village, and he's terrified that he won't be able to complete the ritual and will then lose his ability to shift.

He doesn't answer Serim's question because both girls know his feelings about Kyr. There's no way he'd go near him. "You two are so lucky that you're born knowing your animal form," he says instead. "It's not fair." He pulls his feet out of the water and hugs his knees, dark hair falling forward and brushing over his skin. According to legend, it used to be only the females who had the ability to shift. They were born that way, their fangs coming in when they lose their baby teeth and their tattoos growing and changing with their bodies. It was only after years of praying to the Goddess of the Forest that the men were given the ability. But they had to go through the Choosing first.

"Imagine if we still followed the old ways," Serim muses, and Mahli scoffs.

"Yeah, Kyr would never get to shift, then."

The girls laugh, but Jerath secretly wonders whether that would apply to him too. The elders say the Chosen female would only consent to the ritual if the male was worthy. That has changed in recent years, and the ritual is completed whether the male is deemed worthy by the females or not. Jerath can't help but think his lack of interest in the female form would have seriously hindered his chances if they still followed the old ways.

"I'm glad things have changed," he says eventually. "But I still wish we didn't have to do it."

They lie there in silence for a while, watching the clouds as they pass overhead. There's not much either girl can say. Jerath will just have to deal with it when his fangs come in—whenever that might be.

"So," Mahli starts, and Jerath senses Serim instantly bristle at the teasing tone in her voice. "I saw Ghaneth today."

"That's nice," Serim answers, her voice steady.

"Oh, come on, Serim," Mahli coaxes, her tone a little softer. "I know you like him."

Jerath chances a look at Serim, but she has her eyes closed. He catches Mahli's eye instead and shakes his head when she raises an eyebrow. Jerath and Mahli have both been watching Ghaneth, looking for any signs he's come of age, but Jerath saw him only this morning out by the barn and hadn't noticed anything.

It's risky to like a boy who hasn't come of age. They don't yet know their animal form, and only marriage between matching forms is allowed. It's considered safer to stay away from unmarked boys altogether. The Choosing itself is the one and only time it's acceptable.

In reality, not many of the younger generation stick to this rule. They aren't interested in marriage just yet, and since the boys aren't fertile until they get their tattoos, there's no risk of pregnancy and most of them think, *Why not?* Jerath's one of the few his age who is still a virgin, though that is due to lack of opportunity more than anything. He's had the odd quick fumble behind the barn, but nothing more.

Neither Jerath nor Mahli would ever tell anyone about Serim's feelings for Ghaneth. They all keep each other's secrets without question. But Jerath can tell that Serim is reluctant to admit to anyone—even her best friends—that she does like Ghaneth. A whole lot more than she should.

"Mahli," Serim warns, opening her eyes and glaring at her friend.

"We won't tell anyone," Jerath cuts in. "You can trust us." Serim looks between the two of them, and Jerath smiles softly as he sees her resolve start to crumble. He knows from bitter experience how hard it is to keep your feelings all locked up inside, and he doesn't want Serim to have to do that.

She stares at Mahli for a few seconds longer and then lets out a long, deep sigh. "Yes, okay. I do like Ghaneth. I like how his smile makes my belly all warm and tingly, how his eyes are the bluest of any I've ever seen. I really wish that it was his Choosing instead of Kyr's."

Wow. Jerath stares at Serim, openmouthed. He never expected her to admit it, let alone in such detail. Mahli just smiles in triumph and starts to speak, but Serim cuts her off. "But it doesn't matter. He probably won't be a match anyway."

"You don't know that," Mahli protests. Her green eyes automatically drift to the tattoo that curls around Serim's left shoulder and disappears under the back of her dress. Jerath looks too, with more than a little bit of envy. His own back is still bare, a wide expanse of soft, pale skin that's ready and waiting to be covered with his own cat, whichever one it might be.

Serim's tattoo is that of a sleek, black panther; the tail loops over her shoulder and comes to rest along her collarbone. The body spans the middle of her back, and the head—jaws open and teeth bared—sits at the base of her spine. The whole tattoo is black, except for the eyes. On Serim's panther the eyes are a vibrant blue, standing out in stark contrast. Jerath hasn't failed to notice how similar they are to Ghaneth's eyes.

"How old is he now?" Mahli asks. "He must be nearly—"

"He's eighteen and four months," Serim interrupts, then immediately blushes when Mahli raises a knowing eyebrow. Boys usually get their fangs as soon as they turn eighteen. Jerath is nearly nineteen and is already getting teased by some of the younger boys. "It's not like I'm counting or anything," Serim mumbles, looking away.

Mahli laughs, and the sound rings clear and true throughout the forest. "Of course not," she answers, still smiling. "Come on, you two. We'd better be getting back," she adds, getting to her feet and holding out her hands to help Serim and Jerath up. "I have chores to do."

"Can we shift and run part of the way?" Serim looks at Jerath with pleading eyes. "It's such a beautiful day and I feel all restless." Mahli nods in agreement and Serim bats her eyelashes. Jerath just smiles and rolls his eyes. He doesn't really mind when they change; he's just a little jealous he can't. "Only for a little way, I promise," she adds.

Jerath nods and turns away as the two girls take off their dresses. He's seen the two of them naked plenty of times. They all grew up together, for one thing, and since Jerath doesn't like girls that way, both Mahli and Serim are very liberal with their clothes around him. He just doesn't like to watch when they shift. There's something very personal and intimate about it and he's so desperate to have that for himself, watching them makes it ten times worse.

He hears the soft growls behind him and slowly turns back. It never ceases to steal his breath away when he sees them—especially Serim. Her panther is big, coming up to the top of Jerath's thighs. Sleek black fur covers her muscular body, and when she turns her head, her bright-blue eyes shine out at him. Mahli's cat is a lynx, so totally opposite to Serim's panther. She's smaller than Serim. Her fur looks just as soft, but instead of black, it's a pale-brown color, dotted with black spots and edged in white. Her tail is short, she has tufts of black hair on the tips of her ears, and her eyes are a lovely burnished amber. They're both beautiful, and Jerath can't help but be awed as they stalk toward him.

They curl around his legs, purring. The deep rumbling sound vibrates through Jerath's hands as he strokes their flanks. Serim butts her head against his fingers and he scratches behind her ear. To an outsider, it would look like madness to pet a wildcat in such a fashion, but when the body shifts into this wild, untamed animal form, the mind remains the same. Well, more or less, from what the girls tell him. According to them, although they feel like themselves, there's also a wild edge to it all that makes them more daring and adventurous than they would normally be. Jerath can't wait to find out for himself.

They let him stroke them for a couple of moments more, and he buries his hands in their soft fur. "Go on, then," he says and gives them both a pat on their behinds. "Show me what you've got." Serim turns and growls at him. Even in this form she manages to look unimpressed. Jerath laughs. He wouldn't be surprised if she rolled her eyes too. They give him one last look before bounding off through the trees and out of sight.

He walks over to their discarded clothing and reaches down to scoop it up. He folds their undergarments inside the dresses to try to preserve at least some of their modesty. With the bundle of clothes tucked under his arm, he heads back toward the village. It's about a twenty-minute walk, but Jerath sets a leisurely pace, giving the girls time to play and get all that excess energy out of their systems. He can hear them, crashing through the woods with no thought to stealth, but he can't see them through the thick trees.

He wonders how long he'll have to wait until he can join them. Until he can shed his human form and really feel what it's like to race through the forest with animal speed and careless abandon. He's old, by his village's standards, for an unchanged boy, but it's not unheard of for a boy to be so late developing. There was one from the neighboring village who didn't come of age until he was nearly twenty years old, but that was a very rare case and Jerath prays to the Goddess of the Forest that he won't have to wait *that* long.

It's not just the ability to shift that will come with his fangs—assuming he can perform the ritual, which is another concern entirely—but for the men it means improved strength and agility. Jerath isn't weak; he works hard at his chores in the fields and around the village, and his body is lean and toned without any trace of fat. But he isn't as strong as some of the other boys, and he is also clumsier than most.

It's not just the younger boys who have started to tease him either. It's not really malicious and most of them don't mean any harm by it, except maybe Kyr. Although Jerath thinks that's more to do with his friendship with Serim than anything else. At first he just laughed along with them, but the older he gets, the more it bothers him.

Jerath sighs and kicks at a large stone on the path in front of him. It skitters into the undergrowth and disappears from view, and he realizes the forest is suddenly quiet. He can't hear Serim and Mahli anymore, and his spine bristles with anticipation. He's almost outside the village now, and the girls will need to shift back and dress before they go any farther. They do this every time, but it still makes Jerath's heart beat faster as he waits for them to pounce.

He stops and carefully places the clothes on a large rock off to the side. He turns in a circle, straining to look through the trees, but he can't see or hear any movement whatsoever. They've gotten better at stalking him over the last few months.

"What are you waiting for?" he whispers into the silence, knowing they can hear him well enough. "I have chores to do too. Can't wait around here all day for you two laz—" A huge black blurring shape flies out between the trees and knocks him flat on his back, winding him.

"Ugh! Stop that!" Jerath tries to push the black panther away as she purrs and licks his face with her huge, rough tongue. "Serim!"

Mahli's lynx is right behind, and she comes up to snuffle at his ear. He's laughing now, batting at them with his hands, but they're far too strong to be moved if they don't want to be.

"Enough! Enough!" Jerath splutters, and both cats finally back away and let him sit up.

He wipes at his face with his sleeve and glares at them. "You two are the worst friends ever," he grumbles, but there's no anger behind it. He loves it when they do this, and they all know it. "Now shift back and get dressed. We're late enough as it is."

Jerath rubs at his face some more, making sure to get all the cat drool off his skin as the girls hurry to get back into their clothes behind him.

CHAPTER 2

THE village of Eladir is nestled at the foot of the Arachia Mountains. The four peaks tower over the village and protect it from being attacked from behind. It's a beautiful sight; the tops are covered in snow for most of the year, only thawing briefly during the summer months.

Jerath's village is the largest in the surrounding area, with over three hundred people. The houses spread far out from the center, and each year they have to chop down a bit more forest to accommodate new families or new arrivals. The neighboring villages of Westril and Lakesh only number four hundred between them, so the Choosing ritual and many of the other rituals involve all three villages.

The girls, fully dressed and more or less respectable now, walk alongside Jerath as they enter the village. Jerath spots Ghaneth and some of the others chopping wood outside one of the smaller barns, and he pokes Serim in the ribs and points over at them. "Look."

Ghaneth has his shirt off again, and Jerath has to admit he's a good-looking boy. He can definitely see why Serim likes him so much. Serim, Mahli, and Jerath all stop to watch as Ghaneth hauls the axe high and swings it down in one easy movement, splitting the piece of wood cleanly in two. He piles the pieces next to him and then starts all over again.

"Wow," Mahli whispers in awe. "He's very strong."

They all stare at the play of muscle across Ghaneth's back, at the way he pauses and wipes the sweat from his forehead. Jerath grins widely when Serim's breath catches and she licks her lips.

Ghaneth must feel them looking and turns his head in their direction, his eyes fixed solely on Serim. His gaze trails lazily over her from head to toe, and Jerath sees her blush when Ghaneth's gaze settles on the tail edges of her tattoo. For a moment he just stares at it. A look of longing crosses his features before he snaps out of it and smiles softly, hefting his axe again and returning to his task.

"Serim." Jerath tugs on her sleeve when he realizes she's still staring. "Come on."

Serim shakes her head and starts to walk. "Sorry," she whispers, and Jerath reaches out to squeeze her hand.

"For what it's worth"—Mahli nudges Serim with her shoulder—"Ghaneth will definitely be choosing you when it's his time."

"Yeah," Jerath agrees. "Did you see the way he looked at you?"

Serim grins, casts one more glance in Ghaneth's direction, and then hurries along with her friends.

THEY reach Mahli's house first and she waves good-bye before disappearing inside. Jerath and Serim walk in silence until they arrive at Serim's door. Her home is bigger than it looks from the front. The back extends farther out than some of the surrounding homes, and Serim's mother is very proud of the extra space it gives them. The low roof is packed tight with rushes, and the slightly curved walls are smooth and well maintained. Jerath has spent many hours helping to keep it that way since Serim's father died. They all have.

Serim reaches for the door and pauses as she turns to Jerath. "Are you coming in for a bit?"

He looks up at the sky. The sun is still bright, and he knows there's a good few hours of daylight left—plenty of time to get his chores done. Besides, Kinis might have been baking, and she makes the tastiest bread in the village.

"Yeah, okay." He reaches to open the door for Serim and steps aside to let her past. She snorts at his obvious display of chivalry as though it's totally wasted on her, and enters the house. Jerath follows, smiling fondly.

They find Serim's mother wrestling with a huge bunch of wildflowers and trying to find something to put them in. "Secret admirer?" Serim asks, smirking. Jerath hurries to take them from Kinis so she can search with both hands.

Kinis smiles her thanks at Jerath and then eyes her daughter before replying, a sly smile on her lips. "Definitely an admirer… only not so secret… and not for me."

Serim groans loudly and Jerath instantly knows who the flowers are from. It's Kinis's turn to smirk.

"You know," she begins as she wipes her hands on her skirt, "you could do a lot worse than accepting Kyr's offer." Serim tries to interrupt but Kinis holds up her hand. "His father is well respected in the village and it's not a promise, Serim. You don't have to marry the boy. Just accept the honor of helping him through this to find his animal form."

Serim huffs but stays quiet. She glances at Jerath with pleading eyes and he shuffles uncomfortably. Both their fathers were killed in the raids over five years ago. Their families are very close as a result, and Kinis is like a second mother to him. Jerath knows her well enough to realize this is one argument he shouldn't get in the middle of. He shakes his head a little, indicating that Serim is on her own with this one, and she shoots him her best death glare.

"You're aware that every girl is expected to go through at least one Choosing," Serim's mother says softly, and Serim nods. Jerath can see the restraint on Serim's face as she struggles not to scoff. According to Serim and Mahli, every girl from the age of *ten* knows this. The boys tend to find out a little later, but Jerath's known how the ritual works since he turned fourteen. "He's a good-looking boy, Serim. They might not all be as easy on the eye as Kyr."

Kinis turns to fix her knowing eyes on Jerath. He fidgets and shoves his hands in his pockets, suddenly finding the floor very interesting. "Don't you agree, Jerath?" she asks, and her tone forces him to look up and meet her gaze. His own mother knows of his preferences, but as far as he's aware she hasn't told anyone else. But Kinis is very perceptive, and it wouldn't surprise Jerath in the least if she suspected he liked boys.

"I guess he's okay," Jerath mutters, and Serim elbows him sharply in the ribs. "If you like that sort of thing, that is."

"What? Arrogant, mean, and full of sh—"

"That's enough, Serim!" Kinis snaps. She appears less than impressed with the pair of them. Serim looks suitably ashamed, mumbles, "Sorry, Mother," and Jerath decides this is the perfect time to leave.

"I think I'd better be getting back home." He smiles apologetically at Serim. She shakes her head, but smiles too so he knows she's not too mad at him for running off and leaving her.

"Yes, Jerath." Kinis takes the flowers from him and places them on the table. "I'm sure Helan is wondering where you are."

Jerath says his good-byes, arranges to meet up with Serim later—as long as they've both finished their chores—and slinks out of the house.

JERATH'S mother is outside hanging up washing when he gets home. They have a piece of thin rope tied between the side of their house and the large sturdy tree next to it, and Helan is busy laying the wet clothes over the line to dry. The afternoon sun is still warm and Helan wipes her forehead when she's finished, a light sheen of sweat clinging to her brow.

"Jerath!" She smiles, walks over, and hugs her son. "How are the girls? Did you have fun down by the lake?"

He relaxes into her embrace and breathes in the comforting scent of orange and ginger. For just a second he can forget about everything else, and he holds on for as long as he can get away with.

"The girls are fine," Jerath eventually answers. He steps back and follows his mother into their house. It's not as large as Serim's, but it's just as well kept and Jerath loves it. "And yeah, the lake was good." He sighs, remembering how Serim and Mahli looked in their shifted forms.

"Are you sure?" Helan stops and turns to look intently at Jerath's face. "You don't sound very happy."

Jerath smiles at her. He doesn't want her to worry, and even though he's envious of them sometimes, he really did have a good time with Serim and Mahli. "No, really. It was fine."

Helan raises her eyebrow, clearly indicating she doesn't believe a word he's saying. Jerath sighs again, pulls out a chair, and slumps down into it. "They shifted on the way back to the village, that's all." He looks up at his mother and she smiles at him, but it's tinged with sadness this time. "You know how I get sometimes."

Helan comes up behind him and wraps her arms around his shoulders. "Your time will come, Jerath. Have faith."

"I know it will. It's just, with me liking… *you know*… and the ritual…." He knows his mother will understand what he means without him having to spell it out.

Helan gives Jerath's shoulders a squeeze and then moves around the table to sit opposite him. "Jerath…." She reaches out and takes his hands in hers. "I know it's hard, and every day I wish your father was here because he would have been so much better at this than I am, but you have to trust that everything will be okay."

Jerath's heart aches at the mention of his father, especially when he sees the matching expression on his mother's face.

"You're not the first boy to have been in this situation and I'm sure you won't be the last. But there hasn't been anyone in the villages' history who has failed to complete the ritual."

Jerath squirms in his chair. How can he explain to his own mother that his biggest concern is getting hard enough to actually attempt the ritual? None of the girls in their village, or girls in general, do anything for him, and the prospect of embarrassing himself like that is something he tries very hard not to think about.

"But what if…." He feels his cheeks heat up, but swallows his pride and carries on. "What if I *can't*?"

Realization dawns on Helan's face, and Jerath wishes he could disappear under the table. "Oh, Jerath." She squeezes his hands and smiles at him. "There are berries and potions that can help you with that."

Jerath must still look skeptical because Helan shakes her head and sighs. "Do you remember Dalen's coming of age?" she asks, and Jerath nods. Dalen was from Westril, just to the east of Eladir. “Well, I’m sure you know that he was about as interested in girls as you are?” She waits for Jerath to nod again. “And he completed the ritual just fine.” She grins then and winks at Jerath. “With the aid of a particularly potent lava berry potion, that is.”

Jerath’s cheeks are on fire now; discussing sex rituals and potions with his mother is one of those things that should be avoided at all costs. But at least he now knows he should be able to participate in his Choosing when the time comes, even if it does mean he has to use sex berries to do it.

“So I don’t want you to worry anymore, okay?”

Jerath promises to try and when Helan suggests he go and finish his chores over at the barn, he can’t leave fast enough.

“HEY, Jerath.” A couple of the older boys greet him as he approaches the largest barn. It’s where they keep the animals and the village’s supply of firewood. One of Jerath’s weekly chores is to help chop the huge pile of wood collected earlier in the month. It’s late summer now, so they need to stockpile enough to get them through the coming winter.

“Hey.” Jerath smiles at them and goes to grab an axe from the tool store. He needs to spend at least an hour here if he wants to do his fair share, so he gets going straightaway. He hefts his axe high and swings it down, cutting cleanly through the wood, before grabbing another piece and doing the same thing again.

After about half an hour, Jerath starts to sweat and his shirt sticks to him all along his back. He stops, rests his axe against the chopping block, and peels off his shirt.

“Still no fangs, Jerath?” Kyr’s voice just behind him makes Jerath startle, and there’s a ripple of laughter. He turns around slowly, not surprised to see Kyr and two of his friends standing there. “And therefore no tattoo either.”

Jerath rolls his eyes. “You know very well I don’t have them yet.” The two boys with Kyr are Jakob and Darek, neither of whom has come of age yet either. Jerath tries hard to keep his voice calm. He doesn't want to give them the satisfaction of reacting. "And I'm pretty sure that none of you three have tattoos either."

Kyr sneers at him. It shows off his fangs, and he runs his tongue over them just to emphasize the fact that he has them. "Yeah, but I'm going to get my tattoo in less than a week." He gestures to the two boys beside him. "And these two aren't even eighteen yet. How old are you now, Jerath?"

Jerath ignores him and picks his axe back up. He readies another chunk of wood on the block and swings.

"Nearly nineteen, by my reckoning." Kyr is still talking and Jerath groans under his breath. "You might be the first one to never actually get his fangs. Imagine how—"

"That's enough, Kyr."

Jerath turns around at the sharp reprimand and sees one of the older boys, Caleb, walking toward them and looking angrily over at Kyr.

"Leave Jerath alone. He's working." Caleb stands in front of the three boys and scowls. "Which is more than I can say for the three of you. If you need something to do, then I've got plenty of jobs for you."

Kyr shakes his head, looks suitably chastised, and slinks off with his two friends following close behind. Jerath smirks, enjoying the rare spectacle of Kyr being put in his place. "Thanks," he says, and smiles at Caleb.

Caleb nods. "Don't let him get to you. That boy's an idiot sometimes, but relatively harmless." He flashes Jerath a grin and goes back to his own pile of wood.

The rest of the time passes in comfortable silence, and by the time Jerath's pile has all been chopped, his muscles ache and he's in need of a wash. He puts his axe away in the store and heads home, hoping his mother has some water heating so he can have a hot bath.

"UGH!" Serim grouses and collapses onto Jerath's bed. "I passed Kyr on the way over here. He's such an ass!"

Jerath hums his agreement while he attempts to dry his hair. He's bathed and dressed now, standing in his room as Serim sighs dramatically and covers her eyes.

"What did he say?" Jerath gives his hair one last rub and then gives up on it.

"The usual rubbish."

Jerath pushes his door closed and joins Serim on the bed. His room isn't overly big. There's enough room for a bed and a small table next to it, but it's his and he loves having this little bit of privacy. He looks over at Serim expectantly and she pulls a face.

"You know what I mean—*Oh Serim, how lovely you look today. I hope you liked the flowers, although they could never compare to your beauty.*" She imitates him almost perfectly and Jerath bursts out laughing. "As if any girl in their right mind would be impressed with that sort of talk!"

"I'm sure some might be."

"Well if they are, then they deserve Kyr." Serim shudders next to him and Jerath can imagine just what she's thinking about.

"So." Jerath pulls his knees up onto the bed and leans against the wall. "I had a very embarrassing talk with my mother earlier."

Serim smirks and rolls onto her side to face him. "Oh, tell me all about it. I could use cheering up."

Jerath takes a deep breath and proceeds to relay the entire conversation in all its mortifying details. Predictably, Serim laughs at parts of it, but she's more than a little interested in the sex berries. Jerath wonders if he should be concerned when she asks if he knows where to find them.

It's nearly dark outside when Helan pokes her head around his door and tells them it's time for Serim to go. She gets up off the bed and bids Jerath good night, but pauses before she leaves his room.

"It'll be okay, you know." She blushes a little, which is so uncharacteristic for her. "The ritual, I mean. Me and Mahli wanted you to know…." She ducks her head and toes the ground. "It might be a little weird at first, but either one of us would be honored to help you through your Choosing."

Jerath feels a lump in his throat. He doesn't know what to say to that. Yes, it probably would be a little weird to have sex with one of his best friends, but the fact they would be willing to do that for him makes his chest ache. He jumps off the bed and wraps Serim up in a big hug, burying his nose in her thick, dark hair. "Thank you."

She hugs him tight for a few moments more, then smiles and bids him good night. If Serim notices that Jerath's eyes look a little watery, she doesn't mention it, and he loves her just a little bit more for it.

CHAPTER 3

JERATH'S eyes snap open. He's breathing heavily and his body is slick with a soft sheen of sweat. He looks around his bedroom, trying to get his bearings, and his heart sinks. *Just a dream.* It was all just a dream.

It's still dark outside his window. It must be the middle of the night and Jerath knows he needs to get back to sleep; he has an early start in the morning. The aftereffect of his dream is still evident under his sheets, the outline of his erection reminding him that he woke up before the main event.

Jerath sighs and scrubs a hand over his eyes. He can still feel the warm, hard body under his hands. The way the muscles bunched and rippled as Jerath licked over them. It was so real that when he first opened his eyes, he fully expected to feel the scrape of fangs across his tongue.

Jerath can't get a clear picture of the face from his dream. But he can remember the smooth lines of his body and the soft skin as it rubbed against him, the hard length rutting into his hip and the sticky trail of precome that leaked out between them. Yes, Jerath can remember all of that, and his cock twitches under the sheets as he pictures it again.

He can't help but slide a hand down under the covers and wrap it around his length. Jerath has to bite his lip. He wants to moan out loud because it feels so good, but his mother is next door and there's no way he wants her to know what he's about to do.

He slowly strokes up toward the head, twisting his wrist and sliding his thumb though the wetness there. He sucks in a breath when his nail catches on the sensitive skin, and his back arches off the bed as he pushes into his fist again and again.

Jerath pictures his dream, his mystery man buried deep inside him as they complete the ritual. He feels the familiar tingling at the base of his spine; it travels up through his balls and draws them in tight. As his cock tenses, painting white-hot stripes across his stomach, Jerath imagines his fangs sinking deep into a soft, willing neck and the stinging sensation of his animal tattoo as it covers his back.

His breathing is harsh in the quiet of his room and the afterglow of his orgasm is bittersweet. He knows it will never happen like that, but in the safety of his bedroom he can still dream.

THE sun has barely risen when Jerath wakes again and rolls out of bed. He hesitantly runs his tongue over his teeth just to check. It's highly unlikely he'd have slept through his fangs coming in—it hurts, by all accounts—but he still feels the small stab of disappointment when his teeth are the same as they were yesterday. Especially after his dream. Jerath sighs but forces himself not to dwell on it. There's nothing he can do about it anyway.

He stretches his arms high above his head, waking his tired muscles in preparation for the day ahead. He has to be up early to tend the animals for the next few days. They work on a rota system in the village, sharing out the work and changing the jobs every week. Jerath is beyond thankful for this because he has no desire to spend his life mucking out pigs and cows. He has two more days left of this rotation and he can't wait to finish. The only upside to barn duty is that Jerath gets to finish early in the afternoon and has the rest of the day off.

Serim and Mahli have to go fishing over at one of the breeding pools later, and Jerath has plans to tag along and watch them work. He can doze in the sun in between laughing at them as they moan and curse about handling the fish. Always one of his favorite pastimes.

He's careful not to wake his mother as he moves around getting breakfast. She worked late into the night and needs to sleep later than this. After a quick meal of bread and cheese, Jerath gathers his plate off the table and places it carefully on the side of the sink. He'll help wash up later.

He pulls on one of his old tunics. It's a little tatty and stained, but cleaning out the animals is dirty work and anything he wears will be ruined by the end of the day. He shuts the door quietly and walks through the peace and quiet to the barns on the far side of the village.

It's tough getting up with the sun, but Jerath loves the tranquility that comes with it. There aren't many others up at this hour, and instead of the usual hustle and bustle it's soft murmurings and hushed voices. He can hear the birds in the trees as they welcome in the day. He tilts his face up to the sun as it creeps higher in the sky, breathing in as much clean air as he can, while he can.

THERE are already a couple of people at the barn when Jerath gets there. He smiles when he recognizes one of them as Ghaneth, and walks over to him.

"You're up early," Jerath says when he's about a foot away. Ghaneth looks up, startled, but smiles back when he sees who it is. Jerath doesn't know him as well as some of the other boys, but well enough. He's one of the few who has never teased Jerath about his lack of fangs or the fact his two best friends are girls.

"Something woke me up." Ghaneth bares his teeth, and Jerath notices the elongated canines that shine brightly in the morning light.

Ghaneth grins at him and, despite feeling jealous all the way down to his toes, Jerath grins back because he knows Serim will be overjoyed with this news. He's also happy for Ghaneth and refuses to let his envy take anything away from Ghaneth's excitement about coming of age.

Jerath immediately steps closer and pats him warmly on the shoulder. "Congratulations," he says and he means it. He hesitates before saying what's on the tip of his tongue, but figures Serim will thank him after she tries to kills him. Probably. "You know"—Jerath looks Ghaneth straight in the eye to judge his reaction—"Serim will be thrilled to hear that you'll be going through the Choosing this full moon. She likes you."

Jerath smiles softly when he sees the blush creep across Ghaneth's cheeks. His blue eyes shine, and Jerath can totally appreciate the way they stand out against his pale skin and dark hair. Serim has excellent taste.

Ghaneth manages a shy smile and whispers, almost too quietly for Jerath to hear, "I like her too." Jerath is both happy and relieved to hear Ghaneth say that, even though it's glaringly obvious.

"What about Kyr?" Ghaneth blurts out. "He's been telling everyone that Serim will be his partner for the Choosing." His eyes have lost some of their sparkle and Jerath hates to see it, especially over such a blatant lie.

"Well, he's wrong," Jerath hisses. "Serim would never agree to that, and Kyr must be blind and stupid if he doesn't realize it."

Ghaneth grins. "Well, I don't know anything about his eyesight, but he's definitely stupid." They both laugh.

"Seriously, though." Jerath places his hand on Ghaneth's arm. "You should approach Serim. It'll make her very happy." Ghaneth nods, his cheeks pinking up again, and Jerath drops the subject so as not to embarrass him further. "Come on, then. Let's get started."

They both make a face as they enter the barn. Jerath will never get used to the smell.

THE sun is past the highest point as Jerath makes his way back from the barn. Everywhere is a hive of activity as the villagers make preparations for the upcoming Choosing. The ritual will be held in Eladir, and the neighboring villages of Westril and Lakesh will travel here to take part. Jerath is looking forward to the prospect of new people coming to the village. They don't interact with their neighbors often, and only those of age are allowed to observe the rituals. Even though Jerath won't get to watch—not that there's much to see anyway, as most of the actual ritual takes place in private—he still hopes to meet some of the new arrivals.

Jerath idly wonders if maybe this time there may be someone for him among the visitors, someone who may feel as he does. He realized a long while ago that he's unlikely to find anyone in his own village. The thought of leaving his home, his family, and his friends isn't pleasant, but the alternative isn't appealing either. Jerath doesn't want to spend his life watching others fall in love and find their other halves; he wants that for himself, even if it means he has to look elsewhere.

The ceremonial circle is set apart from the village itself, in the large grassy area just in front of the tree line. As Jerath reaches his house, he can just about see the edges of the circle, and not for the first time he wishes they were preparing it for him instead. The grass has been cut. Three great piles of the cuttings are waiting to be carried away to the waste barrels and turned into mulch.

There are eight tall wooden poles, set in equal spaces around the edges of the circle. The garlands of flowers and vines will hang from these, but they won't be put up until the morning of the ritual.

Jerath takes one last look before turning and entering his house. He needs to wash and eat before he meets the girls. There's no way they'll come within twenty paces of him while he smells like this. His mother is out helping with the preparations, so he strips as soon as he closes the door. He tosses his clothes out the back of the house so they don't make the inside smell.

It takes Jerath just over an hour to clean up and prepare some food. He's clearing away the remains of his sandwich when there's a knock on his door.

"Jerath?"

There's another knock and Jerath hears his name again. He laughs and shakes his head—Serim is so impatient sometimes. He makes her wait a few seconds more before yanking the door open and smiling innocently at her.

"Very funny," she mutters, and breezes past him into the house.

"I thought we were meeting at the edge of the village?" Jerath asks as he closes the door behind her.

"Change of plan." She sits down at the table and huffs out a sigh.

"What's wrong?" he asks. "And where's Mahli? Isn't she supposed to be helping you?"

"Yes, but they needed extra help with some ceremony…." Serim waves her hands in the air. "*Stuff.* Apparently there's another one whose fangs have come in."

"Yeah, I know." Jerath can't stop the huge grin that spreads across his face as he thinks about Ghaneth.

"Oh no, it's not one of Kyr's little followers, is it?" Serim wrinkles her nose at the thought.

"Guess again."

Serim looks up at him, staring intently, and Jerath can almost see her mind working. "Just tell me who it is, Jerath. And why are you smiling like that anyway?"

"Because the answer is going to make you very happy."

Serim scoffs at him. "The only thing that would make me happy is if it was—" She sucks in a breath and jumps out of her chair. "It's Ghaneth, isn't it? Please, please, please tell me it's Ghaneth."

She's practically jumping with excitement and Jerath laughs at her expression. "Yes, it's Ghaneth. His fangs came in overnight."

Serim lets out a very undignified squeal and jumps on Jerath so hard he stumbles as he tries to catch her in his arms.

"I told him you'd be happy."

"Wait…. What? Jerath!" She eases herself out of his grip and slaps him on the arm. "You did not!"

"Yes, I did. He likes you too, so just relax." Jerath rubs the top of his arm where it smarts still. "We can go see him if you like?"

"Definitely not!" Serim gestures to her clothes. She's dressed in what Jerath can only describe as old rags, and her long, thick hair is piled high on top of her head in a ratty-looking bun. "I'm dressed for fishing, Jerath. There is no way I want Ghaneth to see me like this. Especially not now!"

Jerath grabs Serim's hand and picks up the bags and wrappings she brought for carrying the fish back afterward. "Let's go, then. The sooner we get your chores done, the sooner you can go see Ghaneth."

Serim eagerly agrees, but insists on sneaking out of the village, hiding behind houses, bushes, and even a line full of drying clothes. All so they don't run into Ghaneth. Jerath is openly laughing at her by the time they make it to the relative safety of the woods, and she glares at him and sticks out her tongue.

"Last one to the lakes has to gut the fish!" Serim shouts over her shoulder as she tears off into the trees.

"But it's not even my job!" Jerath complains. He grumbles under his breath before chasing after her. The breeding pools are at least an hour away, and there's no way Serim can run all the way unless she… *oh*, she's such a cheater. Jerath spies a bundle of clothes on a rock ten paces ahead of him and he stops to pick them up. "Serim!" he shouts into the trees. "Serim! That's not fair, you know!" He hears a low, rumbling growl off to his right, and he swears it sounds like she's laughing at him. "I've a good mind to leave your clothes here!"

He shakes his head, vowing that there's absolutely no way he's gutting any of the fish Serim catches, and traipses after her through the woods.

BY THE time Jerath reaches the fishing lakes, Serim is asleep. He huffs as he spots the black panther sprawled out on one of the large rocks around the edge of the water. She's lazily soaking up the late afternoon sun, and Jerath knows that if he runs a hand over her sleek fur it'll feel warm.

"Thanks for waiting," Jerath grumbles.

Serim swishes her tail in a dismissive manner, and Jerath swats at it as he climbs up onto the rock beside her. He loves Serim's panther form. She's so strong and powerful, her muscles bunching and relaxing under his fingers as he strokes down her flank. But at the same time she remains soft and feminine. Her fur is smooth against his skin, and her eyes are the most beautiful color Jerath has ever seen.

They lie there for a while, enjoying the sun and the peace and quiet, but the sun is starting to drop and Serim needs to catch some fish before they can head back to the village.

"Serim?" Jerath yawns and stretches, trying to wake himself up a bit. "You need to change back and get to work." He hops down off the rock and places Serim's clothes in the spot he just left. "I'll go get the nets out while you change."

Serim gnashes her teeth at him and Jerath takes it to mean, "Yes, okay."

There are four fishing lakes in total. The people of Eladir need the fish when the autumn and winter months are approaching and hunting is scarce, and they're very careful not to overfish.

The nets are kept in a small wooden building set about ten feet back from the water. It's never locked and Jerath pushes it open, gagging slightly at the strong fishy smell that wafts out at him. It's almost as bad as the barn.

He locates the nets and chooses one of the smaller ones from near the bottom. Since there's only him and Serim, they won't be able to carry that many fish back. He hoists the bundle of ropes onto his shoulder—hoping the awful smell will wash out because, unlike Serim, he's not wearing his old clothes—and heads back to see if she's shifted yet.

"Hey." Serim smiles as she walks over to help Jerath with the net.

"Nice to have you back."

"Yeah, sorry about that." She looks a little sheepish. Jerath knows that, as a rule, Mahli and Serim try not to shift too much in front of him. He's told them it's okay and he doesn't mind, but they still don't do it as much as they could.

"It's fine, Serim." He smiles at her, and she grins in return. "Let's get these in the water."

Serim takes one side, Jerath the other, and they walk backward away from each other until the net is spread open between them. On the count of three, they throw it out into the lake and watch as it lands, perfect and untangled, then sinks down to the bottom.

There are four ropes attached to the net, each one long enough so when the net sinks, there's plenty of rope left on the surface to pull the ends together and haul in the catch. Serim and Jerath carefully lay the ends down and secure them around several of the trees. Then they wait.

The fish will all have scattered as soon as the net hit the water. Jerath has been on fishing duty a couple of times before and he knows from experience it'll be at least half an hour before they start to return. Serim throws a handful of bait into the water to encourage them, and Jerath climbs back onto the rock. He pulls his knees up to his chest and sighs.

"Jerath?" Serim clambers up next to him, not half as agile in her human form but still more graceful than Jerath. "Is everything okay?"

"Yeah." He scrubs a hand over his eyes. "It's just…." Jerath pauses. "You know…." He's tired of all this—being envious of his friends and feeling left behind as more and more of the boys his age get their fangs. He doesn't want Serim and Mahli to have to censor themselves around him, and he doesn't want to keep going on about it all the time either, even though he knows they don't mind.

Serim doesn't say anything; she just nudges him and places her head on his shoulder. It's exactly what he needs right now and he turns his head to place a barely there kiss on her forehead.

"Thank you," he whispers.

"HERE you go." Serim grins as she wipes off Jerath's hunting knife and hands it back to him. "All done."

"Finally." Jerath jumps off the rock and helps Serim put the wrapped and gutted fish in the carrying sacks they'd brought with them.

"It would have gone a lot quicker if you'd helped instead of watching." Serim huffs as she pulls her sack tightly closed, and Jerath laughs.

"Hey, I did my fair share of smelly, disgusting work at the barn this morning. Besides…." Jerath brandishes his knife before hooking it into the sheath behind his back. "There was only one knife."

"Yes, well…."

Jerath laughs again because there's nothing she can say to that. It was Serim who forgot her knife, after all. He hoists one of the sacks onto his shoulder and starts to walk off. "Last one back to the village has to pack them in the ice hut."

"Hey!" Serim calls as Jerath strides into the trees. "That's not fair!"

Jerath smiles to himself as he hears Serim hurry to catch up.

They're about ten minutes into the forest when they hear it. Serim tenses next to him, and there's something off in her expression. Her senses are far more acute than Jerath's, even in her human form, and her reaction makes him suddenly nervous. He would normally go and investigate the unusual noise, but instead he grabs Serim's hand and pulls her off the path and back into the forest. He puts his finger to his lips to shush her as she opens her mouth, and hurries to crouch down behind a small cluster of rocks.

Serim points to her ear, for Jerath to listen, and he nods in understanding. They keep still and silent, not making even the slightest sound, and soon enough they can hear the crunch and shuffle of people walking through the forest. *Lots* of people.

Serim raises an eyebrow, a look of "What's going on?" written across her face. Jerath has no idea. Apart from him and Serim, he wasn't expecting anyone to be out here. The footsteps are getting louder and Jerath hears a voice barking orders.

"Hurry the fuck up!" someone shouts.

There's a loud crack followed by a grunt of pain, and something cold sits uncomfortably in the pit of Jerath's stomach. He easily recognizes the sound of a whip. Slender fingers slide through his as Serim grips his hand tightly. Jerath feels her trembling, and when he looks over at her, he's met with wide, terrified eyes.

"Try that again and I *will* kill you." It's the same voice. It sounds cold and angry and it's not one that Jerath has ever heard before. He squeezes Serim's hand.

"*Ghaneth…* you need to do as he says." It's a pleading whisper, almost too quiet to hear but still horrifyingly familiar. "I think he means it."

Jerath's heart stops. No… it can't… no. That was Kyr's voice and he was obviously talking about *their* Ghaneth. As much as Jerath dislikes Kyr, he would never ever want him to come to any harm. And Ghaneth… *no*.

Serim's hand vibrates in his grasp and she's the palest he's ever seen her. Her eyes are starting to turn blue, and Jerath realizes with a jolt that she's about to shift. He squeezes her fingers tighter, frantically shaking his head. These people have managed to raid their village and take prisoners, which means there are obviously too many of them for one panther to take on. If Serim shifts now, they'll kill her on sight.

Jerath pulls her against him and crushes her into his side. He strokes her back, his hand rubbing up and down her spine as he tries to calm her. The men have almost passed them now, so Jerath risks a quick peek over the top of the rocks. There are more than he thought.

He can see at least thirty young men being marched along as prisoners, and Jerath can tell that not all of them are from his village. They must have raided Westril and Lakesh too. There are about twenty men guarding them—that Jerath can see anyway. They're wearing clothes Jerath doesn't recognize and their accent is unfamiliar. He hates to think where they're taking Ghaneth, Kyr, and the rest of them.

Jerath and Serim sit huddled behind the rocks until the footfalls can barely be heard anymore.

"We need to get back to the village. Now." Serim jumps up and starts pacing. Jerath can tell she's desperate to shift and run ahead. She'll be much faster that way and he has no intention of holding her back. They need to know what's happened and that everyone else is okay, because Jerath refuses to think of the alternatives.

"Go," he says.

She stops midstep and spins round to look at him.

"Go," he urges. "I'll be as quick as I can behind you."

Serim tears off her clothes. She doesn't give Jerath a chance to look away first, but under the circumstances neither of them have the time to care. With a quick nuzzle against Jerath's palm, Serim races off into the trees.

Jerath shoves her clothes under his arm and hoists one of the fish sacks over his shoulder again. He looks with regret at the other one; he hates the idea of wasting all that food, but two bags will slow him down too much. He sighs and heads off after Serim, back to their village, dreading what he might find when he gets there.

CHAPTER 4

JERATH'S legs are protesting violently by the time he makes it back to the outskirts of his village. He's out of breath and sweaty and his clothes are starting to stick to him in the most unpleasant way, but Jerath hardly notices. He looks around for Serim, but he can't see any trace of her.

He crouches low, taking cover in the tree line that borders the village, and tries to make out what's going on. The village itself seems deathly quiet, and Jerath tries to swallow but his mouth is so dry it almost hurts. There's a gentle rustle of leaves behind him, and Jerath whirls around in time to see a very naked Serim crawling toward him on all fours.

He stares at her for a second before turning back to watch the village again. A soft but very pointed cough has Jerath's head whipping around again. "What?" he mouths at her.

She nods at the bundle of clothes wedged under his arm.

"Oh, right. Sorry," he whispers.

She rolls her eyes and shakes her head as he pushes them into her hands so she can hurriedly get dressed.

"Come on, then." Jerath starts to get up. He's impatient to check on his mother. He wants to check on Mahli and Kinis too, but his mother is his first priority.

"Wait," Serim hisses. She pulls him sharply back down and Jerath frowns at her. "We can't go in there."

"Why not?"

"Because of that." Serim puts her hands on either side of Jerath's face and gently moves him so that he's looking over toward the barns.

Oh.

Jerath would never normally curse, but fuck it all. He can't believe this is happening.

There are strangers wandering out of the barn, men Jerath has never seen before. They're dressed in much the same clothing as the raiders who passed them earlier by the lakes. More and more of them appear, and Jerath can clearly see they are armed.

He turns away and slumps on the ground, burying his face in his hands. He sits like that for a few silent minutes, the enormity of the situation only just starting to sink in.

"Our mothers could be—"

"They're alive," Serim interrupts. She peels Jerath's hands away from his face and gets him to look at her. "I could smell them, Jerath, Mahli too. I don't know what's happening to them, but they're alive and unharmed, so that's… that's something."

She looks close to tears and Jerath grasps her hands in his. He tugs her closer until she settles into his lap and he wraps her up in his arms. "Yeah…," he breathes into her thick hair, now falling in disarray down her back. "That's something."

"What do we do now?" Her voice is muffled by his clothes, but Jerath hears the faint traces of desperation in it.

They can't stay here. There are armed men in the village, and Jerath has no wish to become one of their prisoners. He's even less inclined to find out what they might do with Serim. But neither of them has ever left the village before—not overnight anyway. The thought is terrifying, and he can tell by the way Serim goes stiff in his arms that she feels the same way.

"We have to leave and try and get help," he says eventually.

Serim pulls back so she can see his face. "To Westril or Lakesh?"

"We can't go to either of them," Jerath says. "The prisoners weren't just from our village, Serim. I think they went to the others first. We can't risk it."

"So what do you suggest?" she asks.

There's only one other place they can go, and Jerath knows that Serim realizes this too, so he just raises an eyebrow.

"But we haven't been in contact with the Southern lands in over five years." Serim looks resigned as she speaks.

The last time they'd seen the Southerners was when their village had been attacked by raiders from one of the more northern villages. The Northern and Southern lands are separated by the River Valesk. It's wide and long and flows directly down from the edge of the Arachia Mountains. Jerath had never known anyone to cross it before. But it was a particularly bad winter that year and food was scarce, Jerath remembers. Both their fathers were killed protecting the village's meager supplies, and the thought of asking the Southern lands for help again dredges up all sorts of awful memories. Jerath and Serim weren't old enough to be involved with the fighting then—not like now—and Jerath can't really remember much about the Southern men who came to their village and offered their help.

Serim shifts off his lap and sits beside him again. "How do we even find them?"

Five years ago the Southern men had been hunting out on the plains that lie beyond the forest of Arradil. They'd strayed into the forest and run into some of the villagers who'd managed to escape. Jerath still doesn't know why they offered to help—no one talks about it even after all this time—but they did. With the aid of the Southern hunters, the villagers were able to rid themselves of the men who raided their homes—but not without cost.

"I guess we just head south and hope to run into them."

"What if we run into those others first? That's a great plan, Jerath." Serim glares at him and Jerath glares back.

"Do you have a better one?" he snaps and immediately regrets it as Serim's face crumples.

She's normally so strong and feisty. Jerath hates seeing her like this.

"We need to get them back," she whispers.

"I know. But we'll need help for that too." It's all too much for Jerath to think about.

They need to help free their village from the armed strangers. They need to rescue their friends and the others who've been taken prisoner, but they have no idea where they're being taken. Jerath feels everything slipping through his fingers and he needs to stop it before he falls apart.

"We're going to leave and head south until we find help." Jerath is surprised at how confident he sounds, when he's anything but that. His heart is pounding and his palms are slick with sweat.

It seems to be just what Serim needs, though. She nods at him and slowly gets to her feet before shaking her whole body out and turning to look at him with fierce determination in her eyes. There's the Serim that he knows and loves. The one he needs right now.

"Let's go," she says and stalks off into the trees with Jerath scrambling after her.

THEY only manage to get in a couple hours of traveling before the sun begins to drop low in the sky and darkness starts to creep in. It's worse under the cover of the forest, and Jerath is well aware that it's dangerous to travel at night. They need to stop and make camp.

"Serim?"

She pauses in front of him and sighs. "Yeah, I know. We need to stop." She looks up at the sky through the thick branches overhead and then at the surrounding forest. "Not here, though."

Serim has much better instincts than Jerath, even when she's in her human form, and he trusts her to find them somewhere relatively safe. There are dangerous creatures this far out in the forest—not as many wildcats as there used to be, but there are still plenty. They wouldn't hurt Serim, but Jerath hasn't come into his fangs yet and would be considered fair game. There are also wild boars and bears, and Jerath has no wish to meet any of them.

He follows closely behind Serim as she searches for somewhere to rest.

“Here,” she says eventually.

Jerath surveys the area she’s chosen. It’s a small clearing, about ten paces across, but there are two large boulders at the edge that will give them a modicum of shelter. Jerath walks over and leans against one of them. He’s so tired he could probably sleep standing up. He unhooks his waterskin from his belt, thanking the Goddess that he thought to take one on their fishing trip, and has a small sip. It’s enough to wet his mouth, but no more. He offers it to Serim and she does the same. There’s no telling when they might find more drinking water, so they need to conserve what little they have.

Jerath’s stomach grumbles loudly and, for the first time since they left the lake, Serim laughs at him.

“Why don’t you start a small fire and we can cook a couple of those fish?” She waves at the bag by his feet and Jerath nods. His stomach growls even louder with the promise of actual food.

It doesn’t take him long to strip some branches and get a fire going. They have limited supplies with them, but as Jerath sits and stares into the surrounding dark of the forest, he’s beyond grateful that he brought his knife. Serim has claws and teeth to protect herself, but Jerath only has his hands otherwise.

Jerath keeps the fire small. He’d love nothing more than to pile it high with the dried branches they’ve collected and bask beside the glowing warmth, but they can’t afford to attract attention. Especially not in the dark, when they can’t see. The fire is big enough to cook the fish, though, and provide a little bit of heat.

They both sit huddled around the flames, watching the fish roast with agonizing slowness. Jerath has his arm around Serim, her body a comforting warmth at his side.

“What do you think they want with them?” she asks.

“The rest of the villagers or those they took?”

“Both.”

Jerath sucks in a breath. He’s been trying really hard not to think about this, but there’s really only one reason to take young men from a village and march them away to who knows where. “The men will probably be used as slave labor, I guess.” From what Jerath had seen, there were no women among the prisoners. "But I have no idea why they're still in the village."

Serim shudders and sighs. "You know how slaves get treated, Jerath."

"Yeah." The odd escaped slave has come to their village over the years. None of them had been shifters, but Jerath remembers them all as being thin and badly beaten. He has no idea where they came from because none of them ever wanted to say. Jerath just assumes they were still terrified of their captors, and no one ever pushed for information. The elders try to heal them as best they can, but sometimes even that's not enough. "I know."

Serim falls silent after that and Jerath is grateful; he really doesn't want to dwell on what might be happening to the people of his village. It will be hard enough for him and Serim to make the trip south as it is—they only have the clothes on their backs and barely any supplies. They can't afford to worry about everyone else too.

The fish is surprisingly good, despite its lack of seasoning or accompaniments. That's probably due to the fact they were both starving, but Jerath isn't complaining either way. His full belly has made him sleepy, and he yawns and stretches before inspecting the ground for somewhere to bed down. The options are limited. Jerath looks longingly at the fire. It's going to get cold tonight, and the meager flames aren't nearly enough to keep them both warm.

He can feel Serim watching him, and she abruptly stands and starts to peel off her clothes.

"Um… Serim?" She ignores him and carries on undressing. "What are you doing?" Jerath moves nervously, his mind full of naked bodies snuggling together for warmth. He's cold but he's not sure he's ready for that. Especially with the way he's been waking up in the night recently. Serim doesn't need to see him after one of his dreams, let alone be lying naked next to him. Jerath flushes at the thought.

Serim's soft laughter brings him out of his internal panic. "Relax, Jerath. I know what you're thinking." She folds her clothes and places them carefully on the rocks behind them. Jerath quickly lowers his eyes. "I just think it'll be safer if I shift. I'll be much more aware of our surroundings while we sleep and I can keep us both warm with all my fur."

Jerath does relax then, and when he looks up Serim has vanished and her beautiful, black panther is staring back at him.

Jerath hurries into the trees to take care of the necessary bodily functions and then settles down on his back beside the fire. Serim prowls around the perimeter of their camp and Jerath assumes she's doing much the same thing, but for scent-marking purposes. The scent of a black panther should keep most things away.

Serim pads back over to him and settles her bulk down along the ground. She presses herself right up to Jerath's side, and he can already feel the heat from her body seeping into his skin. It's not long before his eyes fall shut and sleep pulls his exhausted body into unconsciousness.

A SHARP, stabbing pain in Jerath's gums startles him awake and he sits bolt upright, clutching his mouth. It's still dark and it takes him a second or two to realize where he is and what's going on. He gingerly runs his tongue over his teeth, and then it's all too clear what woke him up.

His fangs have come in.

No! No, no, no!

He's waited months and months for this and it has to happen now—at the worst possible time. The full moon is tomorrow night, they're miles from their village, and there's no hope of performing the ritual there, even if they could make it back in time. He'll just have to wait and pray that everything is okay by the next full moon, because that will be his last chance. Jerath refuses to accept that he might lose his ability to shift when it's so tantalizingly close. Sometimes he wonders who he offended in an earlier life, because this really isn't fair. At all.

He finally notices that Serim is nowhere to be seen. Jerath's heart rate spikes, his initial thoughts full of all the bad things that could have happened to her. But then he spots her blue eyes glowing in the dark as she walks back over to him, and he relaxes. He keeps his mouth closed, though. He has no other secrets from Serim, but for some reason he's not ready to share this with her just yet.

She tilts her head at him, probably wondering why he's awake. Jerath lifts the waterskin, indicating he woke up thirsty, and takes a small sip. Serim eyes him curiously and Jerath gets the feeling she doesn't believe him. She can't call him on it, though, so he puts the waterskin down beside him and settles back on the ground. Serim takes up her previous position again, her warm fur a comforting presence against his skin, but it takes Jerath a long while before he can drop off again. He's never kept anything from her before, and guilt is starting to seep in and irritate his insides.

It's just that this was supposed to be something to celebrate. If it had happened yesterday, he would have rushed to tell Serim and Mahli and they could have started planning for the ritual—which would have raised all sorts of issues, but he would still have been excited. But now… now there is nothing they can do, so he just wants to pretend it never happened.

"JERATH?"

"Hmm…."

Cool fingers stroke across Jerath's forehead and he bats them away with his hand. Soft laughter washes over him and the fingers are back, on his cheek this time.

"Jerath… wake up."

Jerath opens one eye and squints up at Serim's smiling face. She's dressed and looking far too fresh for someone who spent the night in the forest as a panther. He covers his mouth, pretending to yawn, and mutters out a "Morning."

"Finally!" Serim grins and gets to her feet. "Get up. I made breakfast."

She turns and gestures to the fire, where two pieces of fish are roasting on sticks. "Fish again?"

"It's all we've got." Serim pulls the two sticks away from the flames and hands one to Jerath. "Make the most of it. The rest of the fish will be spoiled by tomorrow and then we'll have nothing."

Jerath sheepishly accepts the fish and mumbles his thanks.

They eat in silence. Only when the fish bones have been picked clean does Serim sigh and lean on Jerath's shoulder. "Do you think they're all okay? Our mothers, Mahli, and the others?"

Jerath swallows thickly. "I don't know." He slips his arm around her and pulls her close. "I hope so…."

"Yeah… me too."

He places a gentle kiss on her forehead and gives her shoulders a squeeze. "Come on, we need to get moving." He stands and holds his hand out for her.

"Thank you, Jerath." Her voice is low and gravelly, and Jerath can tell she's fighting back tears as she takes his hand.

He's not far off himself. He misses Mahli and his mother so much and he can't bear to think they might be in danger. But they need to keep going. They need to go and find help and they both need to be focused if they're going to make it.

He smiles at her, big and wide, doing his best to reassure her. "It's going to work out all right, Serim. It's got to."

Serim doesn't say anything. She still has hold of Jerath's hand and she's staring at him, openmouthed. To be more precise, she's staring at his teeth.

Oh.

Jerath quickly claps a hand over his mouth but Serim shakes her head and peels his fingers away.

"Jerath?" She reaches up and runs her fingertips over his new fangs.

They're still sensitive and he flinches a little.

Serim snatches her fingers back. "Sorry… I forget how it feels for you at first."

Jerath licks over his gums, his tongue soothing the tender skin around his teeth.

"When did this happen? Why didn't you tell me?"

She looks confused and a little hurt, and Jerath's shoulders slump with the weight of his guilt.

"Jerath?" Serim lays her hand on his arm, her touch gentle and her voice reassuring.

He raises his head and meets her eyes. "Last night. I woke up with the pain and you were gone… so I…." He takes a deep breath and Serim rubs his bicep, urging him to continue. "I didn't tell you, because it doesn't matter."

"What? Of course it matters, Jerath." She grips both his arms tight, and looks at him with wide eyes. "How can you even say that?"

"Look where we are!" He shrugs out of her grasp and waves his arm out in a wide circle. "Miles away from our village. The full moon is tomorrow, and there's no way we'll find a village elder to perform the ritual before then. I'll just have to wait for the next one." It suddenly dawns on him what else he needs and he flushes and lowers his gaze. "Besides, I still need to find a partner to help me through it."

He scuffs the ground with his boot and studiously avoids Serim's eyes.

"Oh, Jerath." Her voice is soft this time and she gently lifts his chin back up. "We don't have to wait. Do you not know anything about the Choosing?"

"Yes, of course I do!"

"Then you know that the presiding elder is there only to make the ritual easier to perform. The incantations need to be said while the union is in progress." Jerath's cheeks get even redder and Serim grins at his embarrassment. "Both parties involved are usually too busy at that point, so one of the village elders recites the words to complete the ritual."

"So?" Jerath must still be half asleep because he still doesn't get it.

"So…" Serim's lets out a long suffering sigh, but her eyes are full of warmth. "It means that I can perform it. Girls are taught the words as soon as we can speak, so I know them off by heart. We can still do the ritual tomorrow night, Jerath."

"But, that would mean…." The words stick in Jerath's throat. Serim is one of his best friends, and although both she and Mahli already willingly offered to help him, he has never actually thought about it in great detail. Until now.

"Yes, it would." Serim steps into his space again and cups his cheek. Her hands are cool and feel wonderful on his overheated skin. "It'll be okay, Jerath. You'll just have to trust me." She looks determined and not at all unsure or embarrassed, and Jerath relaxes into her touch.

"I do trust you." He trusts her with his life, so of course he'll trust her with this too. He just hopes he doesn't mess it up. "It's just I've never… and I don't—"

"Jerath." Serim cuts him off before he can get into a panic. "It's me, remember? I know all this." She reaches up on her tiptoes and kisses him softly on the cheek. "We'll work something out."

She smiles at him and steps away. "Besides, we still have two days of walking to do before then, so stop worrying and let's go."

Jerath nods, relieved to be dropping the subject for now at least. They grab the few things they have and head south again.

THEY walk all day. The sun is warm when it breaks through the trees, but the forest is still too thick in places to let it through. They break for lunch and eat more of the fish. They have to eat it raw this time, since they don't want to waste time building a fire. Jerath moans that he doesn't want to eat fish again for at least three months. Serim laughs and informs him that unless they find something else to eat, they'll be having it for supper as well.

They don't find anything else and so fish it is. They can't exactly catch anything, since the only weapon they have is Jerath's small hunting knife—useful for gutting and skinning, but not for actually catching things. The other alternative would be for Serim to hunt as her panther, but she'd have to leave Jerath's side for far longer than either of them is comfortable with at the moment. When the fish run out, though, she may have to.

"How far do you think we've come?" Jerath asks. They've both finished off the last of their fish and are lying beside the small fire Jerath made.

"I'm not sure exactly, but the edge of the forest is about two days' walk from our village, so we'll probably reach the plains sometime tomorrow." Serim shifts onto her side to face him. "I think we should stay in the forest to complete the ritual."

It's the first time they've talked about it since this morning, and Jerath starts to feel uncomfortable all over again.

"The Goddess of the Forest needs to bless our union and allow your animal form to come through, so I don't think it would be wise to try and do it out on the plains." Serim looks thoughtful, not a trace of embarrassment to be seen anywhere. Her easy manner makes Jerath relax a little. If she's really okay with doing this, then he should be too.

"Yeah, I think you're right." Jerath has enough bad luck as it is; he doesn't want to invite any more. "Can we afford the time, though?" he asks, fidgeting slightly. "Shouldn't we focus on finding help first?" He wants to find his animal form more than anything, but not at the expense of the others' lives.

"It will be much safer for us both if you can shift, Jerath." She reaches out and squeezes his hand. He nods in return and they let the subject drop.

They settle down for the night again, just like before: Serim in her panther form, pressed along the length of Jerath's body to keep him warm.

This time when Jerath wakes in the morning and runs his tongue along the smooth surface of his fangs, a frisson of excitement flows through him. Tonight is the full moon. He can feel the slight tingling in his blood that happens every month at this time, but tonight will be different. He has waited months and months for this day, and it's finally here.

Jerath can't help but wonder what form his animal will take—panther, lynx, tiger, or jaguar? Jerath will be happy with any of them. He just wants that tattoo on his back and to experience the shift for the first time.

"Someone's happy this morning." Serim is just pulling on her tunic when Jerath looks up at her.

"Yeah." He grins, unable to keep it in, and Serim smiles in return. "I'm a little excited about tonight, I guess." He realizes just how that sounds and tries to backpedal immediately, "I mean about getting my tattoo… not… you know, the other thing." Serim raises an eyebrow. "No! I didn't mean I wasn't excited about that too, I just—"

Serim is openly laughing at him now, and Jerath knows his face must be the reddest it's ever been and he wishes the ground would open up and swallow him whole. "Oh, Jerath. Fortunately for you, I know just what you mean. Otherwise a girl might be offended by that."

He smiles up at her and some of his embarrassment fades. It really is a good thing she knows him so well. "Sorry." He pushes himself off the ground and brushes the bits of dirt and leaves from his clothes.

"It's fine. I know the union part isn't ideal for you—and honestly, if you were overly looking forward to that, I might be a bit freaked out myself—and you should be excited about getting your tattoo." She picks at a stray twig Jerath has missed. "Shifting is… it's the best feeling in the world, Jerath. You can run faster than ever, smell and hear a hundred things you would never even notice as a human. All your senses are alive and it's so freeing. I can't wait to share that with you."

Jerath looks at Serim with awe. It all sounds so wonderful and far too good to be true. He's almost certain something will come along to ruin it. Serim must catch the look on his face and she prods him in the belly.

"None of that, either." He makes an "I don't know what you mean" face at her. "Nothing is going to go wrong, so don't even go there," she adds, and pokes him again for good measure.

Serim looks Jerath over from head to toe and frowns.

"What?" he asks.

"Well, not to be rude or anything, but we could both do with a wash before tonight. Our clothes too."

Jerath looks between him and Serim and sees exactly what she means. Their skin is smeared with dirt in places, Serim's hair has leaves in it and the odd twig, and he's sure his doesn't look much better. Their clothes are rumpled and dirty from being slept in, and a quick sniff reveals that they don't smell too good either.

"I think the Goddess would be extremely put out if we did the ritual looking like this," Serim adds.

"Yes, but where can we clean up?" Jerath has never been this far out into the woods before, so he has no idea where the nearest stream or lake is.

Serim grins, obviously privy to information Jerath isn't. "Well, it just so happens that I might know where to go."

"How?"

She pats her nose. "When I scouted around earlier—you were still asleep, by the way—I could smell it."

Jerath ignores her playful dig, but he can't believe that she can smell water. "Really?"

"Yes, really." She doesn't roll her eyes, but Jerath senses it was a close thing. "I told you that our senses are so much more advanced in our shifted form. I can smell the stream, and hear the faint sounds of the water as it rushes over the rocks."

Jerath is still skeptical but nods anyway. "Okay, then." He gestures for Serim to walk in front of him. "Lead the way."

"We have to veer off our path slightly to get to the stream," she says, and Jerath notices that they're now heading in a southwesterly direction. "But it can't be helped."

Jerath hums his agreement and they fall into a comfortable silence once again, both of them careful to avoid any conversation about their families or friends. It's too painful to think about what might be happening when they have no possible way of finding out yet.

CHAPTER 5

"HOW much farther?" They've been walking steadily uphill for the last hour and Jerath's legs are starting to ache. It must be almost lunchtime too because his stomach is making some very angry noises. They ate the last of the fish this morning, which Jerath is sort of thankful for even if it means they have no more food. It was an effort to force it down, and he knows his body would protest if he had to eat any more fish today. Of course he'll probably think differently when they're starving.

"Just a little farther, come on." Serim grabs for his hand and gives it a tug.

Jerath picks up his pace, but doesn't let go of her hand. It feels nice, her fingers entwined with his, and she doesn't seem to mind, so he holds it all the way to the top of the hill.

When they finally reach the top and look down, Serim gasps at the sight. She squeezes Jerath's hand and turns to look up at him with wide, excited eyes. "Jerath, look!"

It's beautiful.

If Jerath could have described the perfect place to go through the Choosing, then this would be it.

The stream Serim mentioned is in fact a small waterfall. It tumbles down over the large rocks, crystal-clear water pooling at the bottom before flowing out in a gentle trickle and carrying on its journey. The pool itself looks to be about ten feet across, and there's a small clearing on the far side. The sun shines through the gap in the trees and bathes the clearing in warm-looking, natural light.

Jerath meets Serim's eyes again and she nods. "It's perfect."

They scramble down the hill together with eager faces. Jerath helps Serim over the slippery rocks, and she bursts out laughing when he slips on the last one and falls backward into the water.

"Fuck, that's cold!"

"Jerath!" Serim gasps.

The icy coldness took him by surprise, so Jerath thinks his outburst is totally understandable. He shakes the water out of his hair and wipes his eyes.

"Come on in." He beckons her. "It's very refreshing." He grins and she laughs again.

Serim climbs over the last of the rocks and lands gracefully on the grass at the edge of the pool. "I will. I just need to get something first."

She wanders over to the bushes at the edge of the clearing, and Jerath takes the opportunity to swim over to the side and throw his hunting knife and waterskin onto the bank.

"What are you looking for?" He watches as she picks flowers and berries and…. "What's that?"

Serim turns around with her hands full and a triumphant smile on her face. "Soap!"

Jerath eyes the collection of flora held tightly in Serim's fists and raises an eyebrow. "Really?"

"You have so little faith in me, Jerath." She tuts at him and makes her way over to the water.

Jerath looks on, fascinated, as Serim scrunches everything together and adds a little water. She works it all between her hands, and sure enough, Jerath sees the unlikely mixture start to froth. Serim's smile is huge now and she has her "I told you so" expression all over her face.

She steps into the water and walks over to where Jerath is standing, the water coming up to his thighs.

"Here." She holds out one hand to him and he scoops the mixture out and holds it gingerly in both of his. "It won't bite." She rolls her eyes, and Jerath can't resist sticking his tongue out at her. "I expected better behavior from someone whose fangs have come in."

Jerath just shrugs and grins at her.

Serim shakes her head and starts to rub the soap mixture under her clothes. "Use it to clean your skin first and then your clothes." Jerath must look as confused as he feels, because Serim pauses and adds, "Like this, look."

She scrubs the top half of her body under her tunic and then pushes her hands below the waistband of her trousers to wash between her legs. Jerath watches, and Serim is so matter-of-fact about it all that he doesn't feel the least bit embarrassed. But then she starts to peel off her clothes.

"Then like this." She rubs the remaining soap into her tunic and all over her trousers.

Serim is totally naked now and Jerath hurriedly looks away and starts to wash himself. He scrubs hard all over his skin, washing off the grime of three days and two nights spent sleeping out in the woods. He glances over at Serim and sees her duck under the water to wash her hair. Her long, dark locks swirl all around her, and Jerath smiles as he notices the contented look on her face.

He strips off his shirt and trousers, then rubs the soap into them like Serim showed him and wades farther out to rinse everything off. When the water reaches waist height, Jerath ducks down until his head slips beneath the surface. He's used to the cold now, and the cool water feels so good against his clean skin.

Serim is laying her clothes out on one of the large rocks when Jerath comes up for air, completely at ease with her nakedness. She tells him to pass his clothes over so she can do them as well, and Jerath does as he's told. The rock is in full sun now and it shines down on their clothes. With any luck they'll dry quickly. Jerath hates having to put on wet things.

When Serim has finished with their clothes, she slips back into the water and swims into the middle of the pool. Jerath dives under the water and comes up next to her, the splash hitting her in the face as he breaks the surface.

She splutters and laughs, wiping the water out of her eyes, and then she smirks at him. "Do you know what else I found over in those bushes, Jerath?"

She looks far too mischievous for Jerath's liking. "No, what?"

"Lava berries."

It takes Jerath a couple of seconds to make the connection, but when he does he can feel the curl of excitement deep in his belly. He avoided thinking about the ritual all morning while they walked. He can't wrap his head around the fact that it's tonight. He's going to have sex for the first time. The fact that it's going to be with Serim is kind of weird, yet also kind of right. He loves her—not in the romantic way, but he knows he'll love her forever.

As he watches her now, big brown eyes sparkling as she smiles at him, Jerath thinks there was never going to be another choice for him. Yes, he loves Mahli too, but he and Serim have a deeper connection he can't really explain. It's just there and Jerath needs it now more than ever.

"Um… that's good, then?" Jerath may be excited at the prospect of finally getting his tattoo, but he's still nervous about actually performing the ritual itself. Serim isn't a virgin like he is. She tells Jerath everything, so consequently he knows about the three boys she's bedded and also what she thought of their performances. He's well aware of what goes where, but he has limited sexual experience, and all that has been with boys. Jerath won't be able to look Serim in the eye if he's terrible at it.

"Yes, that's good." She swims a little closer to him and wraps her legs around his waist.

Jerath's hands automatically go to her hips to keep her steady, but he still gasps in shock when he feels her rub up against him. "Wh-what are you doing?" He stutters a little and blushes. His cock is soft between them, but having something warm pressed against it is definitely making it take an interest.

"We're going to be a lot closer that this later, Jerath. I don't want you to freak out when we start the ritual, so I'm acclimatizing you." She grins at him as if her logic makes perfect sense, and he laughs at her.

"Thank you for being so thoughtf—*Serim*!"

His voice catches as she grinds her hips against him and it feels… nice. It's not the instant heat that flares in his groin when he touches another boy, but it still feels good and he's already half hard.

Serim slips her fingers into his hair, and her expression turns into something more serious. Her eyes are darker and she licks her lips before speaking. "I don't think we're going to have any trouble later." She rolls her hips again to emphasize her point, and Jerath realizes with a jolt that he's going to have to fuck his best friend in about six hours' time. This is actually happening.

Serim is a solid weight in his arms. She's not as soft and feminine as the other girls, but just as beautiful. Her body is lithe, full of hard muscle, and Jerath feels her flat, toned belly pressed against his. He's almost sure that this is helping matters.

"What about you, though?" Her long hair tickles the tops of his fingers and he idly plays with the ends.

"What do you mean?" Serim has her head resting on Jerath's shoulder as she lets him get used to the feel of her body.

"Well, it's not just about me tonight." He swallows. He doesn't relish the idea of discussing this with Serim, but it's all been about him so far, and Jerath is well aware that he wouldn't be Serim's first choice of sexual partner either. "I mean… I know I'm not exactly your type and you have to *come* too." He cringes at his choice of word, but the bite has to happen when the female shifter climaxes. What if he can't do that for Serim? Jerath feels himself softening as the nerves take over. "What if I can't… you know… make you?"

To Jerath's utter mortification, Serim throws her head back and laughs. It's totally not what he was expecting from her, and he can feel shame and embarrassment wash over him. He loosens his arms and is about to push her away when she grabs his chin and forces him to look at her.

"I'm sorry, Jerath." Her eyes are soft as they meet his. "I'm laughing because that is the most ridiculous thing I have ever heard!" She wriggles in his arms and he tightens his grip again. "I like boys—tall, dark-haired, hot boys. And last time I checked—and believe me, Jerath, Mahli and I regularly check—that is exactly what you are."

"Oh." It's the most Jerath can manage because he's a little shell-shocked still.

"I mean, have you seen yourself?" She gestures over his body and he looks down between them. He's not as well muscled as some of the other boys his age, but he's fit and toned. His broad shoulders taper down to a trim waist and slim hips, but Jerath has never considered himself to be "hot." He's far too slim for that.

"Jerath, you are a fine specimen. Both me and Mahli used to have the biggest crushes on you! I can't believe you didn't know that."

"Um…."

"Oh don't look so worried. We both got over that when we saw you making out with Lukas behind the barn that time. What were you then, fourteen?"

Jerath blushes at the memory. That had been his very first kiss.

"But I've never been with a girl. I don't know how to touch you… or what to—"

Serim interrupts him by placing her fingers on his lips. "I'll show you, Jerath. You just have to trust me." She strokes her thumb across his jaw and her voice drops to a whisper. "You may be my best friend, and yes, this is an odd thing for best friends to do, but I will have absolutely no problem completing my part of the ritual."

She places a soft kiss on his lips, then extracts herself from Jerath's arms and swims away.

Jerath stays where he is. He relaxes back in the water and tilts his head up to the sky. It's a clear day apart from the odd cloud scattered here and there, and that means it will be a clear night. For the first time in… maybe ever, Jerath realizes he's not worried about the Choosing. Serim will guide him through it—more than likely with the aid of lava berries—and afterward he will be a shifter. A true member of their village. Jerath closes his eyes and drifts on his back. The night can't come soon enough.

MUCH to the delight of Jerath's stomach, Serim feels it's safe to leave him and she shifts into her panther form and manages to catch a couple of rabbits. He passes her his hunting knife so she can prepare them, while he gets a fire going. Their clothes dried after a few hours in the sun, and Jerath is feeling so much better now that both he and his clothes are clean.

They roast the rabbits on long sticks, and Jerath moans in appreciation when he bites into the tender flesh. "So much better than fish." He licks some of the juice off his fingers and grins over at Serim.

"So much better cooked," she replies.

Jerath stops chewing and stares at her. "Eww, Serim. Tell me you didn't?" He can't believe she ate one raw while running around as her panther. It's not unheard of to hunt and eat as your animal, but most people prefer not to. Rumor has it you can still taste the raw flesh when you change back.

She just shrugs. "I was hungry."

"That's just… ugh!" Jerath pulls a face and goes back to eating his well-cooked, and totally not raw, piece of rabbit.

It's dark by the time they finish eating and clean up. Jerath can see the full moon clearly in the night sky, and his skin prickles in anticipation. There's magic in the air. He looks over at Serim. Her brown eyes are tinged with the blue of her panther, and he knows she can feel it too.

"Are you ready?" Her voice is steady and she reaches out her hand to him.

Jerath takes a deep breath to calm himself. He slides his fingers across her palm, his hand trembling slightly with nervous excitement. "Yes."

Serim leads him into the center of the small clearing. They prepared it earlier. A bed of large, thick leaves lies on the grass, and next to it sits a bunch of lava berries. They'll have to eat them raw, since they have no way of making a potion.

Serim lowers herself onto the leaves, sits cross-legged, and tugs Jerath down to join her. They remain silent as she reaches for the berries and starts to break them off and feed them to Jerath. They taste surprisingly sweet on his tongue and he greedily accepts more from Serim's fingers. He returns the favor, placing the berries in Serim's mouth as she opens up for him.

When all the berries are gone, they quietly undress and place their clothes on top of the leaves as a sort of blanket. They kneel before each other.

“Close your eyes,” Serim whispers.

She closes hers and Jerath quickly does the same. Her soft lips cover his in a fleeting kiss before Serim starts chanting. The familiar words flow soft and low, curling around them both, and Jerath feels the magic of them prick at his skin. He’s never experienced a Choosing before but he knows the words that are used.

When performed properly, the ceremony takes place outside. The village elder recites the incantation with the rest of the villagers who are of age, but the boy and his partner are tucked away in a special hut behind the clearing. The elder is close enough to hear them, so the words can be spoken at the right time, but cannot see them. The ritual union is sacred and private, only to be witnessed by the Goddess herself.

Out here it will be just the same. No one to see them except the Goddess and her forest creatures.

Jerath startles as Serim puts a hand on his chest. Her touch ignites something deep in his groin, and it’s so very different from when they were in the water. It must be the berries taking effect, because Serim’s fingers are trailing a blaze of white-hot heat across his skin. Jerath moans as she rubs her thumb across his nipple. His cock lies heavy on this thigh, already half-hard, and it twitches with expectation when Serim’s hands glide down his body toward it.

She pushes a little, guiding him back down onto the makeshift bed, and Jerath goes willingly. Serim is still whispering words, a stream of beautiful prayers for the Goddess to bless their union.

Serim falls silent. The first part of the ritual is now over, and Jerath’s heart rate spikes. He knows what happens next and his body is coiled and ready. The lava berries are coursing through his system now, setting his skin on fire and making him ache with need. He can feel Serim’s touches deep inside as she runs her fingertips over the taut skin of his belly.

His head is a little foggy, his mind blissfully quiet, and he vaguely registers that this is also due to the berries. But then Serim’s hand closes around the base of his cock, and Jerath feels nothing but the delicious pressure on his sensitive skin. She uses her mouth to get him ready. He lets his eyes fall shut and arches his back, moaning loudly at the feel of the hot wetness wrapped around him.

When Serim pulls away, Jerath's cock is hard and straining against his stomach. He wants to pull her head back down, get her to carry on what she was doing because it felt so good, but somewhere in the back of his mind he knows he needs to let Serim take the lead.

"Jerath."

When he opens his eyes, his breath catches in his throat. Serim is lying beside him and is almost shimmering. Her skin is bathed in a pale-blue light that makes her look otherworldly to Jerath's hazy mind. She looks over at him and reaches out to take his hand in hers. Serim smiles and whispers, "Trust me," before spreading her thighs and placing Jerath's hand between her legs.

She puts her hand over his and guides his fingers until Jerath is rubbing and circling and Serim's breath stutters. He marvels at the sight of her, head thrown back and mouth open.

She starts to speak the incantation again, and her voice is rough with arousal. Jerath feels the words. They heat his body and he wants to… needs to….

"*Serim….*" It comes out as a plea and Serim smiles at him through her words, as though she knows exactly what he needs. It's not like his dreams, where he longs to touch and lick the warm, hard body underneath him. But the feelings are almost as powerful as the berries coax Jerath's body into a heightened state of desire and keep his mind pleasantly empty.

Serim moves his hand so he's no longer touching her and she moves so she's now straddling Jerath's lap. He feels her brush against him and he almost whimpers with the need to be inside her. It's something Jerath never expected to feel. Ever. But the urge is so strong he can barely contain it.

Serim raises her hands to the sky and her voice gets louder and louder. "We beg thee, oh honored Goddess. Take this offered union and bless this male with your most precious gift."

Jerath feels the shift in the air around them. The wind picks up and brushes against his skin. It's like a thousand tiny fingertips all over his body, making his blood boil, and he just wants to take Serim and claim her.

His hands curl into fists at his sides, but the need inside him is growing and growing, and he can't help but grab Serim's hips and pull her roughly against him.

"Serim!" Jerath looks up at her, begging her to help him.

His mind is sluggish and he knows what he wants, what he has to do, but there's something stopping him and he doesn't know what it is. Serim's voice cuts off once again and when she lowers her gaze to meet his, her eyes are the glowing blue of her panther. She growls at him, her teeth elongated and sharp, and he can feel her nails dig into his skin as her hands come to rest on his stomach.

"Take me, Jerath… claim your gift."

Her words ignite a fire inside him. Magic crackles through his veins and burns away the unseen force holding him back. He flips them over, Serim landing on her back and Jerath settling between her legs. He slips his hands under her shoulders and holds her tight. Her eyes are wild as she watches him and he wants to claim her, wants to take what is rightfully his. The wind swirls around them now, licking at their skins and urging them on.

He pauses to glance at her, and when she hisses his name and tells him to hurry, he pushes inside her with one long, hard thrust.

And *oh*, Jerath has never felt anything like this before. He's consumed by Serim's heat and his whole body trembles with the pleasure of being inside her. She's firm under his hands, her body more boyish than soft and feminine. When Jerath closes his eyes it's easy to imagine a flat, muscled chest instead of rounded breasts and that the body underneath him is that of another man. He loses himself to the moment. Serim rolls her hips, her nails dig into his back, and Jerath feels something building inside him.

His mind may be hazy, but Jerath knows it's more than just his orgasm. He can feel it work its way up from his toes. It snakes up the backs of his legs, pushing him to go harder and faster. Serim starts to whisper the final words and the feeling intensifies. Jerath clings on as heat flares up his back and out along his arms to the tips of his fingers.

Serim's legs wrap around his waist and pull him toward her and Jerath knows that this is it. She screams out the last words of the ritual and roughly shoves Jerath's head to the side of her neck. His fangs lengthen and he sinks his teeth deep into her flesh.

Jerath's body shudders as he releases inside her, and he greedily drinks down her blood as she climaxes underneath him. Pain flares hot and sudden across Jerath's back. It's like a lick of fire tearing across his skin and he throws his head back, Serim's blood dripping down his chin as he cries out. He feels the tattoo as it forms, the image of his animal searing onto his skin as the magic flows through his body. It's all he can focus on, the pain so intense that Jerath's vision whites out and he collapses on top of Serim, still buried deep inside her.

JERATH has no idea how much time passes before cool, gentle fingers brush over his cheek.

"Jerath?"

He slowly opens his eyes to find Serim peering down at him. Jerath blinks in confusion. The last thing he remembers is being on top of Serim. "How did I…?"

She blushes a little. "You were heavy, Jerath. I had to… um… move you."

He very rarely sees Serim embarrassed or lost for words, and for a second he can't understand why she would be now. Jerath's mind is beginning to clear, though, the effects of the berries finally starting to wear off, and it all comes rushing back to him in a flurry of very vivid images. Him and Serim… together… the ritual… *sex*.

Jerath remembers the overwhelming need to take Serim and claim her as if she was his, and his cheeks flush hot. He has an awful feeling in the pit of his stomach that he was too rough with her, and his hands immediately go to touch her, to find out for himself if she's okay, but he hesitates. Jerath doesn't know the etiquette for after the ritual. Can he touch Serim? Will she want him to?

He wouldn't have thought twice about it before, but now he's not sure how to act.

"Are you okay, Serim? I didn't...." Jerath swallows down his rising apprehension. "I didn't hurt you, did I?"

"No, Jerath." Her voice is soft, soothing. "You didn't hurt me."

He looks into her eyes and he can't handle the whole awkwardness between them. Serim is his best friend and he needs her. He won't be able to cope with all this without her. Things have to be okay between them.

"Serim… I don't how to do this… how to go back."

She puts her fingers over his mouth. "We can't go back to how things were before, Jerath." He feels his heart sink and opens his mouth to protest, but she shushes him again. "What we just shared was sacred and magical. I can still feel it humming under my skin." She closes her eyes and breathes deeply. "I can smell your animal now, Jerath." Her eyes flash blue. "I can sense it inside you."

Jerath shivers. He can feel it too: something new and exciting, lurking under his skin and just waiting to be released.

"It won't be the same between us, Jerath, it will be so much better," Serim continues. "You are still my best friend, and I love you as I did before." She cups Jerath's cheek in her palm and grins at him. And *there* is the Serim he knows. "But now you can run and hunt with me, and I can show you what it means to be a shifter."

He grins back and feels a weight lift from his shoulders as some of the awkwardness flows away. He's a true shifter now. He has fangs and a—

"My tattoo!" Jerath yells and scrambles to his feet. He tries to see over his shoulder, desperate to know what's on his back. "Serim! Have you seen? Do you know what it is?"

Serim laughs, and it's a beautiful sound in the now-still night. "Come with me." She takes his hand and leads him to the edge of the pool. They're both still naked, but Jerath discovers he's not bothered by this anymore.

The surface is unnaturally calm and the moon is brighter that he has ever seen it. Jerath can see himself clearly in the water and he turns to Serim and raises an eyebrow.

"Can't you feel it, Jerath?" She waves her hand around them, encompassing the pool and the clearing behind them. "The magic lingers in the air—it's all around us."

When Jerath closes his eyes and lets his new senses take over, he almost staggers backward at the flood of information that flows into his brain. He can hear and smell things he never could before, and his skin is alive with the prickle of magic. He snaps his eyes open and turns to Serim.

"Jerath… your eyes." She's staring up at his face, and her smile is blinding. "Look."

He glances down to the water and sees his reflection.

Oh.

Jerath blinks. His eyes are normally green, with the barest hint of golden flecks, but the eyes staring back at him are a vibrant green, glowing brightly in the darkness, and Jerath can't quite believe they're his.

Serim puts her hand on his arm and gently turns him until his back is to the pool. This time when Jerath looks over his shoulder, he can see the clear reflection of his back, and his breath catches in his throat.

"It's beautiful," Serim whispers.

Jerath can't speak. Serim's right—it's the most beautiful thing he has ever seen. His tattoo is a jaguar—sleek and powerful—and covers the lower half of his back. The jaguar is standing, looking out from his skin with its teeth bared. Its tail is up and curls at the end over Jerath's shoulder blade. The colors are breathtaking—the golden markings, edged in black, stand in proud relief against the soft caramel and white of its fur. But the eyes are Jerath's favorite. They're the same bright green as his own were earlier, and they make the tattoo look alive.

Jerath wants to shift. He feels restless in his skin, as though his animal form is prowling impatiently and wanting to get out. "Can I shift now? Or do I have to wait?"

"It's best if you shift straightaway." Serim rolls her shoulders and stretches out her arms as she prepares to shift. "Your body needs to adjust to all the magical energy."

"So I just…." Jerath realizes he has no clue how to actually change into his jaguar.

"Just close your eyes and let it come, Jerath. Picture your tattoo in your mind, and your body will do the rest."

Jerath watches as Serim closes her eyes and takes a long, deep breath. The air around her shimmers slightly, and her body morphs into the majestic form of her black panther. Serim growls and swishes her tail.

"Okay, okay." Jerath makes a face at her. "Don't be so impatient. I've never done this before, remember?"

Serim bares her teeth, but lies down to wait for him.

Jerath closes his eyes. He breathes in and out, focusing on the image of his tattoo, and he can feel a sharp pull deep in his belly. He concentrates harder and follows the lines of the jaguar in his mind. Heat surges up Jerath's spine and spirals out to his fingers and toes. His vision blurs for a second, and then he can see… *Serim*. But he's not looking down at her; they're on the same level now.

Jerath is on all fours and it feels like the most natural thing in the world. He can hear all the sounds of the forest and everything is so much clearer than before. He licks over his teeth and he can taste the magic in the air. Jerath laughs and it comes out like a low rumble in his chest, and he can't help the roar of delight that escapes. Serim pads over and nuzzles at him, and Jerath licks her ears as she rubs against his jaw.

She growls and knocks into him with her shoulder before bounding off toward the trees. She stops and looks back at him, and Jerath sees the anxious twitch of her tail as she waits for him. He growls back and races past her into the forest. Jerath's powerful muscles bunch and release as he runs. The wind rushes past his ears and he's never felt more alive and aware of his surroundings, as he finally, *finally* knows what it is to be a shifter.

CHAPTER 6

"SO…." SERIM stretches out on her back and soaks up the late afternoon sun. "Was it everything you thought it would be?"

Jerath is lying on the grass next to her and he opens one eye to look at her. "The ritual? Or shifting?"

Serim blushes a little. They've somehow managed to avoid speaking about the ritual. After they both shifted last night, they spent hours running and hunting through the forest. Jerath wanted to explore everything and Serim happily indulged him. They didn't change back until the sun was already rising and the pair of them collapsed, exhausted, by the side of the pool.

"Well, I meant shifting." She pauses and bites her lip. "But… um… maybe we should talk about that too."

"Okay." Jerath closes his eyes again. They probably should talk about it, but Jerath isn't sure he can look Serim in the eyes as they do. It was different last night, with the magic still surrounding them, but in the cold light of day Jerath feels the awkwardness creeping back between them. They need to clear the air before it has a chance to settle. "Was it okay? For you… I mean." Jerath swallows his embarrassment. "Was *I* okay?"

He squints at Serim out of the corner of his eye, while still trying to pretend he has them closed. She props herself up on one elbow and stares at him for a while before answering.

"Jerath…." Serim's voice is soft, but Jerath can detect a hint of amusement in her tone so he opens his eyes wide and watches her.

"The berries that we ate were particularly potent. Which is just as well, considering that you don't find girls attractive at all. And I—"

"That's not true!" Jerath interrupts. He thinks Serim and Mahli are beautiful. "I can appreciate how attractive a girl is. They just…."

"Don't do anything for you?" Serim finishes for him, and he nods.

"As I was saying." She looks pointedly at Jerath and he refrains from adding anything else. "I know how you feel about girls, but with the berries I sort of forgot all about that and got swept along with the magic of the moment. Do you know what I mean?"

Jerath nods. "Yes! That's exactly how they made me feel." He sits up and starts to use his hands as he talks. "I mean, my head was all fuzzy and it was like I was there, but not really? If that makes any sense?" Serim nods this time. "And when we were… *you know*… I didn't think of it as being you. Just a warm, firm body, and I actually imagined that you were a boy at one point—"

Jerath's eyes go wide and he slaps a hand over his mouth. He's so used to telling Serim everything that it just all came out. He'll be surprised if she ever speaks to him again. "Serim… I'm so sorry… I didn't mean that I… well… I mean I…."

She lets him flounder a little longer and then bursts out laughing. She holds her sides and has tears rolling down her cheeks. "Oh, Jerath… your face!" She sucks in a couple of deep breaths and manages to compose herself. "I know the berries are good, but they aren't *that* good. You like boys, Jerath. I'm not the least bit offended that you pictured me as a man during the ritual."

Jerath breathes a huge sigh of relief, but he's a little confused still. "You're not?"

"Don't get me wrong, the ritual itself is a very intimate and sacred act and I'm not trying to belittle it in any way. It was amazing, Jerath, and I wouldn't have wanted anyone else to help you through the Choosing."

"But?" he asks, because there's definitely a *but* coming.

"But… I'm only human, and I may or may not have pictured you as Ghaneth at some point."

"Serim!" Jerath glares at her. "I can't believe you let me think I'd upset you!"

She grins at him and he lunges for her. He digs his fingers in between her ribs and tickles her until she's begging him to stop.

"No more… Jerath… please…." She's breathless and writhing around under his hands, and he eventually takes pity on her. "So, in answer to your original question. It was wonderful. You were wonderful. But can we please not talk about it anymore?"

Jerath blushes at her words, but grins too and readily agrees to let the subject drop now. The awkwardness has gone and Jerath knows it won't be back.

They sit in silence and enjoy the sun for a few minutes before Serim sighs.

"I miss them, Jerath." She shuffles closer to him and rests her head in his lap. "I've never gone a whole day without seeing my mother or Mahli, and we've been gone for three nights now." She takes a deep, shaky breath, and Jerath slowly runs his fingers through her hair to try to soothe her.

"I know." He doesn't know what else to say. He can't tell her it'll all be okay, as much as he might want to, so he just carries on stroking her hair.

"I worry about Ghaneth and Kyr too. We have to get them back, Jerath. If they don't complete the Choosing by the next full moon, then they won't ever be able to shift. We can't let that happen."

Jerath pulls Serim up by her shoulders so that he can see her face. "We'll find them, Serim. Even if we have to beg the hunters to help, we'll get them back."

"And our village?"

"Once we have Kyr and the others back, we'll free our village too." Jerath speaks with a conviction he doesn't really feel, but Serim looks at him with such hope and trust and he knows he's going to make it happen, or die trying.

"Yes." She sits up straighter, and Jerath watches with pride and relief as she reins in all her fear and worry. He needs her to be strong.

"You're right." She smiles and her eyes flash blue for just a second. "We're going to make them all safe."

They collect more water from the waterfall, and with one last look around the clearing, continue their journey south in search of the hunters.

THEY make camp later that night at the very edge of the forest. The flats of the plains stretch out before them, and Jerath's uneasy at the thought of so much space. He's always felt safe surrounded by the thick forest, and any land devoid of trees seems so exposed.

He looks back at the fire and catches Serim watching him.

"Nervous?" She passes him some roast rabbit on a stick, and he idly wonders how long it'll be until he's sick of that too.

"A little." Jerath nods and pulls a bit of meat off. He hisses when it burns and sucks his fingers into his mouth. "Ow!"

Serim laughs and shakes her head at him. "What did you expect? It's just come off the fire."

Jerath pulls a face and blows on the meat before trying again.

"There's so much space, isn't there?" Serim looks out at the grasslands as she speaks. "We'll need to take extra care, Jerath. Those raiders might be out there somewhere."

He follows her gaze. "We could travel at night," he offers. "If we shift, we can search for the hunters under the cover of darkness. Won't that be safer?"

Jerath is aware that big cats are hunted outside the forest of Arradil. If they should meet any hunters while still in their animal forms, he and Serim would be fair game. But it seems less dangerous than to risk being caught by the raiders.

"It might be." She finishes the rest of her rabbit and throws her stick into the fire. "Shifting takes a lot of energy, Jerath. We'll still need to rest. And I don't know how safe it'll be to sleep during the day."

He'd not thought of that. They'll be far more exposed in the light and they won't get much farther if they don't stop to rest.

"We can travel at dawn," Serim says. "If we take turns shifting, we should be able to spot any danger before it gets too close."

So that's what they decide to do. They rise the next morning before the sun and tread carefully through the last part of the forest in the dim light. Jerath gives the safety of the trees one last look before walking out onto the grassy plains with Serim's black panther by his side.

They walk for hours. Serim bounds up ahead to check for signs of either the hunters or the raiders and their prisoners; but each time she comes back silent, just the annoyed swish of her tail telling Jerath she's seen nothing.

They manage to find a small grove of apple trees by the side of a stream and decide it's as good a place to stop as any. It's only late afternoon, but they're both tired from the early start. It's Jerath's turn to be in his shifted form, and he stalks off to check the surrounding area while Serim sinks down onto the cool grass and leans back against one of the thick trunks. He prowls over to her after finding nothing untoward and flops down next to her with his head on her lap.

She ruffles his fur, scratching her fingers behind his ears, and Jerath yawns and pushes against her hand. He never thought it would feel this good to be "petted," but it does, and Jerath can't hold back the deep, rumbling purr that reverberates through his chest.

Serim laughs and tickles under his chin. "You're such a softie, Jerath. You won't scare anyone like this."

He bares his teeth and flicks his tail at her, but she just ignores him and carries on stroking his fur. Jerath closes his eyes with a contented sigh and decides that if anyone needs scaring, then Serim will have to do it. Her panther is much more suited to that anyway.

JERATH is dozing in his jaguar form, his head still in Serim's lap, when he smells the unmistakable scent of humans. He flattens his ears and listens. They're coming from the southwest and Jerath can tell that there's definitely more than one. He bares his teeth and growls, low and menacing, and slowly gets to his feet.

Serim's hand drops to the ground and she startles awake. "Jerath?" she whispers. She looks at his stance: teeth bared and shoulders hunched. "What is it?"

Jerath hisses and snarls, his tail twitching back and forth, and looks in the direction of the approaching men.

"We have visitors?" she asks, and Jerath nuzzles her hand in answer.

He's just about to shift back when Serim lays her hand on his back. "Wait." She closes her eyes and sniffs the air. "Southwest and quite a few of them by the sounds of it."

Serim had told him that her senses were heightened because of her animal form, but he hadn't realized by how much before now. He can hear their feet as they march through the grass, their chatter and laughter as they walk closer and closer to him and Serim. Jerath is a little shocked when he realizes that Serim can hear it too.

"They'll be here soon, Jerath. We could hide, but…."

She meets his eyes and Jerath tries hard to convey how much he hates that idea. They need to know if these men can help them, no matter how risky it might be.

"No. We need to find out who they are."

He paces in front of Serim, protecting her as much as he can.

"I need to stay in my human form. If they're hunters from the Southern lands, I'll need to be able to talk to them. But if they're members of the raiding party…." She's quiet for a moment, and Jerath can smell a hint of fear. He pushes up against her legs and whines. "If it's the raiders, then I'll shift and we'll run away as fast as we can."

Jerath snarls and shows his teeth. The last thing he wants to do is run. If it is the raiders, he'll tear them limb from limb for what they've done. He'll—

"Jerath!" Serim hisses. "I can tell what you're thinking, but that's your animal instinct. We can't beat them all, and us getting caught or killed won't help the others."

Jerath struggles to contain his urge to attack. He knows Serim's right but it's hard to let it go. She strokes her hand down the length of Jerath's back and he calms under her touch. They wait in silence. Both have their eyes trained on the trees where the strangers should appear any minute now.

They don't have to wait much longer before several voices can be heard, getting louder and louder until a large group of young men breaks through the trees. Some don't even look much older than he and Serim, and Jerath is almost positive they aren't the raiders. He feels Serim relax beside him, obviously thinking the same thing.

"Who are you?" One of the strangers steps forward. He's tall, with golden skin and almost white-blond hair; he's one of the younger ones. Jerath licks his teeth and lets his gaze sweep over the length of the man's body. He has broad shoulders, and Jerath can see a flat and tightly muscled stomach through the open front of his tunic.

"Jerath, focus," Serim mutters under her breath.

She sounds a mixture of angry and amused, and Jerath knows he'd be blushing right now if he was human. He huffs and flicks her with his tail.

"I am Serim, of Eladir."

Jerath curls around her legs, baring his teeth at the men.

"Eladir?" The young man looks confused. "You're a long way from home."

"You know of our village?" she asks, and Jerath studies the man some more.

He has a dark wooden bow slung over his shoulder and a large, serrated-edged knife tucked into his belt. Definitely hunters. They all look too young to have been with the hunters who visited Eladir before, but it's possible they could be from the same village.

"Yes, we're familiar with the villages of Eladir, Lakesh, and Westril. You're shifters, yes?"

Serim nods, and her hand tightens in Jerath's fur. Not everyone is comfortable with shifters, and Jerath waits to see how they will react.

The young man steps forward with his hand outstretched, and Jerath instinctively crouches low to the ground and snarls. The man falters and holds up both hands instead.

"Hush." Serim strokes her hand down Jerath's flank and looks up at the hunters. "You'd best stay there. We've recently had some trouble and my friend is a little protective."

"Okay, okay." The man looks wary, but doesn't step back. "I'm Meren. And we"—he waves a hand over the men standing behind him—"are all from the Southern lands of Kalesaan. We're on a hunt, looking for food for the winter. What are you two doing so far from home?" Meren's gaze falls on Jerath, and he looks at him with an almost awed expression. "Is she a shifter too?" he asks, before Serim has a chance to answer any of his other questions.

Jerath huffs in amusement.

"Yes, *he* is," she says. "And we're traveling south to find the hunters who helped our village five years ago. They were from the village of Chastil. Do you know it?"

The men behind Meren start to talk among themselves, but it's too quiet for Jerath to hear clearly. Meren holds a hand up and they fall silent. "We are from Chastil. I believe my father may be one of the hunters you're looking for."

Serim gasps and flings her arms around Jerath's back, burying her face in his fur. "We found them, Jerath. We found them." He turns his head and nuzzles at her until she laughs and stands back up.

"I'm sorry," she says, and wipes a stray tear away with the back of her hand. "It's just that we're so glad to have found you. We really need your help."

MEREN'S camp is about half an hour's walk from the apple grove. Jerath and Serim walk beside Meren at the front of the group. Jerath is still in his jaguar form—he doesn't trust them enough to shift back yet—and he listens closely as Serim fills Meren in on what happened to their village and its people.

"What did they look like?" Meren asks. "The raiders, I mean." His eyes flicker down to Jerath as he speaks, and Jerath can already tell Meren's one of those who are fascinated with the idea of shifters.

It makes Jerath feel a bit strange, as though he's something of a spectacle, but regardless of that it's a nice feeling to have Meren's attention. He has lovely deep-blue eyes with dark lashes, and Jerath wonders if they'll still seek him out as much when he's human again.

"They were dressed much like you and your men," Serim answers, and gestures to Meren's clothing. "They carried bows and hunting knives too."

Jerath watches Meren's face for his reaction. Meren frowns and shares a look with a couple of the men on his other side. "They sound like hunters from Kalesaan, but no one I know of would raid a village for slaves."

"Oh… they had whips too," Serim adds, and Jerath feels the anger rush through her body as she no doubt thinks about Ghaneth. Her fingers are hanging down by her side and Jerath nips at them, licking her palm to let her know he feels it too.

"Eww, Jerath." She glares down at him and wipes her hands on her loose trousers, but the anger has gone and Jerath hums with approval. Serim strokes the soft fur behind his ear and whispers, "Thank you," so quietly only Jerath seems to hear it.

"Isn't that weird?" Meren asks. He's watching Serim and Jerath closely, and Jerath can sense his curiosity.

"Yeah." One of the other men joins in the conversation. "Aren't you worried that he might bite you?"

Jerath would raise an eyebrow if he could, because what a ridiculous thing to say. As if he would ever bite Serim.

Some of the others start to speak now. "He's a wild animal, after all. Shouldn't you have him restrained, or on a lead?" The men behind them start to laugh until Meren barks an order for them to be quiet.

Jerath snarls, his sharp teeth glinting in the fading light. He might not bite Serim, but he could quite easily sink his teeth into one or two of the hunters.

"I apologize for my men," Meren says, and Jerath is more than a little surprised to hear him call the group "his men." He doesn't look old enough to be their leader. "They aren't used to your kind."

Serim smiles and Jerath recognizes it as her sly and calculating one. "That's okay. But they'd better not say anything else. Jerath can be quite vicious when he's upset." Jerath growls loudly, just to add weight to Serim's words.

"Sorry." The men look warily at Jerath. "You won't tell him, will you? I don't fancy being on the receiving end of those teeth."

Serim grins and Jerath waits for the punch line.

"I don't have to tell him, he can understand you just fine." Serim tickles Jerath under the chin. "Can't you? You big, vicious meat eater."

Jerath roars, startling the birds and making one or two of the men jump back. Serim laughs loudly at the shocked and slightly pale faces around them, and Jerath rubs up against her thigh.

"I suggest you tell your men to keep a civil tongue in their heads from now on," Serim informs Meren as she keeps a hand on Jerath's back. "You never know who's listening."

Meren smirks and shakes his head. "I think they got the message."

The rest of the walk back to their camp is relatively silent. Jerath feels nearly everyone's gaze on him, but none of them dare to speak and Jerath wonders how awkward it's going to be when he shifts back.

THE camp is much larger than Jerath expected. There are seven tents in total and a large fire in the middle where something—and it's definitely not rabbit—is being roasted. Five more men appear from inside one of the tents and they walk forward to greet Meren. They look a little older than the others; their bodies are filled out with thick muscle and they have the air of experienced fighters. All five of them give Jerath and Serim curious looks. Well, the look they give Jerath's jaguar could be classed as curious, but Serim garners rather more interest. Jerath doesn't miss the way each man's gaze sweeps over her body and lingers on her breasts.

He growls out a warning and walks in front of her, baring his teeth and stopping the approaching men in their tracks.

"I don't think the cat likes you leering at his mate." Meren laughs as the men look between Jerath and Serim with confused expressions. "They're from Eladir," Meren says, and Jerath can see the moment they realize what that means. It seems everyone has heard of their village.

"Shifters?" one of them asks. "A bit far from home, aren't you?" He looks at Serim expectantly, but it's Meren who answers.

"They've had some trouble from raiders." He pauses to take off his bow and prop it up next to one of the tents. "Southern raiders, looking for slaves. Have you heard of any such hunters in Kalesaan?"

The man scratches the back of his neck. "Only rumors, Meren. Your father asked us to keep an eye out for trouble before we left."

Meren mutters something under his breath, which Jerath is almost sure is a string of curses. "I'll take it up with my father when we return." He turns to Serim. "I assume it's my father that you want to talk to? He's the leader of our village now."

Serim looks down at Jerath for confirmation, and Jerath realizes that it's probably safe for him to shift back now. It'll make communicating a lot easier too. He concentrates hard, pictures his human form, and feels the air shimmer around him as he changes.

Jerath opens his eyes to see everyone staring at him. Serim coughs next to him. He turns to face her and is met with a raised eyebrow and an amused expression.

"I think you might need these." She hands Jerath a bundle, and his face heats up in an instant as he recognizes his clothes.

Oh, yes. Shifting back means nakedness. On second thought, maybe he should have done that in private.

The group of men is chatting animatedly between themselves now while stealing glances at Jerath. Hopefully they're discussing his shifting display and not his current lack of clothing.

"Thanks," Jerath mumbles and snatches the bundle of clothes out of Serim's hands. He drops the whole lot on the ground and starts to get dressed. Jerath chances a glance up at Meren, about to ask him about the journey back to his village, but he discovers that Meren is looking at him—well, staring would be more accurate.

Meren smiles when he gets caught out. "You're lucky to have such a fine-looking mate." He addresses Serim before his eyes settle back on Jerath's chest.

Jerath's mouth drops open. Did Meren just describe him as "fine-looking"? He doesn't know whether to be flattered or insulted. He's not livestock; he's human and he's standing right here. Serim laughs at his stunned expression and Jerath glares between the two of them.

"Yes." Serim smirks as she turns to Meren. "He is fine looking." She ignores Jerath's huffs of indignation. "But he's not my mate."

"Oh, I'm sorry." Meren apologizes, and Jerath thinks he looks far from sorry, if the smile tugging at his lips is anything to go by. "I just assumed…."

Serim turns around and lifts the back of her tunic to show off her tattoo. "Jerath." She motions for him to do the same. "We're not matched," she explains, looking back over her shoulder after Meren has had time to look at their tattoos.

"Serim and I are just friends." Jerath turns around and Meren snaps his gaze back up to his face. His eyes are wide, and Jerath wonders if he's ever seen a shifter's tattoo before. Maybe he'll ask Meren about that later. "I'm Jerath, by the way. In case you wanted to talk to me directly or anything." Jerath is quite aware of how petulant he sounds, and not at all like the adult he needs to be if they're going to get Meren's father to help them.

Meren at least looks slightly sheepish, but Serim just raises an eyebrow at him.

"Forgive my rudeness." Meren dips his head slightly in apology. "I'd just got used to talking to Serim while you were shifted." He rubs a hand across his eyes and Jerath sees for the first time how weary he looks. "We've started off badly and I appear to be doing nothing but apologizing. Come, let me make it up to you. If my father learns of my lack of manners, he will not be pleased." He walks toward the fire and gestures for them to follow.

Serim sidles up to Jerath as they walk. "He likes you," she whispers.

Jerath narrows his eyes at her. “Don’t be ridiculous,” he hisses back, and she grins up at him.

“I thought he might swallow his tongue when he saw you naked.” Jerath stumbles over the tiniest rock at her words, and she stifles her giggles with her hand. “And when he saw your tattoo….” She pretends to fan herself with her hands.

Jerath pointedly ignores Serim and keeps walking, but he can’t quite ignore the warm feeling that stirs in the pit of his stomach.

CHAPTER 7

"WHAT meat is that, exactly?" Jerath points to the fire.

One of the hunters is currently carving long strips off the joint of meat and piling it on a huge plate. It smells delicious and Jerath's mouth is already watering in anticipation.

"It's white-tailed deer," Meren answers as he sits down next to Jerath. His hard, muscled thigh rubs up against Jerath's as he shifts position, and Jerath swallows thickly. He can feel the warmth through his pants and he wants to shuffle closer to get more of it, but manages to keep still.

Jerath may be a shifter, but he doubts Meren would appreciate it if he started rubbing all over him like a cat. He focuses back on the conversation just as Serim speaks.

"Aren't we too far north for white-tailed deer?" She accepts a plate of meat from the hunter and pops a piece in her mouth. "*Oh*, it's good." She licks her lips and Meren smiles at her.

"It is, isn't it?" He takes a plate too, and passes one to Jerath. "And yes. We are too far north for most of them, but we found a stray herd a few a days ago." Serim nods and falls silent as she continues to eat.

Jerath picks up a piece from his plate and bites into it. He can't help it—he moans. It's more like a low purr in the back of his throat, but the meat is so soft and tender it practically melts in his mouth. He licks the juices from his fingers, sucking them into his mouth to get every last bit. When Jerath looks up, Meren is staring at him again. His eyes are heavy lidded and he's biting his lip.

The hunter who was carving the meat walks over and sits down opposite them. "A fine-looking man, indeed. Eh, Meren?" He pokes at Meren's foot with his boot.

Jerath stops eating and looks between the two of them, not sure he understood correctly.

Meren coughs and struggles to swallow without choking. "Jerath, let me introduce you to Torek." He points at him and grins. "He's my friend and second-in-command, and he has a smart mouth." Torek looks slightly older than Meren. He's just as tall and broad and has the same golden skin, but with black hair and dark eyes.

Jerath nods in greeting and chooses to ignore Torek's earlier comment for now. "Forgive me for asking, but aren't you both a little young to be in charge of all these men?" Jerath can see Serim shake her head out of the corner of his eye, and he hopes he's not managed to offend them. He's just curious. The elders are the ones who make all the decisions in Jerath's village, but these two look the same age as he and Serim. Much to Jerath's relief, both Meren and Torek laugh and don't seem at all bothered by his question.

"I turned nineteen on the last new moon," Meren replies. "It's customary for the chief's son to lead the hunting party when he comes of age. This is my second hunt." He says it with pride, and Jerath notices how his eyes shine with the light of the fire.

Meren's face is all angles—high cheekbones and a sharp jawline—but his lips look soft and inviting, and Jerath wonders if they taste as good as they look. He realizes a moment too late that he's staring, and Torek's loud laughter has him scooting back a little, away from Meren.

"It would seem that Jerath likes the look of you too, Meren." Torek wipes his hands on his breeches and fixes his gaze on Jerath. "What do you say, Jerath? Will you be warming the bed of our handsome leader tonight? I hear that he's very talented in that particular area."

Jerath feels the heat blooming in his cheeks. He's already warm from the fire, but now his face feels much hotter than the flames. Both men are looking at him, waiting for him to reply, but Jerath can't think of a single thing to say. He's not used to men talking so openly about liking other men, and he's not sure if they're serious or just trying to goad him into saying something incriminating.

Jerath has no idea what it's like in the Southern lands, how they treat same-sex pairings. He doesn't want to get caught out and ruin their chance of getting help for their village. All that aside, he may not be a virgin anymore after the ritual, but he's still inexperienced where sex with men is concerned. He isn't about to jump into bed with the first man that shows an interest. Jerath opens his mouth, but he still has no idea how to reply.

Torek grins and apparently takes Jerath's silence as permission to tease him some more. "Maybe I was mistaken. Do you prefer women or men, Jerath? Meren likes both, don't you?"

Jerath turns to look over at Meren and notices that he's not smiling anymore. Jerath can't quite tell what expression Meren's wearing; it's sort of a mixture between confused and worried. Jerath puts his plate on the ground, ready to get up and walk away if he needs to. He doesn't like the look on Meren's face and he's not sure what's expected of him and he can feel his heart rate spike.

"Stop it." Serim looks between Meren and Torek as she grips Jerath's hand. "I don't know the customs of the Southern lands, but this isn't something we talk about openly in Eladir." She looks accusingly at Meren.

Torek immediately cuts in, his voice full of apology. "The fault is mine. I meant no harm, I swear." He looks over at Meren, who nods back at him to continue. "In Kalesaan it's common for men and women to take partners of either sex into their bed, if they desire. And it is spoken of without shame or embarrassment." He reaches out and puts a gentle hand on Jerath's knee. "I'm sorry if I've offended you. I didn't know this wasn't common practice in the north, I only meant it in jest."

Jerath begins to calm down as Torek speaks. He can't believe that people are free to choose whomever they want in Torek's village, and he feels a stab of jealousy at the freedom they're afforded.

"If this is not your way," Meren addresses him as Torek sits back down, "then we will not speak of it again."

No. Jerath wants to talk about it. He wants to be able to relax and be himself for once, without fear of being judged by his peers for something that comes naturally to him. He reaches out and grabs Meren's wrist. "It's not the way of my village." He takes a deep breath, knowing what he'll be admitting with his next sentence. "But it is *my* way."

It takes a moment or two for Jerath's words to sink in, and then Meren smiles. It reaches all the way to his eyes, and Jerath feels that familiar warmth inside as Meren nudges him with his shoulder. "I look forward to learning more of your ways, Jerath." His voice is soft and it washes over Jerath and makes his skin tingle.

"So, Serim," Torek starts, and he's deadly serious now. "I think I'd like to know a bit more about these raiders."

Meren seems reluctant to look away from Jerath, but eventually turns to include Torek and Serim as he speaks. "Yes. And also what you want from my father."

Jerath tries to concentrate on the conversation. He joins in with Serim to explain that they're hoping Meren's father will help them, as the people of his village did before. But Meren is still pressed up against his thigh and it's very distracting.

By the time they've finished, it's dark and Jerath is yawning. It's been a long day for him and Serim, and it's starting to take its toll. Meren and Torek have agreed to talk to Meren's father and encourage him to help them. It's all they can ask for, and Jerath knows that Serim is as relieved as he is.

They all stand, ready to go to bed, and Jerath feels the awkwardness start to seep in. They've not mentioned the teasing conversation from earlier, but now that it's time to sort out sleeping arrangements, Jerath can sense that everyone is thinking about it.

Although he likes Meren, and has already imagined what it would be like to share his bed, there's no way that's happening tonight, so he speaks up before anyone else has the chance.

"Serim and I will be happy to sleep by the fire, if that's all right?" They're used to sleeping outside, and Jerath has every intention of suggesting they take turns to keep watch. These men are still relative strangers, after all, no matter how trustworthy they appear.

"No," Meren says, and Jerath is about to protest, but Meren smiles and holds up both hands. "You are our guests. Please." He gestures to the tent behind them. "You and Serim take my tent. I will join Torek and the others."

Jerath is speechless again, but fortunately Serim is not.

"Thank you," she says. "That's very generous of you. We will be honored."

She walks toward the tent after bidding the men good night, and Jerath follows her.

"Jerath?" Meren's soft voice stops him in his tracks. "Can I speak with you a moment before you go?"

Jerath turns back and is surprised to see Meren now alone by the fire. He walks toward him and stops a couple of paces away.

"I'm sorry if you felt uncomfortable earlier. Torek meant no harm, but doesn't always know when to stop." He takes a few steps closer and Jerath swallows nervously. "He was right, though, you are a fine-looking man." Meren reaches up and strokes his thumb down Jerath's cheek. His skin feels rough, but his touch is gentle and Jerath leans into it. "And as much as I would like you in my bed tonight, I understand that your ways and mine are very different."

Jerath's heart pounds. How easy it would be to lean forward and kiss Meren, to tell him yes, he'd very much like to join him in his bed. But Jerath is inexperienced and Meren is obviously not. Jerath's not sure he wants to be just another bed warmer for the chief's son, as appealing as that seems at this precise moment. He also doesn't want to leave Serim alone. So he takes a step back.

"Yes," Jerath answers. "They are."

Meren smiles softly. "Night, Jerath."

Before Jerath has time to react, Meren leans in and kisses him. It's just a gentle brush of lips at first. Meren's are warm and soft as they move over his; then he goes to pull away. But Jerath has had a taste now and he wants more. He grabs Meren's hips and tugs him forward until they both gasp at the contact.

Meren brings his other hand up and cups Jerath's face, tilting his head for a better angle. He licks into Jerath's mouth and Jerath moans—a low rumble in his chest. The sound shocks them both and they pull back quickly, lips wet and glistening in the firelight.

Meren looks flushed and his eyes are so dark they're almost black. Jerath wants to kiss him again, wants to feel Meren pressed up against him, but he knows he won't be able to stop there and he doesn't want it to go any further tonight.

"Night, Meren." He steps back to put some space between them.

"See you in the morning." Meren smiles and reluctantly turns away.

Jerath watches him head off to join his men in one of the larger tents, and sighs heavily. He has a feeling these next few days are going to be very interesting.

SERIM is lying on the soft pallet of furs and blankets when Jerath ducks into the tent. He turns away from her before he pulls his shirt over his head, but decides to keep his breeches on. He's half-hard from the kiss and doesn't want Serim to notice.

When he scrambles under the blankets next to her, she's smirking at him.

"What?" He tries to sound nonchalant, but Serim raises an eyebrow and he can't help but grin. "Meren kissed me."

She smiles back and drags him in for a hug. "I told you he liked you." Her breath tickles his ear, and he shivers a little before flopping onto his back and staring up at the canvas.

"What's the point, though?" He sighs and turns his head to look at her. "I mean, once he takes us to see his father, we probably won't see him again."

"You don't know that, and it's not like you have to marry him, Jerath. Just have some fun." Serim looks down at the furs covering them and when she raises her eyes, Jerath can tell that she's on the verge of tears.

"Serim?"

"We don't know what tomorrow will bring, Jerath. I waited for Ghaneth, followed the stupid rules that said I wasn't allowed to get involved before he'd been through his Choosing. And look where that got us." She wipes at the tears that have started to fall. "I may never get the chance again."

"We'll get them back, Serim." He pulls her into his arms and she buries her face in his chest.

"I know we will." She snuggles farther in. "All I'm saying is, don't let anything hold you back from taking what you want, Jerath. Especially not our outdated village traditions." She sniffs a little and lifts her head so that she can look at him. "If you like Meren, do something about it before it's too late."

She settles back down and they lie in silence for a while. Jerath's eyes are closing and he's just dropping off to sleep when Serim's voice jolts him awake again.

"So, do you?" she asks in a quiet whisper against his skin.

"Do I what?"

"Like Meren."

Jerath smiles to himself. He thought she'd let that go far too easily before. "Yes. I like him." He feels her lips curve up in a smile.

"Tell me about the kiss. Was it good? Did he use his tongue, and did you want more?"

"Serim!" Jerath hisses and gives her ribs a poke for good measure. "I'm not telling you!"

"I tell you everything," she huffs.

"Yes, and now I'm scarred for life." He laughs softly as she grumbles and threatens never to tell him anything again. "Fine… yes, yes, and fuck yes."

Serim just about manages not to squeal.

"Good night, Serim."

They fall asleep with Serim still tucked under Jerath's arm and neither one of them thinks to shift and stand guard.

SERIM and Jerath are both up before the rest of the camp the next morning and they take the opportunity to shift and explore. They pad silently past the sleeping tents and out into the surrounding grasslands.

It feels good to run. They race after each other, and Jerath nips at Serim's tail when she sneaks past and flicks it in his face. By the time they make it back to camp, the men are up and about. Serim and Jerath are still in their shifted forms. They get more curious looks as they walk back toward their tent, but thankfully no one tries to attack them.

Meren's just coming out of his tent when they get there and he stops abruptly, staring at them both with a small smile curving his lips. "I don't think I'll ever get used to it," he says. He takes a step toward Serim and raises his hand. "Can I?" he asks before Serim has a chance to growl at him. "Can I stroke you?"

Serim purrs as she saunters over and rubs against Meren's outstretched hand. He grins and his face lights up as he strokes down the sleek fur of her back. Jerath watches as Meren fusses over her, and swishes his tail in annoyance. He knows Serim's panther is beautiful but it doesn't mean that Meren has to ignore him. Jerath flops down and drops his head onto his paws. He huffs out a breath and growls when Serim curls around Meren's legs. She looks back at him, her blue eyes full of mischief, and then saunters off inside their tent.

"Jerath." Meren walks over to him and crouches down, but Jerath turns his face away. "Are you angry with me?" Jerath bares his teeth. "It's just, I've never seen a black panther before, that's all." Meren sits down in front of him and tentatively reaches out with his fingers. "But you… your markings are breathtaking." Meren's fingertips brush against Jerath's ears and Jerath shuffles closer.

Meren runs his hands over Jerath's head and ears. He strokes down Jerath's flank and fists his hands in the thick fur there. When Jerath has finally had enough of being petted, he slowly rises to his feet. Meren looks at him. Their faces are almost level and Jerath can't resist taking a swipe at him with his tongue. He nuzzles at Meren's neck, licking along his collarbone and up behind his ear. He tastes soft furs, grasslands, and underneath it all the warm, musky scent of Meren's skin. Jerath purrs in contentment and licks at him a little more.

Meren laughs and tries to push him off, but Jerath is much stronger in his animal form and he just nudges Meren back down until he's hovering over him. "Okay, okay," Meren concedes and attempts to avoid Jerath's rough tongue. "I promise to pay you more attention than the panther, from now on."

Jerath growls his approval and leaves Meren lying on the floor as he heads into the tent to shift back. He does, however, manage to flick Meren in the face with his tail as he passes.

"HOW long will it take to get back to your village?" Serim asks. She and Jerath are sitting in the middle of the camp as the men around them prepare to go hunting.

Meren walks over and stands in front of them. "It takes two days from here, but we have at least another two days' worth of hunting to do before we can head back."

Serim's face falls.

"If we help you hunt," Jerath says and reaches for her hand, "can you leave in one day's time instead?"

Meren sighs and sits down next to Jerath. "If we get enough meat today, then yes. But I can't go back to my father with less than we need."

"We understand." Jerath stands and tugs Serim up with him. "If it's okay with you, we'll join you in a few moments."

Meren smiles and nods before going back to check on his hunters.

Jerath and Serim quickly return to the tent and shed their clothes, all embarrassment gone, and shift. When they join Meren and the others at the edge of the camp, Meren beckons them over to where he's chatting with Torek. He grins as Jerath muscles his way in front of Serim to get to him first, and Jerath butts against his legs, making him stumble.

"Hey!" Meren laughs and runs his hand down Jerath's back. It feels good, and Jerath wonders what it would feel like on his bare skin instead of his fur.

"When you two have quite finished?" Torek raises an eyebrow at them and Serim huffs out a breath. Jerath knows she'd roll her eyes if she could. "Maybe we can get going?"

Meren smiles widely at his friend, but shouts out orders to the rest of his men and they all set off in search of more white-tailed deer.

THE hunt is very successful, but bloody. Serim and Jerath take down two deer each and the hunters another six. The animals are taken back to camp to be dressed and wrapped, and Meren and a few of the others head down to the nearby river to clean up.

"Are you coming?" Meren walks over to Jerath and waves a finger at all the blood on his fur. "You could wash all that off before you shift back."

Serim doesn't wait for Jerath, she just pushes past him and heads down to the water. Torek laughs and wanders after her. "I guess that's a yes, then."

"Come on." Meren gestures for Jerath to walk with him and they follow after Serim and Torek, side by side.

The water is cool and refreshing and Jerath bounds into the stream, splashing Meren and Torek as he jumps about. The men crouch down and wash their faces and arms, and then wipe the blood from their knives.

Serim is quick to clean herself and head back to the tent, and Jerath decides to let her have a little time alone to get dry and dressed. They may be used to seeing each other naked, but that doesn't mean they don't like their privacy too.

One by one, Meren's men head back to camp until it's just Meren, Torek, and Jerath.

Torek clears his throat and looks between the two of them. "I'll go see if they've started the fire yet." He gives Meren a knowing look and Jerath is so glad he can't blush in this form. They both watch Torek until he disappears over the hill and out of sight.

Meren turns to Jerath and walks out a little farther into the water until he's standing in front of him. "You've missed a bit." He bends down so he can scoop up some water and washes the side of Jerath's neck, working his way up to just behind Jerath's ears.

Meren's hands are firm and strong, and Jerath purrs as he works his fingers through the thick fur. It's the second time today that Meren's hands have been on him, and Jerath has still yet to feel them on his skin. He imagines it now: strong fingers massaging his shoulders, moving down his back and settling low on his hips.

He wonders if Meren would slide them over his wet skin, around and over his stomach before dipping down lower. Jerath is concentrating so hard on the visual of Meren touching his body that before he knows what's happened, he's shifted back and now stands dripping wet and very naked in the water.

Meren freezes and stares at Jerath, mouth open and eyes wide, and he doesn't move for several moments. Jerath starts to feel self-conscious about his lack of clothing and Meren has yet to say anything, and so he moves to cover himself.

Meren reaches out quickly and grasps his wrist. "Don't." He tugs Jerath closer to him and Jerath swallows thickly.

Their bodies are only a few inches apart. Meren is still fully clothed, though, and Jerath's eager to see what's under there. "You have blood just"—Jerath runs his hand down the open front of Meren's shirt—"here." Meren smiles and licks his lips. "And here." Jerath lets his hand drop lower and trails his fingertips over the jut of Meren's hips. "You should take your clothes off and wash them."

Meren sucks in a breath and Jerath can clearly see the growing bulge in his breeches. Jerath doesn't have to look down to know that his own cock is erect. He slides his hand over the curve of Meren's ass and starts to pull at his clothes. He's not usually this forward, but Meren makes him bold.

"Jerath…," Meren whispers, and fists his hands in Jerath's hair. He yanks him closer and kisses him, his mouth eager and insistent. Jerath moans as their hips rub against each other, and he feels that they're both fully hard now.

"These… off." Jerath breaks the kiss, and Meren laughs at they both struggle to get him out of his wet clothes.

Finally they get them all off and Jerath tosses them onto the bank. Meren reaches for him and wraps his arms around Jerath's back. He draws him in and they're kissing again, but it's so much better now Jerath can feel skin on skin.

Jerath slides his hands up into Meren's hair. It's surprisingly soft between his fingers, and he grips it tight and deepens the kiss. He's never kissed anyone like this before. It's hot and dirty, and Jerath lets Meren take control as he maps the inside of Jerath's mouth with his tongue and his hands move down to grip Jerath's ass.

Jerath thanks whichever Goddess allowed him to have this as Meren tugs him impossibly closer, but when he slides his finger down between Jerath's ass cheeks, Jerath tenses. No one has touched him there yet. His first instinct is to freeze and pull away, but Meren smiles against Jerath's mouth and moves his hands back to the safer territory of Jerath's hips.

"Sorry," Jerath mumbles. He breaks the kiss and drops his head onto Meren's shoulder and feels his face heat up.

"It's okay." Meren runs his tongue along the smooth skin of Jerath's throat. "There's no rush." Jerath sighs and lets Meren's touches wash away his embarrassment.

None of the male shifters have facial hair—a fact that Serim and Mahli are constantly thankful for and Jerath never really understood why they were until now. He can feel the scrape of Meren's stubble against his neck and knows it's going to be red enough for people to notice. But when Meren licks and bites, soothing the skin with his tongue afterward, Jerath doesn't care who sees it.

Meren nudges gently against Jerath's throat, and he obliges and tilts it to the side. Meren hums with approval and bites at the top of Jerath's shoulder, and Jerath grins—he thought he was supposed to be the animal here. Meren grinds his hips, and the head of Jerath's cock catches on the skin of Meren's stomach. A spike of pleasure shoots up Jerath's spine and he moans.

The need to touch is almost overwhelming, and Jerath pulls away a little so he can snake his hand in between them. It's not the first time he's done this with another man, but when his fingers wrap around Meren's cock, it feels as though it is. Jerath's not sure why, he's only known Meren for a little over a day, but this time it somehow means more.

Jerath lets out a shaky breath. His nerves start to get the better of him again, and he's about to pull away when Meren's hand covers his.

"Here," Meren whispers. "Let me help." Warm breath washes over Jerath's skin, and it sends goose bumps down his spine.

Meren adjusts his grip and makes him take hold of both of them. He urges Jerath to move with a squeeze of his fingers, and they start off with a slow drag of hands up and down. They do it over and over until they're slick with precome and Jerath feels his orgasm approaching, a tight coil in the pit of his stomach.

"Meren…." Jerath bites his lip in an effort to be quiet. The camp is within shouting distance, and he doesn't want everyone to know what they're up to. "I'm close."

Meren moans, his strokes getting faster and when he bites into Jerath's shoulder and comes over both their hands, Jerath can do nothing but follow straight after him.

"TELL me about your village," Jerath says, and turns his head to face Meren. "Do you have any brothers or sisters? Do you look like your mother or your father?"

They're lying on the bank of the river, the grass is soft underneath them, and the sun is warm on their skin. Meren's clothes are drying on a nearby rock, so they're both naked.

"One at a time, please." Meren grins and pokes Jerath in his side. "My village, Chastil, is beautiful. It's surrounded on all sides by rich grasslands, and in the summer all kinds of wildflowers fill them with color. I have my own house there. It's not as big as some of them, but it was given to me by my father when I came of age."

"You don't live with your family?" Jerath asks. In Eladir it's customary to live with your family until you meet your mate, and Jerath can't imagine living on his own.

A look of sadness flashes in Meren's eyes, and Jerath wonders what he's said to cause such a reaction.

Meren takes a deep breath and closes his eyes. “My mother died when I was very young, before she had the chance to give me any brothers or sisters.”

Jerath twines his fingers with Meren’s and squeezes them a little in silent support. Meren smiles, but keeps his eyes closed.

“My father says I have her eyes and her smile, but the rest is all him.”

Meren opens his eyes then and Jerath’s breath catches. They’re so very blue and Jerath could easily get lost in them. He imagines that Meren’s mother must have been beautiful.

“I’m sorry about your mother.” Jerath inches closer and presses a soft kiss to Meren’s lips.

“Thank you. It was a long time ago, but I still miss her.”

Jerath understands that only too well. “My father was killed five years ago and I miss him every day.”

Meren hooks his arm around Jerath’s shoulders and pulls him against his chest. They lie there in silence and let the warm sun soothe them.

“We’d better head back soon or Torek is likely to come looking for us.” Meren props himself up on one elbow and smiles over at Jerath, all traces of sadness gone from his face. “And we wouldn’t want that, would we?” He looks pointedly at Jerath’s naked body, and Jerath blushes as he suddenly realizes he doesn’t have any clothes. “I’ll need to shift here. My clothes are back at the tent.”

Jerath starts to stand but Meren grabs his hand. He looks up and smiles, before pulling Jerath down on top of him. “I said soon.”

JERATH shifts for the walk back to camp, and when they approach the fire in the middle, most of Meren’s men are seated around it, and Jerath is suddenly very glad that he’s in his jaguar form. The whistles and catcalls that greet them would have had him blushing furiously if he was human. But now he just growls and bares his teeth, secretly pleased that the men shut up quickly and back away as he stalks past them to Serim’s tent.

Once inside, Serim smirks at him and raises an eyebrow. She waits for him to shift back and get dressed before she pats the bed beside her. “Sit and tell me everything.” Jerath tries to look innocent as he drops down next to her. He knows he’s failed when she just smiles and nudges him in the ribs. “Well?”

“Well what?”

“Jerath!”

He grins at her and laughs as she punches him in the arm. “Okay, okay. We kissed.”

“And?”

“And… *other* stuff.” Jerath’s not sure that he actually wants to tell her everything in detail but Serim is insistent.

“What sort of stuff?”

“*Come on*, Serim,” Jerath pleads. “We… you know….”

“Did you two have sex?” Serim’s eyes are wide now and Jerath shakes his head quickly.

“Well, not *sex* sex.” Serim looks skeptical, so Jerath elaborates. “The camp’s not far from the stream, anyone could have come back and found us.”

She nods, but Jerath can tell she’s still eager for details. “Ugh, Serim, you are the worst friend, do you know that?”

She smiles sweetly and slips her arms around his waist. “You love me, though. So just tell me.”

Jerath lets out a defeated sigh. “There was nakedness, and touching, and well… you can guess the rest.”

Serim laughs and hugs him tight. “Yes, okay. I get the idea. I’m so happy for you, Jerath.”

“Yeah, me too.” Jerath smiles as he thinks about Meren’s hands on him and tries not to dwell on what might happen after they talk to Meren’s father. He’s just going to enjoy himself for however long this lasts.

CHAPTER 8

BY THE time Jerath and Serim leave their tent, there's a roaring fire at the center of the camp and a large deer roasting above the flames. Some of the meat has been carved already, and the hunters already seated around the fire dig in as they chat among themselves. They glance up when Serim and Jerath approach, some looking a little nervous after Jerath growled at them earlier.

Although most of the camp are sitting and eating, Jerath can't see Meren among them, but he does notice Torek sitting off to the side on the trunk of an uprooted tree. He nudges Serim and nods over in Torek's direction. She takes the hint, heading over and settling beside him with Jerath following after her.

"Help yourself to some food," Torek says and gestures at one of the men. The man nods and grabs two wooden plates from a stack on the ground next to him.

Serim starts to stand again but Jerath stops her with a hand on her shoulder. "I'll get these, you stay and relax." She smiles up at him and he walks over to collect their food. It smells delicious again, and Jerath's stomach grumbles loudly, causing the men closest to him to laugh.

The man carving the meat—Jerath thinks his name is Harik—raises an eyebrow at him and adds an extra cut to one of the plates. "Sounds like you'll be needing this." He grins and Jerath smiles back in thanks. He hadn't realized just how hungry he was until he'd smelled the meat close up. Harik adds a chunk of bread and a handful of berries before handing them both over.

Jerath thanks him again and takes them back over to Serim. She looks at the meat piled higher on one of the plates, but Jerath's stomach rumbles again and she just laughs at him and takes the smaller portion. They eat in comfortable silence for a while, until Jerath has filled his belly with enough food to keep it quiet and he leans back on his hands to give it a bit of a rest.

Torek and Serim have also finished and both place their plates on the ground at their feet. Jerath still hasn't seen Meren and his curiosity gets the better of him. "Where's Meren?"

Torek smirks before he answers and Jerath gets an odd feeling. "He's sorting out sleeping arrangements."

"But I thought he was bunking with his men," Serim cuts in. "If he needs his tent back, Jerath and I are more than happy to sleep by the fire."

Jerath nods in agreement, but Torek is quick to hold up his hand. "No, the tent is yours. Meren would never see his guests sleep outside, but he's also had enough of sharing a tent with the likes of Harik over there." He points over his shoulder with his thumb. "And I think he might want his privacy back for… *other* reasons." He looks pointedly at Jerath and Serim giggles beside him.

As the implication of Torek's statement slowly sinks in, Jerath feels heat blossom in more than just his cheeks. He's just about to ask Torek what he means by that exactly when Meren appears, plate in hand, and sits down on the log next to Jerath. He's close enough that their thighs are touching, and when Jerath looks up at him, he's smiling widely.

"Hey." He looks at their empty plates. "Have you had enough to eat?"

"Jerath has eaten enough for all of us!" Serim laughs.

"He needs to keep his strength up, though," Torek adds, and the pair of them grin.

Jerath glares at Serim and tells Torek not to encourage her. "Everything okay?" He turns and faces Meren.

"Yes, I have a tent all to myself again." His eyes darken as he looks at Jerath, but he doesn't elaborate further. "So." Meren peers past him to include Serim as well. "I was curious. I know the people of your village have the ability to shift, but are you born that way? Can everyone do it?"

Jerath is a little surprised that Meren doesn't know more about them from his father, but he's more than happy to tell him about their village and its people. "Only the females are born with the ability to shift, and it usually kicks in between their sixth and seventh birthdays. You saw our tattoos, yes?" Meren nods and licks his lips, and Jerath suddenly remembers what Serim said yesterday, about how Meren had looked when he'd seen Jerath's tattoo. He clears his throat and pushes that thought away for later. "Well, all females in the village are born with their tattoo already on their skin, and it depicts which cat they will shift into. The males get their tattoos when they come of age and their fangs have come in."

Jerath shows off his teeth, and Meren raises his hand as though he's going to touch them but he hesitates at the last moment. "Can I?" he asks, and Jerath nods. With careful fingers, Meren traces the tips of Jerath's fangs and smiles as he drops his hand back into his lap. "Those are impressive."

"How do you get your tattoo?" Torek leans forward with his elbows on his knees. "Does it just appear? Or…."

Jerath casts a worried glance at Serim. All of a sudden Jerath can see where the conversation is heading and he's not sure he wants to tell Meren about this particular ritual. But apparently Serim has no such reservations.

"When the males get their fangs, they must go through the Choosing to reveal their animal tattoo."

"The Choosing?" Both Meren and Torek speak at the same time, and lean a little closer.

"It's one of the most sacred rituals of our village," Serim says, and then, much to Jerath's horror, she begins to recite what it entails. "When the moon is full, each and every boy who is of age shall choose a willing female. Together they will consummate their union and invoke the spirits of the forest to bless him with their magic. Only then will his animal form be revealed."

"Consummate?" Meren turns to face Jerath with a confused expression. "So that means you have sex, right?" Jerath nods and sighs as he waits for Meren's next question. "But… I thought you only liked men? Yet you have your tattoo?"

"The only way to gain the ability to shift is to drink the blood of a female shifter at the point of climax," Jerath explains, but Meren still looks confused. "There are berries and potions that can help with… you know… *that* part."

Meren smiles with understanding, and Jerath breathes a sigh of relief that he doesn't have to answer any more of Meren's awkward questions.

But he'd forgotten about Torek.

"So when did your fangs come in? And did the poor girl mind that you needed berries to help find her attractive?" Torek grins at him and winks, and Jerath does his best not to glance at Serim.

He contemplates lying about his fangs. It's not as though they need to know when he went through the ritual. But he doesn't want to taint the growing relationship they're both building with Meren, and the rest of his men, by being dishonest. "They came in three days ago."

He waits for Torek and Meren to fully comprehend what he means, and sure enough, after a moment or two they look from Jerath to Serim and back again.

"You and Serim?" Meren asks.

"Yes."

Torek studies Serim closely and shakes his head. "I can't believe you needed sex berries in order to find a creature as lovely as Serim attractive."

"Thank you." She smiles at Torek. "You don't need to defend my honor, though. Jerath's not interested in girls," she says matter-of-factly and shrugs. "So my attractiveness wasn't the issue."

Torek looks between the two of them curiously and Jerath has no idea what to say now. "It wasn't just me who had the berries," he eventually blurts out. "It's not like Serim finds me attractive either—she's my best friend. And she has feelings for another."

"Another?" Torek looks totally confused now. "Won't he mind that you did this with Jerath?"

"It's an honor to help someone through their Choosing," Serim answers. "Usually only unmated females are eligible and only if they're willing." Jerath notices she leaves out the part about them being assigned in extreme cases, but he isn't about to tell them either. Some things are best left unsaid.

"But I thought Jerath said there was someone else?" Meren joins in.

"Yes, his name is Ghaneth. But…." Serim takes in a shuddering breath, so Jerath slips an arm around her shoulders and pulls her close. "We weren't mated. His fangs had only just come in, and I was waiting for the full moon to see if his animal would be a match for mine. But then he was taken." Serim buries her head in Jerath's chest and takes several deep breaths until she's back in control again.

No one speaks for several long moments, and then Meren's soft voice breaks the tension. "The full moon was two nights ago. What will happen to the ones who didn't get to do the ritual?"

Serim tenses at the reminder and Jerath holds her tighter against him. "If they don't complete the ritual by the next full moon…." Her breath hitches and Jerath strokes his thumb up and down Serim's arm. "They will lose the ability to shift. Forever."

Jerath can tell by the look on Meren's face that he doesn't seem to grasp how awful that will be for them.

"They would be the first ones in the history of our village," Jerath explains. "With no tattoo, there is no way to find a mate, so they will never have a family of their own. I wouldn't wish it on my worst enemy."

Meren finally gets it and he lays his hand on Serim's knee. "Is that why you're so desperate to see my father? You need to get them back home before the next full moon?"

"Yes," she whispers. "We're hoping he'll help us, like your village did before."

"The hunters in my village are expert trackers. But even if my father agrees to help, the raiders who took your people have a huge head start and there's no guarantee that we'll be able to find them." He squeezes Serim's knee before he lets go and sits back.

"We know that, Meren." Jerath rubs a hand over his eyes, feeling the events of the day catching up with him. The sun has set while they've been talking, and he feels tiredness start to settle into his bones. "But we have nowhere else to turn."

Meren entwines his fingers with Jerath's, and Jerath struggles not to look as surprised as he feels. Meren's hand is warm and strong and Jerath grips it like a lifeline.

"I'll do my best to convince my father to help you." Meren strokes the back of Jerath's hand and looks very much as though he wants to lean in and give Jerath a kiss, but he just sighs and looks away.

"I think I'm going to go to bed." Serim ducks out from under Jerath's arm and gets to her feet. Jerath goes to follow her, but Serim smiles softly and shakes her head. She looks between Jerath and Meren and gives Jerath a wink. "Why don't you stay here? I'd like some time alone, if that's okay?"

Jerath knows what she's trying to do, but he's worried about her. He gets up anyway, giving her a fierce hug, and she laughs against his shoulder.

"I'm okay, really, Jerath." She whispers it into his chest so only he can hear. "But I wouldn't mind some time to myself, and by the looks of things, Meren would like some alone time with you." She tilts her head back and looks him in the eyes. "I won't be too upset if I get the bed all to myself tonight."

Judging from the muffled laughter behind him, Serim wasn't being as quiet as she thought she was, and Jerath groans as he leans down and kisses her forehead.

"Sorry." She giggles and Jerath knows that it was totally intentional on her part.

"Good night, Serim." He sits back down and narrows his eyes at her, but she just shrugs as though she doesn't know what he's mad at.

She says good night to Meren and Torek and walks over to her tent.

"Well." Torek stands and rubs his hands together. "As much as I'd like to sit here and force you two to make polite conversation for the next hour or so, I have things to prepare for our journey home tomorrow." He grins at Jerath as he turns to leave. "Make sure he doesn't keep you up too late, we have to be awake early in the morning."

Jerath can't help but blush at that, and Torek laughs loudly as he makes his way over to join the rest of the men by the fire. He watches Torek laugh and joke with the others for a moment or two before looking over at Meren.

Meren is staring at him, and Jerath can't decipher the look on his face. "Everything okay?" he asks when Meren doesn't say anything. "You're very quiet."

Meren swallows and licks his lips. "Would you like to spend the night with me, Jerath?"

Oh.

Jerath fidgets, his hands twisting together as he lets the question sink in. He wants to. Meren is everything he likes. He's tall and strong, but not overly big—Jerath has never been a fan of huge muscles—but Jerath still hesitates. He doesn't know whether it's his lack of experience or something else, but the silence is stretching out between them and quickly becoming uncomfortable.

"Jerath?" Meren's hand settles on Jerath's leg. It's high enough to make Jerath shiver, a lick of heat traveling straight to his groin. "We don't have to do anything." Jerath knows he must look confused because Meren laughs and squeezes his thigh. "I want to, believe me. I *really* do. But I… I just want you in my bed. We have two more nights before we get to my village and who knows what will happen then."

Meren slides his hand farther up Jerath's leg, his thumb rubbing just shy of Jerath's groin. "Please."

Jerath's indecision slips away with every stroke of Meren's thumb. He feels his body react; his heart rate picks up and his cock starts to fill, half-hard already. "Yes." It comes out as barely more than a whisper, but it's enough.

Meren leans forward and brushes his lips against Jerath's in a kiss that's far too chaste for Jerath's liking, but Meren is up on his feet before Jerath can protest or try to deepen it. He offers Jerath a hand up, and when their fingers meet the heat of his touch seeps through Jerath's skin and warms him deep inside.

"Come on." Meren smiles and leads Jerath to a smallish tent on the outskirts of the camp.

It's not as comfortable inside as the one Meren gave up for Jerath and Serim; there's just a bed of furs and blankets in the corner, but that's all they really need. Meren stops in the middle of the tent and turns to face him. Jerath's heart pounds as Meren steps closer, his hands coming up to cup Jerath's cheeks.

This is different from earlier by the stream. They could have been discovered any moment there, but here, in the privacy of Meren's tent, they won't be disturbed and they can take as much time as they like. Jerath swallows down his nerves and shuts his eyes as Meren's mouth closes over his.

It's a soft kiss, unhurried and lazy, and Jerath relaxes into it with a sigh. Meren shuffles a little closer until the hard length of his body is flush against Jerath's, and Jerath feels every solid inch of him. He walks Jerath backward toward the makeshift bed as his fingers trail down Jerath's back and slip underneath the bottom of his shirt.

Meren breaks the kiss and pulls back. "Let's go to bed."

Jerath can see fairly well in the dark since he gained the ability to shift—not as well as in his feline form, but better than when he was human. He takes in Meren's face, eyes dark and heavy lidded, lips slightly swollen. Meren's breathing is faster than normal and Jerath smiles because he did that. He feels the burst of confidence in his chest and steps back to tug off his shirt. Meren stares at him hungrily, reaching for his own shirt, and pretty soon they're both standing there naked.

A gust of wind lifts the tent flap, and they both shiver as the cold air swirls over and around their exposed skins. It breaks the tension between them and they laugh, scrambling to get underneath the furs before it happens again.

"Fuck, that was cold!" Meren pulls the fur up to his chin and shivers again.

Jerath instinctively wraps an arm around Meren's shoulders and draws him in. He pulls him tight against his side, like he's done so many times with Serim, only registering what he's done when he feels Meren's hard length against his hip. Jerath stills, not knowing what to do next. But Meren obviously does and he slides a hand over Jerath's stomach and kisses the side of his neck.

Meren moves his hand lower and strokes teasing patterns over Jerath's sensitive skin, and Jerath moans. He watches intently as Meren licks at his chest, tonguing his nipples until they ache.

Jerath bites his lip as Meren pushes the furs aside and moves down his body. He feels the sharp sting of Meren's teeth as they nip at the taut skin of Jerath's hip, followed by the wet heat of his tongue as he licks over the mark afterward. Jerath writhes under Meren's touch. It's too much and not enough all at the same time, and he moans loudly when Meren's warm breath washes over his cock.

Jerath has only ever done this once, with Serim, and then he was half out of his mind with sex berries. He wants to feel Meren's mouth on him so badly and he pushes his hips up, needing more.

Meren laughs softly at Jerath's frustrated sigh. "Are you always this impatient?" His tongue dips agonizingly close to the head of Jerath's cock, and Jerath answers without thinking.

"It's just… I've never done this… with a man."

Meren tenses and looks up at him with a curious expression. Jerath shifts his hips and tries to coax Meren's head back down, but Meren shuffles back up the bed until he's lying alongside Jerath again. Jerath stares at the top of the tent and wishes he'd kept his mouth shut.

"Jerath?" Meren takes hold of Jerath's chin and forces his head up so their eyes meet. "I don't understand. I thought you preferred men?"

"I do, but…." Jerath sighs again and closes his eyes. "But my village is not as accepting as yours and there's not a lot of options open for someone like me. The opportunities for any type of sex are limited." Meren's hand returns to its place on Jerath's stomach and strokes soothing circles over his skin. "I haven't done much more than kissing… and hands. Apart from with Serim, during my Choosing.

Jerath wonders if he's said too much, if Meren will be put off by his inexperience, and he feels his earlier confidence fading fast.

"Hey." Meren leans in and kisses him. He licks into Jerath's mouth, and it's wet and dirty and not at all what Jerath was expecting. "I'm going to show you what it's like with a man, Jerath." He kisses along Jerath's jaw and down across his throat. "I'm going to show you everything."

Jerath cries out when Meren's lips finally wrap around his cock. His fingers fist in the furs beneath them, and Meren sucks him deep into his throat over and over and it feels so good. Meren's tongue slides up the underside of Jerath's length. He laps at the precome leaking out at the tip and Jerath whimpers, his hips lifting clear off the bed.

Jerath's orgasm starts to build low in his belly. It curls up and around his spine and as Meren takes him deep into his throat again, Jerath is vaguely aware of his claws extending. The ripple of power flows through him as his jaguar stirs just below the surface. When Meren swallows around him, Jerath sinks his claws into the fur and growls out his release.

Jerath's heavy breathing fills the air around them and he lies back on the furs and grins. He can't help it, and when Meren finishes licking him clean he crawls back up Jerath's body, looking rather smug.

"Fuck." Jerath pulls Meren in for a kiss. He can taste himself in Meren's mouth, and it makes him feel dirty in the best of ways. He chases the flavor with his tongue and Meren moans, rutting against Jerath's hip and smearing wetness over the skin there. Meren is hard and Jerath wants to touch him, to feel the weight of him in his hand.

"Can I?" Jerath asks. He starts to slide a hand between them but Meren grabs his wrist.

The sting of rejection hits him hard and Jerath starts to pull away, but Meren just smiles and shakes his head.

"No, Jerath. It's not that I don't want you to, but look…." He lifts Jerath's hand and shows him his fingers—with all five claws still extended and glinting sharply in the dark. "I'd just rather you got rid of these first."

Jerath immediately licks over his teeth to check for elongated fangs, but they're smooth and normal sized. He doubts Meren would've kissed him so hard if they'd still been there. He looks at his hands, unsure as to why his claws are still out. He concentrates on willing them away, but his heart is still pounding from his orgasm and he can't seem to get them to retract. He looks up helplessly at Meren. "I can't do it… I… sorry."

"It's okay." Meren smirks wickedly before kneeling and straddling Jerath's hips. "You can watch, this time."

Meren takes hold of his cock and starts to stroke up and down its length. His long fingers wrap around it in a tight fist, and Jerath's eyes track the movement of Meren's hand as it slides back and forth. It's one of the hottest things Jerath has ever seen—Meren staring down at him and biting his lip while he brings himself off. Jerath inhales deeply and draws Meren's scent into his lungs. It's a heady mix of sweat and sex and *man*, and Jerath wants it to soak into his skin and drown in it. He can feel his animal instincts flaring up, the urge to mark and *be marked* flowing thickly through his body.

Meren's breath catches, his rhythm stuttering to a stop as his whole body tenses. Jerath is powerless to stop the low growl that rumbles out of his chest as Meren throws his head back and comes, thick and wet, over Jerath's stomach.

Jerath barely gives Meren time to finish before he's flipping him over and pressing their bodies together. He keeps his hands away from Meren's skin; his claws are still out and dangerous, and Jerath buries them in the deep furs again. Meren's release is all over both of them now, and Jerath shuffles down until he can lick at the mess on Meren's stomach.

He's not fully aware of what he's doing. The sudden need to taste, to claim, pushes him on and Jerath just lets it happen. He doesn't know if this is normal or not; he and Serim haven't talked about sex since his Choosing, but he's definitely going to ask her about this later. For now, though, he concentrates on getting every last trace of it with his tongue.

Finally, Jerath sits back on his knees and wipes his mouth. His own skin is still sticky and he idly rubs it in with his fingers. His claws have finally gone back in, and Jerath lets out a deep, contented sigh and looks up to find Meren staring at him with wide eyes.

Oh.

Jerath might not be sure whether that was normal behavior for shifters, but from the look on Meren's face, it's probably not normal behavior for humans. He swallows and struggles to find something to say.

"Sorry?" he offers, wondering just when his inexperience is going to stop ruining everything. "I guess that's not normal. I… I don't…."

"Jerath." Meren reaches up and tugs him back down until Jerath is lying on top of him again and then kisses him. It's soft and gentle, and Jerath feels the tension bleed away with each sweep of Meren's tongue. "It's okay to lose control." Meren runs his hands up Jerath's back and Jerath resists purring at the touch, but only just. "I like it."

"Really?" Jerath pulls back and looks Meren in the eye. "Even with the licking and the… um… rest of it?"

Meren grins up at him. "Especially the licking."

Jerath laughs and feels lighter and happier than he has in a long time. But almost straightaway he feels a sudden, sharp stab of guilt. He shouldn't be able to feel like this with everything that's happened to his village.

"Hey?" Meren's soft voice draws him out of his thoughts. "What's wrong?"

Jerath sighs and closes his eyes for a moment. Images of Mahli, his mother, and the men that were taken flit through his mind. "I shouldn't be this happy when my people are still in danger."

Meren takes him firmly by the shoulders and Jerath's eyes fly open. "It's okay to find a little comfort, Jerath. You and Serim are doing all you can to help your village, there's no cause to feel guilty." He kisses Jerath once, a chaste brush of lips, and then pulls him down onto his chest. "Tomorrow, we start the journey back to my home. I promised you that I'd do everything I could to convince my father to help you. And I meant it."

"Thank you." Jerath pulls the covers up, settles against him, and closes his eyes again. He's asleep within moments with the warmth of Meren's arms wrapped tightly around him.

CHAPTER 9

JERATH wakes early again the next morning. Meren is still fast asleep beside him, and since Jerath can't hear anything outside the tent, he assumes the rest of the camp is still asleep too. He listens hard, trying to pick out Serim's heartbeat from all the others. It takes him a few minutes, but eventually he narrows down the familiar thump, slightly faster and louder than all the rest. She's awake and prowling around. Jerath is almost certain she's in her animal form and he itches to join her.

He tries to slip out from underneath the furs without disturbing Meren, but as soon as he replaces the covers, Meren's eyes flutter open and he strains to see Jerath in the dim light.

"Where are you going?" Meren's voice sounds thick with sleep and Jerath smiles. He reaches out and rubs his thumb across Meren's bottom lip.

"To run with Serim. I need to burn off some energy." He flexes his shoulders and hands as if to emphasize the point, and Meren manages a lazy, sleepy grin.

"I could help you burn off some energy." He looks Jerath over from head to toe, his eyes suddenly dark and wide awake. "Much more fun than running."

Jerath laughs and is sorely tempted to climb back under the furs, but he needs to talk to Serim before they do anything like that again. "As appealing as that sounds, I need to see Serim."

"Okay." Meren just smiles, and Jerath gets the feeling Meren knows exactly why Jerath wants to see her. "Be careful."

Jerath nods, letting his mind delve deep inside for his animal form, and feels the now-familiar feeling wash over him. He stretches out his back and his legs, swishes his tail about and shakes his head. It's still new and exciting to be able to do this, to feel the raw power that bunches in his muscles and hums through his veins.

Meren stretches out his hand from under the fur covers, and Jerath saunters over and rubs against it. He licks between Meren's fingers, tickling at his skin, and Meren laughs, snatching his hand back and wiping it on the fur.

"Ugh, Jerath. That's disgusting." Meren grins, so Jerath figures he doesn't really mean it.

He moves a little closer and takes Meren by surprise with a long lick along the side of Meren's neck. Jerath nuzzles up against him and rubs his scent all over Meren's skin, grumbling with satisfaction as their combined smell fills the air.

Meren buries his hands in Jerath's thick fur. He runs his fingers through it, and Jerath contemplates jumping onto the bed so Meren can pet him more easily, but he hears Serim's impatient growl just outside the tent. He gives Meren one last lick, snaps playfully at his fingers when Meren swats at his nose, and leaves the tent to join Serim.

SERIM bumps Jerath with her shoulder, casually sniffing at him, and her whiskers twitch with the feline equivalent of a smile. He knows she's going to tease him mercilessly when they shift back, but for now he just nudges her in return and enjoys the peace and quiet.

They leave the tents behind, stretching their legs as they leisurely bound about through the grass. The sun will be up soon, the sky already shot through with bursts of light, and Jerath loves this time of the day. The air is crisp and fresh, filling his lungs and blowing against his fur. It makes him feel alive.

They run back toward the camp, but Jerath veers off in the direction of the stream. Serim follows and they both shift back and step into the water.

"Oh, that's cold!" Serim shivers violently as she dips down to wash herself.

Jerath laughs at her for a moment, before his expression turns more serious. "I need to ask you something." He turns and ducks his head so she doesn't see him blush. "About sex."

"Is this about you and Meren?"

He looks up and meets her eyes. There's no hint of laughter or teasing in her face and Jerath could hug her for that. "Yes."

"Did something happen, Jerath?"

He gives her a brief explanation, skimping on the details until he gets to the bit about being unable to retract his claws and everything that followed. Serim, to her credit, manages to keep her reaction down to a smirk and a raised eyebrow, but when he gets to the end she's all serious again. In fact, she looks far more serious than Jerath was expecting, and he gets a bad feeling in the pit of his stomach. "What is it?"

"Jerath—" she starts, and then stops. She motions for him to follow her and leaves the water to go sit on the grassy bank. "A reaction like that, Jerath, only happens when we find a match." She pauses a moment for that to sink in, and Jerath struggles to understand what it means exactly.

"But Meren isn't female or even a shifter. How is that possible?" He wades out of the water and sits down beside her.

"I don't know." She reaches out and grasps his hand. "Have you…?"

He knows why she's asking. Serim wants to know if he and Meren have had full sex, because if they were both shifters that act alone would complete the bond, if they were matched. He's also pretty sure there's some biting involved, as there is in the Choosing. This has happened before in one of Jerath's neighboring villages, where they're more relaxed than his own in their beliefs. But the elders of Eladir heavily discourage same-sex matches because they see them as a waste; no children can come of them.

"No. Not yet."

"I don't know what will happen if you do, Jerath. But you can't risk it."

Jerath stands and turns away from her. "We don't know that *anything* will happen."

"But it could." She pulls on his hand and he reluctantly turns to face her. "If you do this, Jerath, and the magic works, you'll become a mated pair. There'll be no one else for you. Ever." She sighs and pulls him back down onto the bank. "Meren comes from the Southern lands, Jerath. He will never leave his home, and neither will you. Does he even know?"

"Of course he doesn't," Jerath snaps and immediately regrets it when Serim shrinks back. "I'm sorry. But how could Meren know, when this is the first I've heard of it? He probably wouldn't want it, Serim, so I don't think there's any cause to worry. Last night was just…."

"What?" She looks at him expectantly, but he doesn't know what answer to give when he's not exactly sure himself.

"I don't know. But I don't think it meant that he wants me forever. We've only just met!" He looks down at the ground, not wanting to face her any longer.

A heavy silence falls between them, and the faint sounds of the camp stirring to life start to filter down to them.

Serim sighs. "We'd better get back; it'll be time to leave soon. But, Jerath?" He meets her eyes. "You need to tell Meren. It's not fair to carry on with whatever this is between you unless he knows what could happen."

Jerath nods. He doesn't want to tell Meren about any of it. He's almost sure that as soon as he mentions *mates* and *bonds*, Meren will run away as fast as possible. Jerath spent so many months longing for the ability to shift, but now he wishes it could have waited just one more month so he wouldn't have this problem.

He lets his jaguar form take over and pads after Serim's panther back into camp.

THERE'S a flurry of activity when they arrive. The tents are being packed away and loaded onto big carts. Jerath and Serim hurry into their tent to get changed so the men can take it down. Meren is nowhere to be found, and neither is Torek, so Serim and Jerath help out where they can to disassemble the camp.

They're ready to leave in just under two hours. They use horses to pull the carts, so Jerath and Serim refrain from shifting for fear of spooking them. The horses have been kept out at the back of the camp, so they've managed to avoid them thus far.

Jerath hasn't seen Meren since this morning and he's starting to wonder if something's wrong. The men are waiting to go and the horses are getting restless.

"Serim," Jerath whispers. He edges closer to her so they won't be overheard. "Have you seen Meren or Torek today?"

"No," she whispers back. "And when I asked some of the men about it, they refused to answer."

Jerath doesn't know what to say to that. He has no idea where they could possibly have gone, but none of the men seem worried about it. Before Jerath can discuss it further, Torek and Meren appear, walking up from the direction of the stream.

Meren's forearm is heavily bandaged and Jerath rushes to meet him halfway. Meren grins when he sees him and Jerath's stomach does an odd little flutter.

"I was worried." Jerath reaches for Meren's bandaged arm to inspect the damage. It's dotted with red where the blood has seeped through, but Jerath can smell that it's already stopped bleeding and started to clot. "What happened?"

Meren gently pulls his arm back and smiles ruefully. "Would you believe Torek did it?"

Jerath turns and growls at Torek, his instincts taking over.

"Hey, it was an accident!" Torek backs up with his hands raised and Jerath snarls at him. All he can think is that Torek hurt his potential mate and he's filled with the need to protect. His body vibrates with the urge to shift.

"Jerath?" Meren steps in between them, his hand coming up and cupping Jerath's cheek. "It's okay. It really was just an accident." He rubs his thumb over Jerath's skin and moves closer until they're only a couple of inches apart. "Jerath?"

Jerath concentrates on Meren's face, on the feel of his hands, and the tension slowly starts to fade. He takes a shaky breath and closes his eyes. "I'm sorry." He covers Meren's hand with his own and links their fingers. "I don't know what happened… I…."

"It's okay, Jerath." Meren leans in and kisses him. "We'll talk about it later. We need to get moving if we're going to make it to my village by tomorrow night." The kiss takes Jerath totally by surprise. He didn't think Meren would be so open about them, and he's still standing there staring after Meren as he walks over to his men and starts barking orders.

It's only when Torek clears his throat that Jerath realizes he's still there.

"I caught him with the edge of my knife while we were taking down the tents. Then we went to wash and dress it by the stream and scout ahead for a mile or so. That's all." He looks Jerath in the eye as he speaks, and Jerath has no reason not to trust him.

Jerath can't believe he acted that way toward Torek. He's never started a fight before in his life, but his instincts took over and he's almost certain he would have attacked Torek if Meren hadn't calmed him down. Jerath swallows thickly and holds out his hand to Torek. "I'm sorry, Torek."

Torek steps forward and takes it. "I may not know much about shifters, Jerath, but I do know how protective they get where their mates are concerned." He raises an eyebrow and Jerath looks at him, wide-eyed. "But Meren doesn't. You need to tell him what's going on, before someone gets hurt."

Jerath wants to ask what Torek knows, and how Meren will react when he finds out, but he's scared of the answer. So he just nods and hurries away to find Serim.

JERATH and Serim walk at the back of the group, away from the horses, as they travel south across the plains. Jerath tells her all about what happened with Torek, and she agrees that he needs to talk to Meren as soon as possible.

He manages to avoid Meren all day while they travel, but as soon as they camp for the night, he knows it's only a matter of time before Meren and Torek join them by the fire. He sits next to Serim as they eat, but Jerath can barely stomach any of the food. He's full of nervous energy and can barely sit still.

"Jerath," Serim hisses. "Calm down."

"I can't." He turns to face her and lowers his voice even more. "How do you think he's going to react when I tell him he's my mate and I want to bond with him for life, Serim?" He puts his plate on the ground and runs his hands through his hair. "I've spent one night with him. One night! He's going to laugh and tell me to go away."

"Is that what you really believe?" she says. "Meren doesn't strike me as being that heartless, Jerath. I think you're doing him an injustice."

"Maybe I am. But you can't honestly tell me that he's going to be okay with it all, can you?"

Serim has never lied to him, and although her next words aren't really what he wants to hear, he's grateful she doesn't lie now. "No, Jerath. I can't tell you how he's going to react. But you need to tell him and let him decide. Not decide for him."

They see Meren and Torek approaching and Serim stands, giving Jerath a pointed look as she does. She brushes the crumbs from her clothes. "I think I'm going to go to bed, it's been a long day." She leans back down to give Jerath a quick hug and a kiss and whispers that she loves him. "Good night, Meren, Torek."

They say their good nights and Serim disappears into her tent. Jerath fidgets, only half listening to Torek and Meren as they discuss tomorrow's journey and what route they're going to take. According to Torek, they should reach their village midafternoon, as long as none of the bridges are out.

He catches Jerath listening and turns to explain. "It took us an extra two days to get home after the last hunt."

"The rivers run high this time of year." Meren continues the story. "They flow all the way down from the mountains, and as the snow melts, the rivers rise. One of them broke its banks last time and the bridge collapsed. We had to double back and find another place to cross. There was a heavy rainfall before we left, so we're going to head for the narrower crossing to start with. It'll take a little longer, but there's less chance of the bridge being gone."

Jerath nods, but doesn't add to the conversation. He has no idea how to get back to their village, so he's reliant on their decisions anyway. And all he can think about at the moment is how to explain to Meren about the bond in such a way that he won't run a mile in the opposite direction.

"I'm going to turn in for the night too." Torek gets to his feet and gathers all of the discarded plates. "I believe you two have things to discuss anyway." He throws a pointed look in Jerath's direction, and Jerath's stomach roils at the thought. The food he just ate is suddenly in real danger of coming back up.

They watch Torek walk away, and then Meren shifts his position so he's now facing Jerath. "Are you ready to tell me what happened earlier, with Torek?"

Jerath sighs and scrubs his hand over his eyes. He doesn't quite know how to start, doesn't know enough about the whole thing himself, let alone how to explain it to a nonshifter. Even Serim doesn't know everything this time.

If he'd gone through the Choosing at his village, like he was supposed to, all this would have been explained by the village elders. He would have been taken aside the day after the ritual and taught all he needed to know by those who had already been through it.

But now, as he sits here and looks at Meren's expectant face, he knows he has to find a way to make Meren understand. That it's instinctual for Jerath, he didn't plan it, and it's not something he can control either. He swallows thickly and meets Meren's curious gaze.

"How much do you know about shifters, Meren?"

"A little more than I did, after talking with you and Serim. But not much really." He scoots a little closer to Jerath so their knees are touching. "I know there are three villages, all closely connected, and that your tattoos depict your shifted form, but that's about it." He scratches the back of his neck as he struggles to think of something else. "Oh, and you have to be mated to someone with a matching tattoo, I think?" He looks to Jerath for confirmation.

"Yes, that's what our village elders believe."

"But?"

Jerath sighs again. There's no easy way to say this, so he just needs to come out with it.

"I don't know how this is even possible, but the reason I almost attacked Torek is because I thought he'd harmed you. I thought he'd harmed my mate."

Meren opens his mouth, then closes it again. He stares at Jerath for so long that Jerath starts to feel uncomfortable and he stares at the ground, picking at the grass while he waits for Meren to speak.

"I don't understand, Jerath." When Meren finally says something, his voice is soft and he sounds as confused as Jerath feels. "We've only spent one night together—not that it wasn't great," Meren adds with a smile. "But I'm not even a shifter…." He drops his head into his hands. "What does all this mean, then?"

"I'm not sure exactly."

Meren's head snaps up and he looks at Jerath with a raised eyebrow.

"I've only been able to shift for three days, Meren. I don't know why I see you as a potential mate, or how it even works with nonshifters." Jerath pauses to catch his breath. His hands have curled into fists at his sides and he forces them to relax. "I just know that I have this urge to protect you, to keep you safe and…."

"And?"

"And mark you as mine," Jerath finishes and feels the blush creep over his skin.

"Is that what all the licking was about?"

"Yeah. I think so." Jerath wants to reach out and link his fingers with Meren's, but he's not sure if the move will be welcome now. He makes do with brushing his knuckles along the back of Meren's fingers. "There's more."

"Go on." Meren pulls both his hands back into his lap and Jerath feels the absence like an ache in his bones.

"Shifters mate for life, Meren. If the bond is formed, then it's forever." He glances up, but Meren isn't looking at him. "For me, anyway."

"What about me?"

"I don't know. I'm not sure this has ever happened before, or if it has, then no one ever talks about it. I don't think it would be the same for you, though."

Meren is quiet again and Jerath waits as patiently as he can. It's a lot to take in and he understands that Meren needs time to process it all, but Jerath hates the growing silence between them. Having Meren so close and not being able to touch him, especially with all the talk of mates and bonds, is torture.

"You said *if* the bond is formed. Does that mean it isn't already?" Meren's voice is stronger this time and he's looking straight at Jerath now.

"No, it's just a potential bond for now." Jerath can sense what's coming next. He sees the question forming in Meren's mind and doesn't bother waiting for him to ask it. "It would only be permanent if I…." He pauses as the words stick in his throat. "If I… fuck you and… um… mark you as mine. I'd also…." Jerath swallows down his embarrassment. "I think I'd probably have to bite you, and you'd possibly have to bite me too." He's not exactly certain about that last part, but when he looks at the juncture between Meren's neck and shoulder, he feels the urge to sink his teeth into the soft flesh.

Meren blows out a breath and jumps to his feet. "Wow, Jerath… that's… *fuck*." He paces back and forth in front of Jerath, hands jammed in his hair.

"It was a shock for me too. I didn't plan this, I didn't know it would happen." Jerath says desperately. "You do believe me, don't you?"

Meren stops and drops his hands to his hips. "Yeah, I believe you." He squats in front of Jerath and places his hands tentatively on Jerath's knees. "It's not that the idea isn't appealing, Jerath. Because I really like you. It's just…." He closes his eyes for a moment before carrying on. "Mates and forever… it's a little more than I was expecting. My father is the leader of our village, Jerath, and there are certain expectations." He lets that sink in, and Jerath feels reality come crashing in around him.

What was he thinking? "Of course." Meren would be expected to marry a girl and raise children to follow after him. He would be chief someday and would never be allowed to have a male shifter for a mate. Jerath draws in a shaky breath and studies the grass again, anything to keep from meeting Meren's eyes. Last night was just a bit of harmless fun, and Jerath needs to accept it and move on. At least the bond was never fully formed.

"Hey?" Strong fingers tilt Jerath's jaw and force him to look up. "It's not what you think, Jerath." Meren's thumb idly strokes along his skin, and Jerath can't help but lean into the touch. "If we did this, if we formed a bond between us, then I wouldn't ever want to be apart from you. I think it'd be the same for you too, yes?"

Jerath nods, not sure where Meren is going with this. "Yeah, it would, I guess."

"Well, I can't leave my home, Jerath, and I don't think I would ever want to. Just like you could never leave yours." Meren's hand slides down and rests on the side of Jerath's neck. It's warm and solid and Jerath wants it to stay there, but Meren is already pulling back. "And I would never ask you to."

Meren sighs and it sounds like *good-bye* and *this is over*, and Jerath's heart sinks into the pit of his stomach. A partly formed bond is painful enough when broken. Jerath is just glad they didn't go any further last night.

"I'm sorry," Meren whispers, and then he's gone—back to his tent, where Jerath definitely isn't welcome tonight.

He's not sure how long he sits there, but by the time he realizes he's cold, Jerath is all alone. The rest of the men have retired to their tents and the whole camp is silent. Jerath shivers as the wind whips over his skin and tugs at his clothes. He doesn't want to go back to Serim's tent. He can't face telling her what happened or the sympathetic looks that she'll give him.

He shouldn't feel like this. He's only just met Meren, but his shifter instincts have latched on and convinced the rest of him that Meren is his mate, and his heart is already heavily invested.

The fire still burns, not as fiercely as before, but it will still offer some warmth. Jerath sheds his clothes quickly and sinks into his animal form, pulling it round him like a blanket.

He pads around the fire on silent feet and settles nearby, close enough to feel the heat but still keeping a safe distance. He lays his head on his paws and watches the flames. Jerath doesn't expect to fall asleep, but it's been a long day and soon enough his eyes drift closed.

CHAPTER 10

"JERATH?"

"Jerath, wake up." There's a hand stroking through the fur on the back of his neck, and Jerath's first thought as he slowly wakes up is that it's Meren and he pushes up into it.

But then he realizes that the voice is all wrong, and when he finally opens his eyes, it's Serim he sees peering down at him. He doesn't have to tell her what happened. He's sure she can sense the dejection rolling off him in waves.

She rubs behind his ears. "Oh, Jerath. Why didn't you come and find me last night?" Jerath closes his eyes and just enjoys her touch. "Come on," Serim continues. "You need to shift back and get something to eat before we head out again." She walks over and picks up his clothes and heads back to their tent. Jerath dutifully follows close behind.

They only see Meren and Torek briefly before the men are ready to move out. It's a little awkward. Torek gives Jerath a small smile and Meren is polite, but it's a far cry from the way he greeted Jerath yesterday. It hurts, but Jerath returns the smiles and pleasantries and acts as though he's fine. The sooner they get the help they need, the sooner they can get back to their home.

Jerath sighs. He can't wait to see his mother and Mahli and Kinis, and to make sure they're all safe, but he won't find a mate there, either. Not a male one anyway.

Jerath and Serim travel at the back of the hunting party again, keeping out of the way and to themselves. Jerath is eternally grateful that Serim doesn't try to talk to him about it. It's pretty obvious that Meren was not onboard with the whole bonding-for-life idea—not that Jerath can blame him—so there's nothing really to say on the subject.

It's late afternoon by the time they reach the river that separates the plains from the Southern lands. The bridge they're going to cross spans the narrowest crossing point, and according to what Torek told him yesterday, it's about an hour's journey from Chastil.

Meren calls them all to a halt and walks back through his men, talking to each group in turn. Jerath shifted into his jaguar form about five miles back. He pads along at Serim's side, his senses alert for any trouble. When Meren gets to Serim and Jerath, he lifts his hand as though he's going to stroke along Jerath's back, but he catches himself in time and crosses his hands behind him. Jerath lets out a low whine and swishes his tail, but it's Serim's hand that reaches out to soothe him.

Meren talks to Serim but his gaze remains on Jerath. "The bridge is still up, but the water level is higher than I was expecting. We need to be careful. I'm not sure how stable the ends are."

Serim nods her understanding and Meren returns to the front.

The horses pulling the stored meat and the camp supplies are led across first—one at a time—and everyone holds their breaths until all the wagons are safely across. The rest of the men start to walk over and the bridge sways and wobbles, but holds firm. Only Serim and Jerath are left to cross.

Jerath growls low in his chest as they approach the bridge. He prowls along the edge of the bank, looking at where the bridge is secured by heavy ropes and timber. It's wider than Jerath was expecting, about ten feet across and thirty feet long. It looks sturdy enough, but something makes Jerath's hackles rise.

Serim ruffles his fur and steps onto the bridge. "Come on, Jerath. If it can hold the horses and all that meat, it can definitely hold us." She starts to walk across and he has no option but to follow.

The men stand around chatting over on the other bank, only a couple of them watching their progress. They're about halfway across the bridge when Jerath notices Torek and Meren talking animatedly at the far end. Torek points at the ropes, then back to the water and shakes his head. There's a faint sound, a low-level hiss and whine, and Meren's eyes snap up to meet Jerath's.

"Run!" Meren steps forward, but Torek immediately pulls him back. "The rope's unraveling! Run!" His words are followed by the sickening sound of rope snapping, and the bridge trembles under them.

Jerath roars, shoving Serim with his shoulder until she starts to run. He bounds along beside her and reaches the other side in three easy strides. He only realizes he's overtaken her when he sees she's not there with him.

"Jerath!" She screams his name, and then everything falls apart.

He whirls around in time to see one side of the bridge drop down by about a foot, and the wide, wooden slats tilt at a crazy angle. Serim struggles to stay upright, but the bridge sways dangerously in the wind. She loses her balance and tumbles over the edge toward the swirling river below.

Jerath charges after her, his claws scratching for purchase in the wood as he skids to a halt where she went over. She's hanging on with one hand, but her fingers are slipping and the terrified look on her face makes Jerath's blood run cold. He can't help her in this form; he needs his hands to grab her and pull her up. It's dangerous to shift like this, but Jerath has no choice. He hooks his claws over the upper edge of the wood, hopes his fingers will be able to catch hold of it when he's human, and shifts.

It's disorienting for the first few moments, as Jerath struggles to get his bearings, but then his hand closes around the wood and he hangs on tight, ignoring the splinters that tear into his fingers.

"Jerath… hurry!" Serim's panicked voice calls from below. Jerath clings to the slanting wooden panels as he inches his way down toward her.

He wedges his hand as far as it'll go in the gap between two of the slats, wraps his arm around the wide panel and holds on for dear life as he slowly extends his hand down to Serim. "Grab it and pull yourself up." Serim is strong, and Jerath is eternally grateful for all the chores they're made to do back home because she needs every bit of that strength as she grabs his hand and hauls herself up his body and onto the bridge.

"Get to the bank; I'll be right behind you." He watches her scramble back over to Meren and Torek, sighing in relief as they pull her onto the bank. He hooks his other arm over the panels and is just about to climb back up when he hears another snap of rope and the whole right side of the bridge falls away, jolting Jerath hard. He loses his grip on the wood and is helpless to stop himself from sliding into the turbulent waters below.

Jerath gasps in shock as he hits the cold water and desperately pulls in a lungful of air before the current drags him under. He struggles to find the surface again. His muscles are stronger since he went through the Choosing, but it still takes everything he has to break free of the water. It rushes into his lungs as he's dragged under again.

He kicks hard for the surface, making one last attempt to get the water out and some badly needed air in. As his head just about clears the water, he's vaguely aware of someone screaming his name, a raw and desperate sound, and he thinks it's Serim, but he's never heard her voice sound like that before. Jerath slips back under, his arms and legs burn with the effort to keep from drowning. He tries to think of a way to get out of this, because there's no way he's going to die here, so far from home with so much of his life ahead of him. He's just about to shift—jaguars are good at swimming and he might stand a better chance despite the risks involved in doing it like this—when he's pulled back sharply as strong arms wrap around his body and crush him against a warm, firm chest.

Jerath holds on tight as he's dragged backward through the water and up onto the grassy bank of the river. He collapses against the body underneath him, gasping and coughing as he tries to breathe and expel water at the same time.

"Jerath! Jerath!" He hears Serim shouting moments before he's covered in hugs and kisses. He lets her gently roll him off his rescuer and onto his side, coughing up more water as she frantically checks him over for any injuries. "I was so scared," she sobs into his shoulder, and Jerath just about manages to reach up and stroke her hair.

When he's finally gotten all the water out of his lungs, Jerath gingerly sits up and bats halfheartedly at Serim's hands as she tries to help him. “I’m okay, Serim.” He pulls her in for a fierce hug before turning to thank whoever pulled him out.

He gets as far as saying, “Thank y—” before Meren has his hands on Jerath’s face and pulls him into a kiss that leaves him breathless all over again.

Meren rests his forehead against Jerath’s. “Fuck… Jerath. I thought we’d lost you.” Jerath pulls back to look at him and sees that Meren has his eyes closed as he speaks, and Jerath watches the way he trembles with each word. “You disappeared under the water and I… *fuck*.”

Jerath puts his hands on Meren’s waist and feels the thick rope still tied around him. “You pulled me out?”

Meren lets out a breathy laugh. “I just jumped in after you.” He waves a hand behind him. “My men pulled us both out.”

When Jerath looks up, there’s a group of men watching them curiously from a few feet away. He smiles gratefully and thanks them for saving his life, before returning his attention to Meren.

“Thank you for saving me.” He tries again, and this time Meren just stares at him and runs his thumb across Jerath’s bottom lip. “But I don’t understand….” He reaches up and takes hold of Meren’s hand. He hopes he won’t have to explain that he doesn’t understand the kissing and the touching after what happened last night, hopes Meren will just know.

“When I saw you fall into the water….” Meren stops and swallows. “I felt… I felt like a piece of me was being ripped apart. The thought of losing you physically hurt, Jerath. I don’t understand it either, but at the moment I don’t really care.” He takes another deep breath and twines his fingers with Jerath’s. “I still don’t think we should bond, Jerath. There are too many reasons why that wouldn’t work. But we can just have this.” He gestures between the two of them. “For now. If you want to, that is.”

Jerath stares at him for a long time. He knows this is a bad idea. It was hard enough to be apart from Meren when they’d only had one night together. Even if they don’t do everything to satisfy the bond, Jerath thinks it will be just as bad when he eventually has to leave. He can feel the magic under his skin already, reaching out to wrap around

Meren and tie Jerath to him. He knows it's probably the worst decision he's ever made, but he lets the smile spread across his face. "Yeah." He pulls Meren closer and kisses him. "I want to."

THEY stay by the river for about an hour or so, judging by the sun's position, while everyone recovers from Jerath's rescue. It's an hour they weren't expecting to waste, and it's nearly dusk by the time they reach Meren's village. Jerath is more exhausted than he's ever been, the events from earlier starting to take their toll, and he leans on Serim while they wait for Meren and Torek to go and see Meren's father.

They've been left to freshen up in Torek's home, a small but well-kept house on the outskirts of the village. Jerath wishes he had enough energy to appreciate the beauty of Chastil, because he's sure it's just as lovely as Meren described, but he's so tired. He and Serim wash up as best they can and then collapse onto two of the chairs around Torek's kitchen table.

"Are you okay?" Serim runs her fingers through Jerath's hair and he rests his head on her shoulder.

"Yes, just really tired. I think I could sleep for a week."

Serim laughs, but pulls him tighter against her. "Don't ever do that to me again, Jerath." She whispers it into his hair and he can hear the tremble in her voice. "Promise me."

"I'll do my best." He stands up and presses a kiss to her forehead. "It's not something I want to repeat anytime soon." He grins and she must feel it because her fingers dig into his ribs, making him yelp.

"So." Serim looks up at him and smirks. "You and Meren, then?"

Jerath blushes and ducks his head, but he can't hide the huge smile that spreads across his face. "Yeah."

"So he's okay with the bonding?"

"No, he still doesn't want that." Jerath refuses to think about that part, though. He has him for now and that's something he never thought he'd get, so he'll take what he can.

"But, Jerath—"

"It's fine, Serim. It's what I want."

She looks as though she wants to say more, but Jerath gives her his best "Please, I don't want to talk about it" look, and she lets it drop. But Jerath isn't stupid enough to think she'll let it go entirely.

They sit in silence for a while until Jerath gets tired of waiting.

"They've been gone awhile." He walks over to one of the windows and peers out, but the area outside is strangely deserted. "Do you think everything's okay?"

Serim joins him at the window. "I don't know. It's far too quiet out there, Jerath. I don't like it."

Jerath shares Serim's unease. Something just doesn't feel right. "Come on." He walks over to the door and eases it open. "Let's go find out."

They hug the sides of buildings as they head to what they hope is the center of the village. Jerath isn't exactly sure when they decided to hide, but his unease is growing and the unfamiliar surroundings only add to it.

There's movement up ahead as Jerath peeks round the side of a seemingly empty building. They haven't seen a single person so far, and Jerath's senses are on high alert. He pulls Serim back against his chest as she leans out to have a look. "Careful," he whispers.

They watch as the men get closer and closer, until Jerath can finally make out their faces. His blood runs cold at the sight, and he growls low and vicious as he recognizes the strangers they saw coming out of the barn in Eladir. The same people who helped kidnap Kyr and Ghaneth and countless others.

"*Jerath.*" Serim snarls his name as she recognizes them too. "Meren is with them."

He scans through the men until he sees Meren. For a moment Jerath is terrified that they've raided his village too and are holding him captive, but Meren is smiling and laughing, and Jerath feels the bile rise up his throat as he struggles not to be sick.

"We need to go. Now!" Serim is already stripping so she can shift as Jerath just stares at the group of men, unable to tear his gaze away. He can't believe he felt the magic of the mating bond for someone who… who…. Jerath struggles to accept that Meren knew all this time. That everything since they met him has been a lie. He thinks about their night together, his stomach churns, and he doubles over and retches.

There's a low rumble from beside him and Serim's black panther nudges his legs. Her tail swishes furiously and her eyes flash. Her whole body is screaming, *Come on.*

Jerath rips his clothes off, not caring if they're ruined, and shifts. He spares one last glance for Meren—his heart shattering as he watches them all together—and then bounds after Serim and out of the village.

CHAPTER 11

THEY run for what seems like hours, but Jerath knows it's only been a fraction of that time before Serim suddenly stops and turns to face him. She immediately shifts and Jerath reluctantly does the same. He feels horribly exposed like this, but it's obvious that Serim wants to talk.

She's chosen a good spot; they're in the middle of a small group of trees, which is rare out on the plains, and Jerath follows her as she climbs up the nearest one to hide in the safety of its branches. It's cold now that they're human again and the bark is rough against Jerath's skin, but in light of what has just happened, he hardly feels it. He doesn't feel much apart from a growing numbness spreading out from his chest.

"What just happened, Jerath? What were those men doing in Meren's village?" Serim's voice comes out urgent and desperate. Jerath wishes he could reassure her, tell her they must have misunderstood and that they should go back, but he just can't.

"I don't know." He rests his head against the thick trunk and sighs. "But you saw them, Serim. They looked comfortable with each other, they weren't strangers. Which can only mean…?" He doesn't want to finish that sentence, doesn't want to say it out loud.

"That they're from Meren's village," Serim finishes for him. She reaches out and takes his hand. "Meren's father… you don't think he's…?"

Jerath hadn't wanted to think about that at all, but now that Serim's brought it up he can see the resemblance between Meren and the older man he was talking to, and the familiar way they interacted. "Yeah… I do."

They don't speak again for a while. The silence stretches between them as they struggle to accept their new circumstances. Jerath had been so happy just a few hours ago. He still had the issue of the bond to deal with, but Meren had wanted to spend time with him and take what they could get while they had the chance. He'd also thought they were about to find a way to help the people of his village. And now? Now it's all fallen apart. Now they're alone again, in a foreign land, and Jerath doesn't think he'll trust anyone new ever again.

"I just don't understand," Serim muses. Her hand is still wrapped in Jerath's, and her head now rests on his shoulder. "Any of it." She moves slightly until she's looking up at him. "I mean, why go to all that trouble to be our friends and…." She doesn't add *lovers*, but she might as well have. "There are only two of us, Jerath. They could have killed us or captured us at any point after we entered their camp."

Jerath doesn't understand either. His mind is stuck replaying every kiss and touch he and Meren shared. He runs them over and over and tries to see the falseness in Meren's actions or the insincerity of his words, but he just can't. Jerath is well aware how inexperienced he is in certain areas, but he always thought he was a good judge of character.

"I know, Serim. None of it makes any sense." He tucks her head into his shoulder and holds her tight—as much for his benefit as hers. "But I know what I saw. What other explanation is there?"

Her only answer is to wrap her arms around him and sigh. Because there is no other explanation. The men who were at Jerath's village are Meren's people, probably led by his father and…. Jerath suddenly sits bolt upright and shakes Serim in the process, nearly knocking her out of the tree.

"Jerath?" she hisses and clings to him for dear life. "What the—"

"What if they're at the village?" She looks up at him in confusion. "Ghaneth and the others? Do you think they've got them back at the village?" He can't believe he didn't think of it earlier. If Meren's father is one of the armed men he and Serim saw at their village before they ran away, it stands to reason the raiders would be from here as well.

Serim's eyes go wide as saucers, flashing blue in the dark as her panther stirs beneath the surface. "Do you think they could be?" Jerath nods and she grips his arms while her body trembles as she fights the urge to shift. "May the Goddess forgive us, Jerath! We just left them." Her nails are now the sharp claws of her cat and they dig into Jerath's skin, but he barely notices them.

"We need to go back." He feels the guilt swirl deep and menacing in his gut. He's ashamed they didn't spare a thought for their people and just ran away to save themselves. "Now."

Serim's grip tightens and this time Jerath does wince but she doesn't let go. "We need a plan, Jerath. We can't just rush in there, no matter how much we might want to." He slumps back against the tree, and Serim relaxes her grip but still keeps her hand on his arm. "There are only two of us."

"We have to do something, we can't just—"

"I know that!" She looks hurt and angry and Jerath immediately apologizes. He should know better; Serim would never leave her people, especially Ghaneth.

"What do we do, then?"

THEY spend the next hour going through idea after idea, but each one seems just as dangerous and foolhardy as the next. They have no idea where Ghaneth and the others are being held, if they're heavily guarded, or if they're hurt. They've avoided thinking about the alternative—as far as Serim and Jerath are concerned, they're all still alive until they see otherwise.

Jerath has his eyes closed, listening to Serim talk through yet another plan of attack, when his spine prickles in warning. He sits up and raises his finger to his lips. It's dark still, only the light of the moon illuminating their bodies, but Serim has no trouble seeing him and stops talking midsentence. Jerath cocks his head to the side and listens. The night is full of noises, nocturnal animals and insects going about their business, but Jerath's listening for something else.

He's just about to accept that he imagined it when he hears it again. It's faint, a way off in the distance still, but he can definitely hear voices. He looks over at Serim. Her face is a mixture of fierce determination and rage and he knows she hears it too.

"They're looking for us," Jerath whispers.

"Let them." Serim's voice is hard and cold, and the look on her face is one Jerath has never seen before.

They both look toward the sound of the voices. Their eyes strain to see in the darkness, and after a few moments, Jerath is able to make out the faint glimmer of torches. They obviously aren't taking any care to be stealthy. Either they don't see him and Serim as a threat or they're just plain stupid. Meren doesn't strike him as being stupid.

They watch and wait as the group gets closer and closer. "What do we do?" Serim's voice is barely a whisper against Jerath's shoulder.

He knows they should attack—they have the element of surprise—but what if it's Meren? He's still Jerath's mate. *Potential mate who betrayed me*, he reminds himself. But the feelings are still there, making Jerath both angry and hurt at the same time. "We wait."

He needs to see it for himself, up close and personal, so there's no trace of doubt in his mind. Serim doesn't answer. She's tense and ready for action, but Jerath senses she's as conflicted as he is.

As the torches get nearer, the voices ring out clearly in the night air. Jerath recognizes Meren and Torek among them as they call out their names, over and over. He feels the familiar tug in his belly. The need to go to Meren is still there. Jerath ignores it.

But then they hear a voice that's impossible to ignore. It rings out clear and beautiful, and Jerath almost loses his balance at the sound of it. His breath catches in his throat and he hears Serim gasp next to him. That's impossible.

"Jerath," Serim whispers. "That was—"

"I know."

Mahli.

She calls out again, telling them it's all right. That everything's okay and "will you please come back because I've fucking missed you and it's too cold to be running about in the plains at night."

Jerath snorts, he can't help it, it's such a *Mahli* thing to say.

Serim looks as though she's about to jump down any moment and reveal their position and he knows just how she feels, but Mahli could be a prisoner too for all they know. He pulls her against his chest and tells her to wait just a little longer.

As the group approaches the trees, Jerath recognizes a few others from his village. They're all walking together, no sign that they're being held against their wills, and Jerath is beyond confused. He glances down at Serim and she shrugs and shakes her head.

"Serim, Jerath?" Mahli calls out into the night, and it's so good to hear her voice after all this time. Jerath's eyes fill with tears. He's missed her so much. Serim sniffles and he squeezes her shoulder in silent support.

"Whatever made you run away, it's not what you think." She pauses about twenty feet from their tree and they get a good look at her for the first time. She's dressed in unfamiliar clothes and has a bow slung over her shoulder, just like Meren and Torek's. Her blonde hair is wild about her face, but she looks… like Mahli. There's no fear in her face. If anything, she looks exasperated as she calls their names again, and Jerath almost wants to laugh at the whole situation. "I've been working with Meren's father, Malek. He and his people want to help us. We know where Ghaneth, Kyr, and all the others are being held, and we're going to get them back."

Jerath wants to believe her, wants to believe Meren and Torek didn't betray them and that it was all just a terrible misunderstanding. He wants it so badly he can almost taste it. But something holds him back from jumping down to meet them.

"Oh for the love of our Goddess!" Mahli shouts and throws her hands in the air. "I know you're around here somewhere. I'm cold and tired and if you two don't come out right this minute, I swear I will shift and hunt you down. And it won't be pretty when I find you!"

Serim is out of his arms before he can stop her. She drops down to the ground with feline grace and barely a sound, but Mahli spins around and screams her name. She grabs two bundles from one of the men and runs toward Serim, then drops them on the ground at her feet.

They hug and laugh and Jerath smiles at their tearful reunion, but he's still reluctant to join them.

He looks back at the approaching group of men and finds Meren almost immediately. He's looking around, searching vainly in the dark, and Jerath's heartbeat falters. Meren is searching for *him*. He can see the look of disappointment when Meren can't find him, and Jerath's hand tightens on the branch beside him.

Mahli eventually pulls back from Serim and wipes at her eyes. "Here." She reaches down and grabs one of the bundles. She holds it out and Serim takes it, untying it carefully to reveal several items of clothing. "We found yours, and the tattered remains of Jerath's, earlier. I brought you both some new ones."

Serim smiles and quickly puts them on.

"Where's Jerath?" Mahli finally asks as Serim gets dressed.

Serim looks at the ground and sighs, but shakes her head. "I can't say." Mahli starts to speak but Serim cuts her off. "He's hurting, Mahli. Give him time."

Jerath feels a fierce burst of love for her as she stands in front of everyone and refuses to give him up, even when she thinks it's the right thing to do. Mahli's shoulders slump and she turns back to Meren and shakes her head.

Jerath watches Meren, unable to look away. He turns to speak to Torek, who squeezes his shoulder, then walks toward Serim and Mahli. Meren's close now, and Jerath wants to reach out and touch him, but he just can't do it.

"Hey, Serim." Meren's voice is soft and uncertain and it sounds so wrong coming from him. "I don't understand what happened."

Serim's shoulders tense and she bristles. "Well, that makes two of us, Meren."

"I left you in Torek's house to go get my father, and when I got back you were both gone." He looks around again and scratches the back of his neck. "What happened?"

"We saw you coming back and…." She stops and clenches her fists, and her chest rises and falls as she attempts to calm down. "The men with you were the same ones who attacked our village."

"What?" Both Mahli and Meren speak at once.

Serim looks at Mahli then, pointing a finger at her as if she's only just remembered. "What are you even doing with them, Mahli?"

Mahli puts a hand on Meren's arm to stop him from whatever he's about to say. "I've got this." She looks at Serim and gently takes both Serim's hands in hers. "Serim, Meren's father and his men came to warn us about the raiders." Her voice cracks, and Jerath wants to pull her into his arms. It must have been twice as awful to have watched them actually being taken. "But they were just a few hours too late."

"Why didn't they go after them then?" Serim snaps.

"Because there weren't enough of them on their own and we still had wounded to tend to!" Mahli shouts angrily, and Jerath flinches at her tone.

"Wounded?" Serim chokes out the words. "Did anyone…?"

"No." Mahli's expression softens. "No one died. But Serim, you need to trust me when I tell you that Malek only wants to help. He and his men are going to take us to get them all back."

Serim looks over at Meren and offers him a tentative smile.

"Just come to the village and we'll explain everything in the morning." Meren smiles back when Serim nods. "What about Jerath? I don't want to leave him out here on his own, but…." Meren sounds defeated, and Jerath has had enough of hiding.

He jumps onto the ground and slowly straightens up to meet Meren's eyes. The initial flash of relief he sees there is soon replaced by hurt and confusion. Jerath swallows thickly as he realizes he's not the only one who feels as though he's been betrayed.

Mahli picks up the second bundle and throws it at him. She waits for him to get dressed before jumping into his arms, and Jerath stumbles back a bit at the force of her hug. She slaps him hard and shouts at him for hiding, but it's mixed in with tears and laughter as she tells him how good it is to see him.

They break apart when Meren clears his throat.

Jerath takes a hesitant step toward him. "Meren, I—"

"Let's get back. It's late," Meren cuts him off with a harsh look.

"Meren… *please*. I'm sorry. I didn't know what to think…."

Meren just shakes his head, then turns on his heel without another word and walks over to join the rest of his men.

"Come on." Mahli follows and pulls Serim and Jerath along with her. "We'll sort out this mess in the morning." She leads them back over to the group of men, where they greet Caleb and a couple of others. Jerath hasn't seen Caleb since that day at the barn with Kyr, and it's so good to see another familiar face. They talk quietly between themselves as they start the long walk back to the village, but Jerath only half listens. He wants to know what happened, of course he does, but he can't concentrate on anything when Meren is so close but ignoring him completely.

Serim notices and nudges him gently. "It'll all work out, Jerath. You two just need to talk to each other, on your own."

Jerath looks at the determined set of Meren's shoulders as he marches on ahead and prays Serim is right.

MAHLI and the rest of the people from Eladir are staying in a group of tents at the far end of the village. There's a fire in the middle—just like Meren's camp when they were out hunting—and Jerath feels a pang of longing.

It's too dark to really see much of their surroundings, but judging from the length of time it took to walk from one end to the other, Meren's village is a lot bigger than he was expecting. Apart from Caleb, there are ten others who have made the journey south and they are all now congregated around the fire. Jerath doesn't know the rest of them all that well, so he sticks by Serim, Caleb, and Mahli.

It was Torek who got them settled in their tents; Meren left them as soon as they arrived back, with a nod and a curt good night. Jerath understands Meren has every right to be angry. It seems to be a huge misunderstanding, mainly on Jerath's part, but Meren won't even give him the chance to explain.

He says as much to Serim, and she then points out that they didn't give Meren a chance to explain either, and Jerath is back to feeling guilty again. The whole thing is giving him a pounding headache, and he just wants to crawl into bed.

He's not exactly clear on everything that's happened since he and Serim left to go fishing, what seems like a lifetime ago, but he's too tired to discuss anything further tonight. Someone has hastily erected an extra tent for him and Serim to share, and Jerath is initially beyond grateful, as the last thing he feels like is being alone tonight. But when he looks over at Serim and Mahli together, chatting animatedly and still with the odd burst of laughter or tears, he knows Mahli needs her more than he does.

"Serim?" He walks over to them and plasters on his best smile. "I'm going to bed. Why don't you sleep in Mahli's tent tonight? I'm sure you've got lots to catch up on."

Serim immediately starts to protest, but Jerath puts his fingers over her mouth. "It's fine, honestly." She looks at him intently for a few awkward moments, and Jerath tries to look as sincere as possible. She must like what she sees, because she beams up at him and whispers, "Thank you," as she hugs him good night.

He gives Mahli a hug too, holds on to her for a moment longer than he normally would, and takes the opportunity to breathe her in.

"I missed you two so much," she whispers into his chest. "I thought they'd taken you too."

Jerath pulls back but doesn't let go of her. "We missed you too." He beams at her, big and wide and it's no effort at all this time.

"Jerath!" Mahli squeals and points at his mouth. "When did you get your fangs and why didn't you tell me?"

He glances at Serim and she grins at him in return. "That's nothing." He lifts off his shirt and turns his back to Mahli and laughs at the shocked noise she makes when she sees his tattoo. He lets her look for a moment longer before he puts his shirt back on and turns to face her.

She looks between him and Serim with narrowed, knowing eyes. "I want to know everything!"

"I think I'll leave that to Serim." Jerath laughs at Mahli's protests and heads off toward his tent. He has no wish to be part of that conversation.

He's almost there when Torek appears out of the shadows. "I know you had your reasons, Jerath. But your lack of trust hurt Meren a great deal."

Jerath stops and turns to face him. He fully expects Torek to be angry as well, but he just looks tired and a little sad. "I need to talk to him, Torek."

"Yes, you do. But he's very stubborn." He shakes his head and smiles ruefully. "According to Serim, you two are very similar in nature."

"I'm not stubborn." Jerath will be having words with Serim in the morning.

Torek laughs and reaches up to pat Jerath on the shoulder. "I'll work on him tonight, Jerath."

"Thank you."

"Don't thank me yet—he's not in the best of moods right now."

Jerath watches Torek leave and then enters his tent.

DESPITE being as tired as he is, it takes Jerath a long time to fall asleep. He tosses and turns. The magic of his bond feels unsettled and antsy while he and Meren are on such bad terms. Eventually, exhaustion wins out and Jerath finally stills underneath the fur bedding.

He has no idea how long he's been out when he hears the faint rustling of someone entering the tent. His senses are aware even when sleeping, and his eyes snap open at the sound. His vision adjusts to the dark almost straightaway but it takes him a moment longer to register who's standing at the foot of his bed.

"Meren?"

"Shh…." He puts his finger to his lips and steps closer. "Torek said we needed to talk."

Jerath takes a moment to catch up. His brain is sleep-muddled and he's still processing Meren's words when he speaks again.

"I shouldn't have come. It's the middle of the night. I just… I needed to…." He looks down at the ground and shuffles his feet. "Yeah… okay. I'm going—"

"Wait." Jerath sits up in bed and the furs pool around his waist. His skin is pale and luminous in the dark. He has no idea how well Meren can actually see, but Jerath doesn't miss the way Meren's gaze flicks down to his chest. "We do need to talk." Jerath gestures to the end of his bed, and Meren hesitates before walking forward and sitting down.

Meren looks uncomfortable, his body tensed as if he's going to jump up and leave at any moment. Jerath knows this isn't going to be easy, but he feels the magic thrum through his veins as the bond settles in Meren's presence, and he knows he has to fix things between them. He studiously ignores the fact that after all this is over, they'll be separating for good. Although it won't be complete, the potential bond will be strong enough to make it incredibly hard for Jerath to leave. But he's willing to face that problem when it happens, because he might never have this again.

Meren stares at him, and Jerath realizes he's waiting for Jerath to start speaking.

"I'm sorry I didn't trust you enough to stay." Jerath holds up a hand when Meren starts to interrupt. "There was a very good reason why we ran, Meren." Jerath closes his eyes for a moment and takes a deep breath. "At least we thought so at the time."

Meren raises an eyebrow, but remains silent.

So Jerath tells him. He explains that the men he and Serim saw in Eladir were in fact Meren's father and some of his men. He tells Meren how they thought the men were with the raiders who took his people prisoner, and that when they saw them here, with Meren, they panicked and fled.

"We didn't know what to think, Meren." Jerath itches to reach out and touch him, but he keeps his hands firmly planted in his lap. "We saw your father and our first instinct was to run away. Do you understand?" Jerath's heart beats furiously. He's said all he can. Now it's up to Meren.

The silence is heavy between them as Jerath waits for him to say something.

"You should have trusted me, Jerath." His voice is soft, but Jerath hears all the hurt behind his words. "I know you haven't known me long, but I thought with the"—Meren waves his hand between them—"bond and everything, mutual trust was implied."

Jerath doesn't quite know what to say, because Meren's right. When shifters bond, the trust between them is complete and unwavering. "Yes, that's true for bonded pairs. But we haven't completed our bond, Meren."

Meren just nods as though he expected that. "I still thought you trusted me, though." He rubs a hand over his eyes, and when he drops it back down, Jerath flinches at the expression on his face. "I trusted *you* enough to believe everything you told me. I brought you to my village to talk with my father, Jerath."

Jerath hangs his head, unable to meet Meren's eyes, because all of that's true. They took Jerath and Serim into their camp, with just their word for what had happened. But a small part of him still feels he had every right to be wary when he first saw Meren and his father.

"I know you did," Jerath answers. "And Serim and I can't thank you enough. But when we saw you and your father together, it seemed like you'd just bought us back here to add to your prisoners." He sighs heavily. "I'm eighteen years old, Meren. This is the first time I've been away from my home, and my judgment may be lacking in certain areas. We thought we were the only hope left for our village, so I think we had every right to be cautious."

Jerath is breathing hard by the time he finishes speaking. He's all worked up and angry, and when he looks down his claws are out and buried deep in the fur blankets.

"Hey." Meren's hands cover his and slowly ease them out of their death grip on the blankets. He's careful not to touch Jerath's claws, just smoothes his thumbs across the back of Jerath's hands until his breathing slows down to a normal pace. "I think you've made your point."

When Jerath's fingers are human again, Meren links their hands. "I'm sorry for the way I behaved when we found you. I was hurt, Jerath." He sighs, and Jerath watches the tension seep out with his exhale. "I couldn't understand why you didn't trust me enough to stay. Especially after… what we'd done. But I understand now." He tugs on Jerath's hand until they're much closer. "You were just protecting your people."

Meren leans forward and tentatively presses his lips against Jerath's, as though checking that he's still allowed to do this. Jerath moans in answer and slides his free hand around the back of Meren's neck so he's left in no doubt. He pulls Meren closer still and slowly leans back until he's lying flat on the bed with Meren on top of him.

"I missed this," Meren mumbles between kisses. He pulls back and strokes along the edge of Jerath's jaw. "When you left… I don't really know how to explain it, but there was something missing. From me."

Jerath can't answer; the words catch in his throat because Meren shouldn't feel any of that. The growing bond between them is definitely the cause for his feelings of separation, but Meren's not a shifter. It shouldn't affect him like that at all.

"When we found Serim"—Meren carries on speaking when Jerath remains silent—"I couldn't see you anywhere, but I had this feeling that you were close."

"It's the bond," Jerath whispers. He rests his hands on Meren's hips, keeping him close.

"How?"

"I don't know." Jerath's mind races as he struggles to think of anything that might explain it, but he can't. "I just…." Meren dips down and mouths along his throat, and Jerath tilts his head, his eyes falling shut as Meren bites and licks at his skin.

"I don't care why it's happening," Meren says. His warm breath tickles over the dampness left by his tongue, and Jerath shudders. "Feels so much better now." He stops touching Jerath long enough to sit up and take his shirt off and goes to carry on, but Jerath stops him with a hand on his chest.

"Everything," Jerath whispers.

Meren pauses, and Jerath tugs on his breeches to show him what he means. Meren grins and hurries to comply. It's cool in the tent, and Jerath pulls back the fur covers, ushering Meren inside as soon as he's naked.

Jerath gasps as Meren's cold body brushes up against him.

"I'm sorry," Meren murmurs, but Jerath hears the smile in his voice. "You're just so warm." Meren slides a hand around Jerath's waist, hooks a leg over one of Jerath's, and nuzzles into the crook of his neck.

Meren's lying half on top of Jerath now, and Jerath feels the hard line of Meren's cock as it presses into his hip. He eagerly slides his hand up Meren's thigh, higher and higher until his thumb brushes the coarse hair of Meren's groin. Jerath didn't get to touch Meren last time they were together. His claws came out as his body struggled with the shift, but he's determined to control it this time. He moves his hand a little farther and wraps his fingers around Meren's length. The skin is soft under his fingertips, and Jerath strokes lazily up and down.

Meren moans. He leans up on his elbow, and when he looks down into Jerath's eyes, Jerath knows he should stop this. They're getting dangerously close to the bond becoming permanent. It's already starting to affect them when they're apart, and he fears it'll get worse the more intimate they are with each other. But then Meren kisses him. His warm, wet tongue pushes into Jerath's mouth and the magic hums between them, flowing through the kiss, and Jerath doesn't have the strength to stop.

"Like this." Meren kisses the words into Jerath's skin. He takes Jerath's hands in both of his and lifts them above Jerath's head so he can move fully on top of him. They rut against each other in a delicious slide, and Jerath bites his lip in an effort to keep quiet.

Meren shifts slightly so Jerath isn't supporting all his weight, and rests on his forearms. He slowly rolls his hips; they're both slick with precome and Jerath can feel it on his belly, sticky and warm. He reaches for Meren and pulls him down into a kiss. It gets a little messy as their rhythm falters, and Jerath struggles to keep his mind on the kissing as Meren reaches between them and takes them both in his hand.

His long fingers glide easily up and down, and it only takes a few strokes before Jerath arches his back and comes with a muffled cry against Meren's shoulder. He holds on tight as Meren fucks into his own hand. The urge to bite him is almost overwhelming, and Jerath feels his teeth elongate, the sharp tips brushing along his bottom lip.

Meren stutters above him as he climaxes, and Jerath turns his head to the side to avoid the temptation of Meren's throat. He breathes in deeply and tries to calm himself down, but the scent of sex hangs heavy in the air, and Jerath hisses as his claws extend into the blankets once again.

Meren must sense his distress and lifts up to plant soothing kisses along his jaw. "Hey… it's okay, Jerath." He cards his fingers through Jerath's hair and scratches at his scalp. "It's okay." He leans down to the floor of the tent and grabs something to wipe away the mess. Jerath hopes it's nothing of his because his available clothing is extremely limited at the moment.

When they're as clean as they're going to get, Meren throws the article of ruined clothing to the far side of the tent and settles back down beside Jerath. The scent isn't as strong now, and Jerath begins to relax, his teeth and claws disappearing with each deep breath.

"It's going to be worse," Jerath says into the darkness, unable to help himself. "When we have to part after all this is finished." He turns to face Meren and finds dark eyes looking back at him. "If we keep doing this, it's going to hurt so much more."

Meren doesn't say anything. He just places his fingers over Jerath's mouth, and Jerath doesn't need him to speak to understand: *Don't say any more*. Then Meren pulls him close. *I know.*

CHAPTER 12

WHEN Jerath wakes the next morning, he stretches out his hand and frowns when he feels an empty space next to him. He sits up and rubs the sleep from his eyes just as the tent flap rustles and Meren ducks back inside.

"Morning." Meren's smile is infectious and Jerath grins back at him. "Come and get something to eat, we've got a lot of planning to do today." Meren passes him his clothes and watches as Jerath throws back the furs and dresses quickly. "My father and the others are waiting for us by the fire."

Jerath swallows thickly. When he originally thought about asking Meren's father for help, he wasn't involved in a potential bonding with his son and heir. "Um… Meren?" Jerath leans down and pulls on his boots. "Have you… does your father know about us?"

Meren's smile falters a little but doesn't disappear completely. "I haven't told him." Jerath sighs and slumps back on the bed. "I just didn't see the point in bringing it up, since we'll be parting ways after this is finished."

Oh, of course.

Jerath understands, he does, and he knows it's the only option for them. It just hurts to hear it. "Shall we go?" he asks instead.

"Jerath—"

"No, it's fine." Jerath stops and takes a deep breath before pulling Meren into a fierce kiss. "I understand."

They take a moment to just breathe each other in, and Jerath fists his hands in Meren's shirt. He wants to rescue his people more than anything, but at the same time he wants to drag out the time he and Meren have together. Things are moving far too quickly and Jerath feels it all slipping away. He steps back and manages a small smile. "Come on, then."

Meren looks as though he wants to say something, and Jerath raises his eyebrow expectantly, but Meren just shakes his head and leads the way out of the tent.

THERE'S a roaring fire going in the middle of the temporary camp, even though it's the middle of the morning, and another huge roast is turning slowly over the flames. Jerath scans the faces gathered around the fire, and he tenses when his gaze lands on the older-looking man at the center.

He's dressed like Meren, and Jerath sees the strong family resemblance—the same build and blond hair, except for a touch of gray around his temples. "I assume that's your father, then?" Jerath gestures over to where the man is sitting, and Meren smiles.

"Yes. Let me introduce you." He strides purposefully over to him, and Jerath swallows his apprehension and follows after.

"Father." Meren places a hand on his father's shoulder in greeting. "This is Jerath."

He doesn't say anything more than that, and Jerath gets the distinct feeling that this isn't the first time they've talked about him. Jerath resists the urge to fidget as Meren's father turns to face him fully and looks him over before speaking.

"Good to finally meet you, Jerath." He stresses the word *finally*, but Jerath is grateful when he doesn't bring up anything about them running off. "Won't you join us?" He points to the empty space beside him, and both Jerath and Meren sink to the ground, accepting the plates of meat, bread, and fruit that come their way.

Jerath glances around as he eats, and catches both Serim and Mahli smiling at him from the other side of the fire. They look far too knowing and happy, so he deliberately shrugs as if to say, "What?" Serim shoots him her *Really, Jerath?* expression back. She pointedly looks between him and Meren and waggles her eyebrows. Jerath sees Mahli wink at him, and he's unable to stop the blush that covers his cheeks. He sometimes wonders why he has them as friends.

Jerath's still glaring at the two of them when Meren nudges him in the side, and he suddenly realizes Meren's father has asked him a question. "I'm sorry, sir, what was that?"

"I was just saying that your mothers asked me to keep a lookout for you both. I only wish I could let Helan and Kinis know that you two are safe."

Jerath startles a little at that. "You know my mother?"

"I knew your father too." He reaches out and clasps Jerath's bicep. "He was a good man."

Jerath blinks furiously as his eyes tear at the unexpected mention of his father. It may have been five years since his death, but the pain is still as raw as it ever was. "Is she okay?" Jerath manages eventually. His voice sounds a little rough, but at least he keeps the tears at bay.

"Yes, worried about you, but otherwise unharmed."

Jerath feels the barest touch of fingers against the back of his hand as Meren offers him what comfort he can. It's enough. The warm touch radiates throughout Jerath's body and eases the tightness settled in his chest. He flashes Meren a small, grateful smile and finishes off the rest of his food.

As soon as everyone's finished eating, Malek—as he insists Jerath call him—calls for quiet, and they start to plan the rescue of Jerath's people.

Malek explains again, for the benefit of Serim and Jerath, that there were rumors concerning one of the southern villages. Some suggested they were heading to raid the northern lands for shifters, in order to sell them as slaves. Others suggested the raiders wanted to use them as some sort of sacrifice. Whatever the reason, it was wrong and Malek took a small group of his men to try to warn Eladir and the other villages. But they were hours too late.

Jerath knew most of this from talking to Mahli, but he hadn't realized they were after shifters specifically. He clears his throat and everyone turns to look at him. "Not all those taken have the ability to shift." A feeling of dread settles in the pit of his stomach. He doesn't want to think of what might happen if and when the raiders discover this.

Malek nods, his expression grave. "Which is why we need to act as soon as possible."

"Do we know where they are?" Jerath asks. He can feel his jaguar lurking under his skin, wanting to get out and avenge his fellow shifters. He quickly glances down at his fingertips, and lets out a relieved breath to see that they're still clawless.

"Yes." Caleb cuts in, and Jerath senses his animal is just as desperate to be let out. In fact, as he looks around at the other shifters, they all look tense and eager for action. "We tracked them to a village three hours west of here."

Jerath is about to ask what they're waiting for and why they haven't rescued them already, but Caleb speaks again as if he can tell what Jerath's thinking.

"There were too many of them for us to attack, Jerath. We needed to wait for Meren and the hunting party to get back first. The plan is to attack at dawn tomorrow."

Malek stands and walks among everyone as he talks. There are as many women as men seated around the fire, all dressed in breeches and tight tunics, and Jerath wonders how many of them will be going in the morning. "They're seasoned fighters," Malek says. "And there are a lot of them." He looks over at Meren. "It won't be easy, and there are bound to be casualties on both sides, but we will get them back."

Jerath listens to them talk and plan and wonders, not for the first time, why Meren's father has agreed to help them. He could very well lose some of his people in the fight, and although Jerath is beyond grateful for all their help, he doesn't really understand why they've offered.

Malek is in deep discussion with Caleb and some of the other shifters, and so Jerath takes the opportunity to ask Meren. "Why is your father doing all this?" he whispers.

Meren turns to look at him and frowns. "What do you mean?"

"Why is he helping us when it could get some of your people killed?"

"Because it's the right thing to do, Jerath. And you asked for our help." He sighs and scratches at the back of his neck. "I'm not really sure of all the details, but I think our villages made some sort of agreement five years ago. But regardless of that, we would have helped you anyway."

"Thank you." Jerath wants to touch him, so very badly, but he slips his hands under his thighs instead. Meren nods and smiles. His gaze flicks to Jerath's mouth, and for a split second Jerath thinks he's going to lean forward and kiss him, but then Meren abruptly stands up and smoothes out his clothes.

He gives Jerath a rueful smile. "I'm going to go and sort out some things for tomorrow, before I give everyone here something to talk about."

Jerath watches him walk over to his father, who is now speaking with his own men. The shifters are off to one side, talking among themselves. Everyone looks on edge as they prepare for battle, and as Jerath looks around at the assembled people, he can't help but wonder who might not make it back tomorrow. It's a horrible thought.

Jerath swallows and chances a glance over at Serim. She looks fiercely determined as she grips Mahli's hand and listens to Caleb talk. His stomach churns with the realization that it could be any of them.

THEY talked strategy for most of the morning and well into the afternoon. The shifters will all be in their animal forms—they're more dangerous that way—and will each accompany a group of Malek's people. Jerath is with Meren and a group of ten others, some of them from the hunting party. They've been over their roles again and again, until everyone knows exactly what they need to do.

Serim is with Torek, and Jerath is relieved she's with someone they know and trust. Mahli seems to be happy with her group too, so Jerath just has to believe she'll be okay. He can't afford to think otherwise.

They need to be up before the sun tomorrow, so as soon as the sky begins to darken, people start to leave the fire to try to get some sleep. Jerath suspects it will be a restless night for all of them.

"We're going back to the tent to rest." Serim bumps him with her shoulder as she and Mahli stand up. "We'll see you in a few hours."

Jerath is up and has them both wrapped in his arms before Serim finishes speaking. They hug him back just as hard. "Promise me you'll be careful tomorrow." He whispers it into Serim's hair, but loud enough for Mahli to hear too.

"Same goes for you, Jerath." Mahli squeezes him tight. "I don't want to have to tell your mother that I let you get hurt."

Jerath laughs and some of the tension leaves his body. He drops his arms and steps back a little. "See you in the morning."

He watches them head toward their tent and then looks around to see if he can spot Meren. He sees him talking to his father and Torek. Jerath doesn't want to interrupt them. He can't say what he needs to in front of them anyway, so he sits back down and waits for them to finish.

Eventually Meren catches his eye and smiles. Jerath tracks his movements as he turns back to talk to his father, pats him on the arm, and walks over to where Jerath sits waiting for him.

"Hey." He nudges Jerath's boot with his foot. "Waiting for me?"

Jerath smiles up at him. "Yes."

Meren glances back over at his father and Torek. "Give me a moment to collect what I need for tomorrow, and then I'll come to your tent. Is that okay?"

"Yeah." Jerath stands up and they just look at each other. His fingers twitch with the urge to pull Meren closer, so he makes it easier on both of them and walks away.

JERATH'S not exactly sure how long he's been waiting for Meren, but it seems like ages. He paces across the small floor space in the tent, unable to think of anything but what might happen tomorrow. He's never had to fight before. He's only hunted small animals as his jaguar; never *people*.

He's not ashamed to admit that he's scared, and not just for himself either. He can't bear the idea of anything happening to Serim or Mahli, or any of them for that matter. And then there's Meren.

If Meren is hurt or… Jerath can't even think the word. If he's injured at all, Jerath will kill whoever is responsible. He feels it deep in his bones, the need to protect is so strong. He won't want to let Meren out of his sight for even a moment. Jerath also knows if they're successful tomorrow, then he'll be heading back to Eladir. And that's what scares him most of all.

There's a noise outside his tent, and Jerath turns to see what it is just as Meren ducks inside. Jerath's on him before he even takes two steps forward. He fists his hands in Meren's shirt and pulls him into a kiss. It's hard and desperate. All Jerath's fears about tomorrow pour into it as he clings to this moment as long as possible.

All too soon, Jerath has to stop because his lungs are burning. He breaks the kiss and rests his forehead against Meren's.

"What's wrong?" Meren cups Jerath's face and strokes along the edge of his jaw. "Not that I object to being greeted like that, but…."

"I just…." Jerath draws in a deep, shuddering breath. "It's going to be dangerous tomorrow. People could get hurt. *You* might get hurt. I can't… if anything happened… I…." Jerath buries his head in Meren's neck.

Strong hands rub up and down his spine, and Jerath tries to calm himself.

"It's going to be okay," Meren murmurs against his hair.

"You don't know that."

"I'll have you there to protect me, what could possibly go wrong?" Meren's tone is light as he attempts to ease the tension, and Jerath's head snaps up to glare at him.

"Don't joke about this, Meren. I need you to promise that you'll be careful and not get hurt, because it would kill me if anything happened to you." The words sound strange as they come out, and Jerath licks over his teeth to feel the sharp edges of his elongated fangs.

His claws press into Meren's clothing and he quickly snatches his hands away.

"Hey." Meren reaches for him, but Jerath backs away.

"It's the bond." Jerath feels it pulsing around him, urging him to take, to claim. If they complete the bond, Jerath will be calmer and stronger and better able to protect Meren tomorrow, but he refuses to say any of this. Meren made his feelings clear.

"It's okay." Meren moves closer and Jerath lets him. The magic hums contentedly as Meren's arms wrap around him and hold him close. "It's okay. I feel it too." Meren kisses up the side of Jerath's throat, and his skin burns with each press of Meren's lips. "I don't know how, but I feel it."

Jerath lets Meren walk him backward toward the bed. When it hits the back of his knees, Jerath climbs onto it and pulls Meren with him. They're clumsy with their kisses, Jerath shuffling back up to the top of the bed and Meren scrambling after him. Jerath doesn't care, though; he feels the weight and warmth of Meren's body as it covers him, and the magic of the bond curls around them both.

"You need to promise me too," Meren says. He lifts himself up onto his elbows and presses a chaste kiss to the side of Jerath's mouth. "I know you want to get your people out of there, Jerath." He stops for another kiss. "But please don't do anything rash."

He looks more serious than Jerath has ever seen him. "It would kill *me* if anything happened to *you*." He dips his head and kisses Jerath properly this time, and they cling to each other as if this is the last time they'll get to. That thought alone makes Jerath flip them over, shimmy down Meren's body, and tug at the laces on his breeches.

"Jerath… you don't have to." Meren's hand rests on Jerath's shoulder as though he's going to push him off, so Jerath bats it away.

The laces come undone easily, parting to allow him access to Meren's already hard length. It springs free, and Jerath slides his hand around the base and brings it toward his mouth.

"Teeth?" Meren mutters it like a question, and Jerath runs his tongue across his teeth to check, but they're thankfully back to normal. He looks up and flashes them at Meren, grinning when Meren grunts and pushes him back down.

Jerath strokes his thumb over the smooth skin and elicits a throaty moan from Meren when he leans forward and licks at the head. He circles it with his tongue, collecting the precome and savoring the way Meren tastes. He wants more, wants to have Meren fill his mouth and then swallow him down until he's gasping Jerath's name. He knows it's the bond magic pushing him on and making him bold, but he doesn't care.

Jerath opens his mouth. His lips are wet and slippery as he takes as much of Meren's cock as he can manage. Meren is thick and long, and Jerath feels the stretch as he slides down until his lips meet the edge of his fist. He sucks and strokes, swirling his tongue as he moves up and down.

Meren's hips push up off the bed, and Jerath is quick to pin him down with his free hand. He holds Meren in place, loving the way Meren squirms and tugs on his hair. When Meren gets impossibly harder and his legs tense, Jerath moans around him, and then Meren is coming. Jerath's name falls from his lips as he releases into Jerath's mouth.

Jerath rests his head on Meren's thigh, breathing deeply as he lets Meren recover. He's surrounded by Meren's scent, but it's strongest here. Insistent fingers pull at his hair again, this time trying to get him to look up.

"Come here." Meren smiles lazily and Jerath crawls back up the bed to lie alongside him. "That's better." He slips his hand over the front of Jerath's breeches and palms his erection. Jerath hisses and arches into his touch.

"I heard that shifter mates can sense each other's feelings, is that true?" He rubs his hand back and forth, and it takes Jerath a moment or two to answer.

"Yes… well, sort of." Jerath closes his eyes and lets the magic wash over him. He imagines what it would be like if he and Meren were fully bonded. "They can feel base emotions, like fear and happiness."

"What about if they get separated? Can they find each other using the bond?"

"I don't think it's true in all cases, but it can happen. With some bond mates, if they're separated they can sense their mate's exact location, if close enough."

"I want that." Meren's voice is soft but firm. Jerath's eyes snap open and he stares at Meren long and hard. "With you, Jerath. I want that with you."

"But after—"

"I don't care about *after*. We'll work something out… somehow." Meren's eyes are wide and pleading and Jerath's heart stutters in his chest. "When we fight tomorrow, I need to know that you're okay at all times, and if you're not, then I need to know how to find you."

"The bond is for *life*, Meren. Life. It won't ever go away." Jerath closes his eyes and forces himself to be the voice of reason, even though he wants to drag Meren close and complete the bond right now. "We hardly know each other."

"I know what I feel, Jerath." He reaches for Jerath's hand and pulls it to his chest. "I may only have just met you, but you're all I think about, all I want." He presses their palms flat over his heart. "I know this is right, Jerath, because I can feel it *here*."

Jerath is lost for words. If they do this, then he will be mated to Meren for the rest of his life, and Jerath never thought he'd find that. By rights, a mated pair should have their union blessed by the elders of their village, but Jerath doubts the elders of Eladir would even allow it. The fact that Meren isn't a shifter is bad enough, and coupled with the fact he's a man… well, Jerath can just imagine how it would go down. He knows he should say no, make Meren understand all the reasons why this is such a bad idea, but he doesn't want to. Anything could happen tomorrow, and Jerath wants to live in the now. They can face the consequences later. Together.

"Okay."

Meren's smile is blinding, and Jerath knows without a doubt, despite what others may say, this thing between them is *right*. He smiles back, curls his hands in the front of Meren's shirt, and reels him in for a kiss. Meren slips his hand between them again, massaging Jerath's crotch, and his cock strains against the material.

"We're wearing far too many clothes, then." Jerath looks down his body and raises an eyebrow. Meren just laughs at him and starts to undo his shirt.

Their clothes come off in a flurry of movements, arms and elbows everywhere as they hurry to get naked. Meren scrambles under the thick furs and holds the end up for Jerath to slide in after him. Jerath has been hard for what seems like forever, and he can't help the low rumble that escapes when Meren wraps his hand around him. He surges forward, capturing Meren's mouth in a hard and desperate kiss. He can't help it; now they've decided to do this, Jerath's instincts are in overdrive with the need to make Meren his.

He pushes Meren onto his back and wastes no time reaching down and feeling him. Meren is half hard already, and Jerath smiles against his shoulder. He licks and mouths at the skin there, barely resisting the urge to bite. He needs to be inside Meren before he does that.

Meren spreads his legs wide and Jerath slots himself between them. They brush against each other and it's too much but perfect all at the same time. Jerath trails his hand down between Meren's legs and passes over his hole, the pads of his fingertips rubbing over the sensitive skin.

"The oil… from the lamp." Meren gestures in the vague direction of the lamp at the side of the makeshift bed, and Jerath nods in understanding. He may not have done this before, but Jerath knows how things work. Although he and Balent never went any further than using their hands, they talked about it sometimes. Balent liked to experiment, and Jerath was eager to hear all about it. He tried fingering himself once and quickly learnt that nothing was going in there without a little help. He leans over the side and collects some of the oil on his fingers, and quickly brings them back to Meren's entrance before it drips off.

Jerath slides a finger inside him. It's warm and tight and Jerath growls at the feeling. He slowly works it in and out, watching Meren the whole time. He adds more, slicking Meren open with slow, easy thrusts, and the noises Meren makes have Jerath aching to get inside him properly. Jerath curls his fingers, and Meren pushes back against his hand, cursing loudly.

“Fuck! Jerath… I’m ready… do it now.”

Jerath stills and swallows thickly, willing himself to calm down. He pulls his fingers out and smears more of the oil over his erection before guiding it into position. Jerath hesitates for just a moment. He looks up and meets Meren’s eyes as though to ask, *Are you sure?*

Meren bites his bottom lip, eyes half lidded and dark with need, and nods.

Jerath pushes forward, slowly easing his way in until he’s buried deep inside. He has to stop. Has to take several long, shuddering breaths because it’s intense and overwhelming and the magic is surging through his body. He daren’t put his hands on Meren. His claws are fully out now, so he places them either side of Meren’s head.

“Okay?” Jerath bites back the urge to just thrust as hard as he can.

“Yes… *fuck*, yes.”

Jerath slowly pulls out and slides back in. It’s a teasingly slow pace, and Meren lets out a frustrated moan before he wraps his legs around Jerath’s back and urges him to go faster. Jerath leans down and kisses him, while his teeth are still human, and starts to pick up the pace.

He draws his hips back and fucks into Meren hard, over and over, and Jerath feels it building between them. Meren gasps. He’s staring at Jerath’s eyes, and Jerath can well imagine what they look like—glowing and animalistic.

Jerath feels a twinge in his jaw and he licks over his teeth to find they’re fully lengthened and painfully sharp. He needs to bite Meren, but he’s not sure how it works with Meren not being a shifter. Usually shifter mates bite each other to cement the bond. But Meren doesn’t have fangs, so Jerath improvises.

He moves so he’s balanced on one arm and brings the other to his mouth. He bites into his wrist, letting his fangs pierce his skin just enough to let the blood flow, then offers it to Meren. “You need… to drink.” He gets the words out between thrusts and can feel his orgasm building fast. “Do it… *now*.”

Meren grabs Jerath’s wrist and brings it to his mouth. He draws the blood onto his tongue, then swallows it down, and the pain shoots straight to Jerath’s groin. He lets out a low, rumbling growl.

"Enough."

Meren pulls back, licking the blood from around his mouth, and Jerath leans down to kiss him. He runs his tongue over Meren's lips, capturing the last traces of blood, and moans. He can feel it now, his body is alive with magic and it pulses through his veins with a white heat. It surrounds them both. He can almost see it in the air as he thrusts into Meren again and again, and then it shatters inside him. He buries his head in the crook of Meren's neck and bites. His sharp fangs sink into the soft flesh and he comes, drinking down the warm blood as his release pulses out of him.

Meren cries out Jerath's name, along with a string of curses as he follows soon after. His body trembles with the aftershocks as Jerath carefully extracts his teeth and collapses on top of him. The steady pulse of magic wraps around them like a soft, warm blanket, and Jerath feels whole, for the first time in his life.

The bond is complete.

CHAPTER 13

"I WAS talking to my father earlier." Meren turns to face Jerath and entwines their fingers.

"What about?"

"My people and your village mostly, and the northern lands." Meren smiles and leans in for a quick kiss. "He was telling me some very interesting stories. I'm not sure how much truth there is to them, but apparently these stories have been passed down through generations."

Jerath props himself up on his elbow and grins. "Tell me." He wants to learn all he can about Meren and his people, especially if it involves his own village too. He's getting tired and they really need to get some sleep before tomorrow, but he's far too curious to go to sleep now.

"Well, according to legend, my people originally lived in the forests of Arradil as well."

"Really?" Jerath interrupts, unable to help himself. "I've never heard that before."

"Yes. Apparently, they used to hunt in the forest and pray to the Goddess. They only killed what they needed: meat to survive, and fur to keep warm. But after one particularly harsh winter, food was scarce and the wildcats of the forest became so few that the Goddess sought the hunters out."

"What happened then?"

"She asked them to leave the forest and head south to Kalesaan, to make a new home where the wild animals were still plentiful. In exchange for this she promised to gift them with exceptional hunting skills and to allow them to still worship her and perform their rituals, even when they were no longer in her forest."

Jerath shifts closer and wraps his arm around Meren's waist. "Maybe that's why you can feel the bond so strongly. If we both worship the Goddess of the forest, then maybe she blesses this union after all."

"It's just a story, Jerath." Meren looks a little skeptical, but Jerath is almost certain there's an element of truth to the tale.

"You can sense my feelings though, can't you?"

"I think so. Let me…." Meren closes his eyes and Jerath concentrates hard. He lets his gaze roam over Meren's body, lingers over his firm, well-defined stomach and chest. The heat of arousal stirs low in Jerath's belly. He imagines all the things he wants to do with Meren and lets the feeling build and build until Meren's breath catches and his eyes snap open.

"Yes." He looks at Jerath. His eyes are dark and full of want, and Jerath doesn't have time to answer before he's roughly pulled in for a kiss. Meren rolls him over, pinning him to the furs beneath. "I can feel you, Jerath." His eyes are bright, full of wonder, and Jerath smiles up at him.

He reaches up and cups Meren's face. "I can feel you too." It's like a comforting warmth in his chest at the moment, full of excitement. Jerath knows Meren's happy, can sense it, and it's so much better than he ever imagined. "As much I would love to explore this all night with you." He sinks his hands into Meren's hair and kisses him again, before turning serious. "We need to sleep. Tomorrow—"

"Don't." Meren kisses him again, then shakes his head. "Just sleep."

They settle themselves under the covers. Meren wraps himself around Jerath's back and holds him close. It's not long before Jerath hears soft snores as Meren drifts off to sleep, and he can let his worries surface without fear of Meren sensing them. Tomorrow will be tough to get through. They don't know for certain how many men will be waiting for them, or even if all the prisoners are still alive. Jerath's animal stirs, restless at the thought, and he knows the shifters will be hard to restrain if any of them have been injured.

Meren sighs in his sleep, nudging Jerath out of his dark thoughts, and he wonders if Meren's subconscious has picked up on his feelings. He takes a deep breath, tries to banish it all from his mind, and closes his eyes.

The morning comes all too soon.

"JERATH."

Jerath drifts awake as he hears the tent rustle. Someone enters and whispers his name again.

"Jerath."

He opens his eyes and blinks a few times until he focuses on Serim's face peering down at him.

"Hey." She keeps her voice low, so as not to wake Meren. "Everyone's awake. It's time to get ready, Jerath." She doesn't bat an eye at Meren being in his bed. Her face lacks the usual teasing smile she'd normally have for him.

He nods and she quietly backs out of the tent.

Meren's lying on his back with one arm above his head, and he looks so peaceful Jerath doesn't want to wake him. But he has to.

"Meren." Jerath leans over and kisses him softly. "Wake up." Jerath shakes his shoulder a little and Meren opens his eyes, smiling up at Jerath until he realizes why they're awake.

"Fuck." Meren scrubs a hand over his eyes and sighs. "*Fuck.*"

He sits up and the fur blankets slip down to his waist. Jerath whines softly and reaches out so he can run his fingers along Meren's exposed skin. He wants nothing more than to pull him back down and stay there forever.

"I know." Meren gives him a soft smile and takes hold of his hand. "I *know*, Jerath."

They don't say anything else, and the silence hangs heavy between them as Jerath watches Meren get dressed. There's no need for Jerath to do the same. He'll be in his animal form from the moment they leave the village. Meren sits to pull on his boots, and Jerath feels a wave of fear and worry wash over him. He can't be sure if it's from him or Meren, but he draws Meren to him and hugs him tight. "Be careful."

Meren nods against his shoulder. "You too."

They stay like that far longer than they've got time for, until Meren eventually moves away and stands up. "I need to go back to my tent. My bow is there."

"See you out by the fire."

Jerath watches him go and his heart already aches. He refuses to think about how bad it will be if they have to part for good. He closes his eyes and lets his jaguar take over.

NEARLY everyone is gathered by the fire when Jerath pads over on near-silent feet. There's no sign of Meren or Torek yet, but he spots Serim's panther and Mahli's lynx with the other shifters and stalks over to join them. They must make for a strange sight—this many big cats standing together in the middle of a village. The hunters are clearly used to them by now; apart from the odd curious glance, no one pays them much attention. They can't do anything other than wait at this point, since they're unable to communicate, but they did all their talking yesterday. Each of them knows exactly what they have to do.

Jerath reaches Mahli first and nuzzles at her. She turns and licks at his neck, greeting him with a rumbling growl. Serim sidles up next to him and knocks him gently with her shoulder. It's still dark out and her blue eyes glow brightly, but Jerath sees the fear and nerves hiding in their depths. He whines and she dips her head and rubs at his chest. Jerath sends up a silent prayer for the Goddess to watch over all of them. They're going to try to rescue more of her children today, so surely she'll keep them safe.

Malek arrives, flanked by Meren and Torek, and calls for everyone's attention. They break off into their assigned groups, and

Jerath gives one last look to his friends before padding over to join Meren.

He walks up alongside him and Meren rests his hand on top of Jerath's head. He strokes from his ears down the length of his back in long, firm strokes, and Jerath calms a little under his touch.

"That's better," Meren whispers, and Jerath nudges against his thigh. He flicks Meren with his tail and gives a satisfied huff at the small smile it produces.

Malek reminds them all once again of the dangers, warns of underestimating the raiders, and prays that the Goddess will see them safely home. Jerath hopes that she's heard all their prayers as they silently set off into the darkness.

IT TAKES them longer than Jerath would like to reach the outskirts of the raiders' village. The shifters have no trouble seeing in the dark, but Meren and his people don't have the added bonus of cat's eyes. The sun is just about to rise; a red-and-golden glow barely tints the horizon when Malek raises his hand to call them all to a halt. He gestures for them to take their positions, and each group splits off in varying directions.

They're far enough away from the village boundaries that they won't be heard, but everyone moves with stealth and Jerath is amazed at how little noise they make. The plan is to circle the village and come at the raiders from all sides, but they have no real idea how big it is. Malek's hope is that they have enough people to cover the perimeter, and as Jerath follows Meren along the south side of the village, he thinks they may just be in luck.

He can see the groups left and right of them. They're a fair distance away, but they're in sight nevertheless. Malek's instructions were clear: wait for the first rays of the sun to break through and then attack. When the prisoners are found, the shifter with that group will roar out a warning to let the other groups know. When they've all been freed, the shifter will roar again, and at that point everyone is to retreat and meet up at the designated spot a few miles away from the village.

It sounded so simple when they talked it through last night. But now, as they wait for the sun to rise, it feels anything but. There are so many things that can go wrong, so many ways for this to fail, and panic flares in Jerath's chest.

"Hey." Meren crouches down next to him and lays a calming hand on his shoulder. He ruffles the fur on the back of Jerath's neck, running his fingers through it over and over. "We go in, we find them, we get out. Easy."

He sounds so sure and confident. Jerath can sense his nervousness underneath his words but makes no attempt to acknowledge it. Meren needs to appear strong and fearless for the sake of his men, if nothing else.

Jerath butts against Meren's hand and then settles down on the ground to wait the last few minutes before the sky lightens and the attack begins.

He senses it before it happens. The air changes temperature by a degree or two, and Jerath hauls himself up and growls. Meren turns to him and his voice is so low Jerath has to strain to hear it. "Remember what we said." His tone is laced with desperation and Jerath wants to whimper but he holds it in. "Be careful… I need you to be careful."

Jerath growls again and he hopes Meren interprets it as "the same goes for you too."

The first bursts of sunlight start to break through the darkness, and Meren signals his men to get ready. When the first ray hits the village, Meren hisses for them to attack, and they race off toward the village on silent feet.

They reach the outer edges without being detected. From what they can see, most of the inhabitants are still asleep, and Jerath hopes that maybe they can do this without any fighting at all. But then they hear the thunder of footsteps, followed by the unmistakable sounds of battle.

Meren abandons all pretense at being stealthy. He and his men are armed with both bows and swords, and Jerath watches with grim resignation as Meren shoves his bow over his back, draws his sword high in the air, and charges forward. Jerath is glued to his side, teeth bared and ready to attack as they slip between the crudely built homes.

They spill out onto a clear stretch of what looks to be a road through the village. Jerath senses movement from behind them and spins around. He growls out a low warning as ten angry-looking raiders come barreling toward them, swords already drawn

"This way!" Meren yells, and his unit turns as one and prepares to fight. Those at the back draw their bows and take aim, and a flurry of arrows fly overhead. Two of the raiders fall down dead and another clutches at his thigh as he stumbles, but Jerath has his sights set on the man in the lead. He recognizes him from that day in the forest and his animal side takes over, the desire for revenge thick and heavy in his veins.

He leaps for the man's throat, slaps his sword arm away with his front legs, and growls with satisfaction as he feels the bone crack under his paws. Jerath knocks him to the ground and sinks his teeth into the soft skin at the side of the man's neck. He bites hard, tearing at the flesh, and the dying man's good hand scrabbles for purchase in Jerath's fur, desperately trying to pry Jerath's jaws open and away. But he's no match for the raw power of Jerath's jaguar form, and soon enough his strength starts to fade and his arms falls weakly to his sides.

"Jerath!"

Meren's voice snaps him out of his bloodlust, and Jerath carefully extracts his teeth from the body of the raider. He looks up to see that Meren's men have dispatched the rest of the raiders without incurring any serious injuries, and Jerath breathes a sigh of relief as his gaze sweep over Meren's body and finds him relatively untouched.

"Which way now, Meren?" One of his men steps forward as Meren wipes the blood from his sword. Fighting can be heard in both directions along the road, and Jerath listens harder to see if he can sense who may need help more. All he can make out is the harsh cries of battle, and it's impossible to separate the raiders from their own men.

A loud roar splits through the sounds of fighting, and Jerath recognizes it immediately.

Serim.

She must have found the prisoners. Before Jerath can even start to feel any relief, another of Serim's roars fills the air, but it's full of anguish and pain and Jerath instinctively knows she's found Ghaneth. And that he's hurt.

"Go." Meren urges as he meets Jerath's eyes. "We'll follow you."

Jerath turns and races down the road toward the center of the village. He can hear the fighting as they get closer. It's a mixture of shouting, cursing, and the odd snarl. Jerath can't tell who's winning from this distance, but when they round the last bend he almost stumbles over the lifeless body of a lynx. His heart stops beating for the entire time it takes him to realize it's not Mahli.

But it's still one of his people, and he snarls with rage.

"I'm so sorry." Meren is beside him then, firm, comforting hands on the back of his neck. They scan the scene in front of them, gazes darting over the fighting to see where they need to help out most. Jerath easily spots the prisoners—corralled in the center like animals. Caleb and his group are fighting to get to them, and from what Jerath can see, they're more than holding their own. He searches for Serim, unable to see her among the mass of bodies.

"Over there!" Meren points over to the edge of the group of prisoners, and Jerath whines in panic as he sees her. She's standing in front of Ghaneth's prone form, snarling and braced for attack as three of the raiders advance toward her. Jerath wants to go and help her, but they suddenly have raiders coming at them from two sides and he knows he needs to stay and help fight.

He looks back at Serim as she bravely faces the three men down. Her tail swishes furiously and her ears are flat to her head. Jerath's torn between his best friend and his mate. The pull to stay and protect Meren is almost too strong to ignore, but Serim is going to *die* if someone doesn't help her. He can't see Torek or any of her group, and the raiders are almost upon her and Ghaneth now. Jerath tries to contain his feelings of desperation, but Meren senses it anyway.

"Go help Serim." Meren's voice is strained as he fights off an attack. Jerath leaps and tears the man's arm from his shoulder and spits it out at his feet. Meren finishes him off with a dagger to the throat and turns to push Jerath away. "Go!" Jerath growls his refusal; Meren and his men are outnumbered. "Now, Jerath! She's going to die! We can handle these." He shoves Jerath again before taking his bow and firing at the oncoming raiders. He takes two more of them out. "Go!"

Jerath swallows down the pain of leaving Meren's side, pushes the need to protect him down and out of sight as he races over to Serim.

She's backed right up against Ghaneth. There's one man lying unmoving on the ground, but the other two are closing in, and there's a deep gash across Serim's left shoulder. It's bleeding heavily, and there's already a sizeable pool on the ground at her feet. She's limping, favoring her right side, and the two raiders try to capitalize on that. One draws her out by going for Ghaneth while the other slips in to jab at her flank. She howls in pain as the blade finds its mark, and Jerath roars.

She's got nowhere left to go, and the raiders grin as they approach her from opposite sides. "Not so fearless now, are you, Blackie?" Serim hisses and snaps her teeth. Jerath knows the exact moment she sees him because her blue eyes flash and he swears he can see her smile. He lunges for the man on the left and bites out his hamstring while Serim takes the other from the front. Her claws tear into his belly and he screams in agony, but Serim's limping badly now and she can't get in a killing blow quickly enough.

Jerath hurriedly finishes off his man, snapping his neck in one clean move, and rushes to help Serim just as the raider manages to raise his sword arm and take a swing at her. It would have sliced down the middle of her back, but Jerath is much quicker. He leaps in front of her, knocking the blade flying, but it glances off his side and nicks the top of his back leg. He lets out a yelp, but the pain is easy enough to ignore.

He turns and growls as the man scrambles to back away. Jerath can taste the blood and flesh still on his teeth, and he must look a terrifying sight because the raider tries in vain to get to his feet. His wounds from Serim's claws are too severe, though, and he stumbles to his knees with a cry. Jerath tears his throat out before he can make another sound.

Serim has collapsed on the ground, and Jerath pads over, licking at her wounds and nuzzling under her chin. She whimpers back and looks over her shoulder at Ghaneth. Jerath follows her gaze and is shocked at the sight. They've only been gone just over a week, but Ghaneth looks awful, as though he hasn't eaten in days. He has bruises all over his face and arms and four long angry welts across his back. Jerath's anger flares deep inside him and he wants nothing more than to kill every single one of the men who did this. He wants to hunt them down and rip them apart with his teeth and—

"Jerath… hey… calm down." It's Meren's voice that pulls him back from the edge. His firm, soothing hands on Jerath's back that rein in his temper and make him focus. "I could feel your anger all the way over there."

Torek is with him, and together he and Meren lift Ghaneth up. He's barely conscious, so they have to carry him over to where the other prisoners are being escorted out of the village. Some of the raiders are still trying to fight, trying to prevent their escape, so Meren and Torek hand Ghaneth over to a couple of men from Caleb's team and return to the fray.

Jerath nudges Serim to her feet. She's still unsteady, but the bleeding has slowed down considerably. He watches her back all the way out of the village. Meren, Torek, and the rest of the men follow behind. Jerath roars as loud as he can to signal the safe extraction of the prisoners and hopes the others can hear. He hasn't seen the other groups, but has to trust they're okay. Mahli is somewhere in this village, and Jerath refuses to believe that anything bad has happened to her.

He nudges at Serim again, urging her to move faster. They need to get out of here and put some distance between them and the raiders before they meet up with everyone else. She huffs at him, but dutifully picks up her pace. Jerath doesn't miss the small whimper that escapes her every time she puts her right front foot down, though.

They're almost at the outskirts of the village, and Jerath finally begins to relax as the raiders fall behind, obviously deciding the prisoners aren't worth pursuing. He looks at Serim and sees her gaze fixed firmly on Ghaneth as he's half carried up ahead of them. Jerath wants to give her a hug and tell her it'll all be okay but he can't, so he settles for licking her ears and rubbing his head under her chin. She purrs in response, leaning on him for a moment before straightening up.

Jerath's just turning back to look for Meren and Torek when a sharp, sudden pain rips through him and he stumbles to the ground. It hurts so much Jerath expects to find a gaping hole or at least an arrow poking out, but when he looks down at himself there's nothing there. His mind scrambles to catch up but he's hit with another wave of pain, and his heart stutters as he realizes what it is.

Meren.

CHAPTER 14

JERATH feels cool hands stroking his face. He must have blacked out because he's on his back and staring up at the early morning sky. He turns toward the soft voice whispering his name and sees a human Serim looking down at him. It's not until he raises his hand to touch her injured shoulder that he realizes he's shifted back too. And then he remembers.

He sits bolt upright, his hand rubbing against his chest where the pain tore through. "Where's Meren?" he gasps, frantically looking around, but he can't see him anywhere. He remembers how much it hurt and he knows Meren's injuries must be bad. He needs to find him now. He goes to stand up, but Serim pushes him back down.

"Just wait, Jerath." She looks at him with pleading eyes, her voice full of concern. "You've been out of it for nearly an hour," she says, looking up at the sun. "You need to take it steady."

Jerath notices she's dressed in one of the hunters' shirts, and when he looks down his body, he sees that he is too. Not that he cares much for his modesty at this point. "Where is he, Serim?" Her reluctance to tell him is making him nervous, and he's getting an awful feeling deep in his stomach. "Is… is he…?" He can't say the word, but Serim understands and she shakes her head quickly.

"No, Jerath. He's not… dead."

But he's not good either. Jerath can hear it in her voice. He tries to sense Meren's emotions across the bond, but there's nothing. It's like an empty void, and Jerath tastes bile at the back of his throat. "But?"

Serim sighs. "It's bad, Jerath." He jumps to his feet and Serim doesn't stop him this time, but she catches hold of his hand. "He took a dagger to the chest. One of the raiders threw it at Torek's back, and Meren pushed him out of the way." She tugs on his hand, and he pulls her up alongside him. "Come on, I'll take you to him."

Jerath lets her lead him past the groups of people scattered around. Someone must have carried him, because they're now at the meeting point and it looks as though all the groups made it back. But not all made it back alive. Jerath shudders as he spots a line of still, lifeless bodies off to the left, set apart from everyone else. He can see at least two shifters, and he wonders who didn't make it back while feeling guilty that he's glad neither of them are Mahli.

"Where's Mahli?" he asks.

Serim points over to the right where most of the shifters are gathered, along with the rescued prisoners. "She's safe."

Jerath relaxes a little at that, but his body is still taut with tension. He hardly even notices the cut on his leg.

They eventually reach a small group of people gathered around in a rough semicircle. Jerath spots Torek and Meren's father—both their faces are pale and worried-looking. Caleb's also there, and he walks forward to meet them. He halts Jerath with a hand to his chest, preventing him from getting closer, and Jerath can't help the snarl that escapes him. He needs to see his mate.

"Hey, calm down." Caleb steps back and raises his hands. "I just need to talk to you, Jerath."

Jerath sucks in a lungful of air and tries to control his breathing, but it's hard. He can smell Meren now. The scent of sickness and death hangs heavy around him, and Jerath wants nothing more than to push Caleb out of the way and go to him. "Talk."

"Torek said that you bonded with Meren." He talks quietly so they aren't overheard.

Jerath shifts awkwardly, not knowing how Caleb will react. He's not sure he can handle it if Caleb tells him it's wrong, not with his mate lying injured and so near to death.

Caleb scrubs his hand over his eyes. "He's lost a lot of blood, Jerath. If you've bonded with him, then you can give him some of yours."

"Yes," Jerath answers almost immediately. "Will my blood heal him?" Shifters heal a little quicker than humans, and though Meren isn't a shifter he is Jerath's mate, so maybe the same rules apply.

Caleb sighs and shakes his head. "I don't think it works quite like that, Jerath. He's still human." Jerath's heart sinks and Serim steps closer, wrapping her arm around his waist and squeezing gently. "I've been studying with the elders of our village," Caleb continues. "And from what I understand, your blood might just keep Meren alive until we can get him back to Chastil and let the healers there take care of him."

"What do I need to do?"

Caleb gestures to where Meren is laid on the ground. The others move out of the way as Caleb and Jerath kneel down beside him. Jerath strokes his thumb across the pale skin of Meren's cheek. It's drained of all its color, and he looks nothing like the man Jerath knows.

"Bite your wrist." Caleb's voice is soft and Jerath does as he's asked. He lifts his arm and sinks his fangs into the soft flesh on the underside of his wrist, barely feeling the sting. The blood starts to pool and slides over Jerath's skin before dripping onto the ground. "Now, hold it over his mouth." It reminds Jerath of when they bonded and he barely stifles a sob.

Caleb pulls gently on Meren's jaw until his mouth falls open, and Jerath holds his bleeding wrist just above Meren's lips. The blood drips onto his tongue, and Meren instinctively swallows. He moans and pulls a face at the taste, screwing his nose up. He tries to turn away, but he's too weak. Caleb just holds his head in place and Meren gives up trying to move.

Jerath lowers his wrist a little, and his blood continues to flow into Meren's mouth. Meren drinks and drinks, and ever so slowly, the color starts to come back to his cheeks. It's only faint, but the deathly pallor has gone and Jerath wants to cry with relief.

"That's enough." Caleb draws Jerath's wrist away and tells him to lick it so that it heals.

Jerath's a little light-headed after giving so much blood, so he stretches out alongside Meren and closes his eyes to rest for a while. His hand brushes against Meren's and he carefully links their fingers. The contact is soothing. Even if he can't feel Meren through the emotional ties of the bond, he can still feel him like this.

Jerath hears them talking around him, but his mind feels a little fuzzy and he can't concentrate on what they're saying.

"Hey, are you all right, Jerath?" Serim whispers it next to his ear and it tickles. He bats her away clumsily and she huffs at him. Jerath opens one eye and squints at her. She's looking at him intently, and he's not at all surprised by her next words. "I thought Meren didn't want to complete the bond?"

Jerath sighs and turns away from Serim to look at Meren's unconscious form. He manages a small smile as he remembers the previous night. "He changed his mind."

"But, Jerath—"

"Not now, Serim." Jerath faces her again and raises his hand when she starts to interrupt. "I know what you're going to say, but *please*… just… not now."

She stares at him for a moment or two longer and then finally nods.

"Thank you." Jerath relaxes a little, because that is the last thing he wants to discuss right now. There are people still talking nearby, and he waves his hand above him in the direction of their voices. "What are they talking about?"

Serim smoothes his hair out of his eyes as she talks. "They want to move Meren and get him back to the village, but he's too badly injured to be carried. They sent two people back to get one of the wagons as soon as it happened, but it'll be at least another two hours before they get back."

Jerath doesn't want to ask, but he needs to know. "Does he have that long?"

"He does now," she answers, and Jerath hears the smile in her voice.

Serim sighs, her hand still carding through Jerath's hair, and he remembers she should be taking care of someone else instead of being here with him. His eyes fly open and he grabs at her hand. "Where's Ghaneth? Is he okay?"

Her smile grows even wider. "He's still hurting, but he's much better than when we found him."

"You can go to him, Serim. I'll be okay here."

"I'll stay for a bit longer," she says, and lies down next to him. "Ghaneth was asleep when I left him. They gave him water and a little food and it wiped him out."

Jerath's eyes are getting heavy, and he doesn't fight the sleepy feeling that comes over him. He vaguely registers Serim leaning over to kiss his forehead before he slips into unconsciousness.

"JERATH."

Someone shakes his shoulder gently, and Jerath's eyes snap open to see Torek. He's not holding Meren's hand anymore and when he reaches out he can't feel him at all. Jerath scrambles to sit up and when he can't see Meren anywhere, he grabs Torek's shirt and pulls him close.

"Where is he?" It comes out low and feral-sounding, but Jerath can't help it. He's barely keeping a rein on his urge to shift and protect his mate as it is.

"They've already loaded him onto the wagon." Torek speaks in soft tones and doesn't make any attempt to remove Jerath's hand. Maybe Torek understands more than Jerath gives him credit for. "Come on, they're waiting for you."

Jerath lets go of Torek's clothes and pushes himself up onto his feet. He feels much better now, the light-headedness has all but disappeared, and he walks quickly after Torek.

Meren is wrapped up tight on a deep bed of furs. Thick blankets are packed around him to keep him as steady as possible during the journey. He still looks pale and near to death, and Jerath's chest tightens painfully at the sight. He tries to sense Meren's emotions again, searching for any sign he's in there somewhere, but there's nothing.

He takes a shuddery breath and startles when soft hands slide into both of his. Mahli and Serim crowd him from either side, offering their comfort, and Jerath squeezes their hands tight. He needs them now, more than ever, and he's beyond grateful they both seem to realize it and don't let go of him when the wagon starts to move.

It takes two hours to get back to Chastil. Jerath walks next to Meren the whole way, still flanked on either side by his friends. The rest of the people from Jerath's village are scattered around them, and he chats to a few of them as they walk. Ghaneth and a couple of the others are also traveling in wagons, and Serim keeps a close eye on them, going over to check on them every so often. Ghaneth is still asleep, so she stays by Jerath's side.

He can see Kyr up ahead, walking alongside Ghaneth's cart, and Jerath is relieved that Kyr hasn't tried to talk to him yet. He's not sure how he'd react if Kyr came over now and started to annoy him as usual. He doubts it would be pretty. He idly wonders if Kyr can sense it, because he's glanced back at Jerath several times already but hasn't said a word.

The familiar outskirts of Meren's village come into view, and Jerath breathes a little easier. Meren's still in a bad way, but at least now his own people can start to care for him. Caleb and Torek look after the rescued prisoners, ushering them through the village to the makeshift camp on the other side. They need food, water, and somewhere to clean up and rest. Jerath knows he should probably go and help, they're his people after all, but there's no way he's leaving Meren's side. Serim gives him a quick hug and follows after Ghaneth, leaving him with Mahli.

Meren's father helps get his son off the wagon and into the small house in front of them. They're met by two women. Both are older than Malek, and Jerath assumes they must be the healers. They have long, silvery hair and are dressed all in white, and have an air of calm confidence about them as they lead the way into the house.

"I think this is Meren's home," Mahli whispers as they follow them inside. "Malek showed us around when we first arrived here."

Jerath has almost forgotten that Mahli had been here before him, and that she appears to be on a first-name basis with Meren's father.

He looks around as they enter. It's nice, surprisingly spacious inside, but Jerath feels wrong being here for the first time when Meren's unconscious.

They take Meren through into what looks like his bedroom, but when Jerath goes to follow, Malek turns and puts his hand on Jerath's chest to stop him. Jerath snarls and Malek immediately snatches his hand back.

"I'm not exactly sure what's going on between you and my son." He pauses, staring intently at Jerath as though he can will the answers out of him. "But I have my suspicions."

Jerath's surprised Torek hasn't told him, but then again Meren probably asked him not to say anything and Torek would never betray his friend. Malek continues to stare, and Jerath waits for the inevitable look of disapproval. But it never comes.

Malek smiles warmly and clasps Jerath's shoulder. "What you did for him"—he looks pointedly at Jerath's wrist, where the puncture marks are still visible—"allowed us to get him back here, and have a fighting chance at saving his life." His hand tightens and Jerath sees all his own pain reflected back at him. "Thank you. My son is lucky to have you as his mate."

Mahli gasps next to him, and Jerath realizes she didn't know he and Meren have bonded. He thought Serim might have filled her in, but he should've known she'd consider it his right to tell Mahli.

Mahli reaches out for Jerath's hand and twines her fingers with his. Jerath is lost for words and Malek's looking at him expectantly, but he's so shocked at the easy acceptance of his and Meren's relationship that the words just stick in his throat. Mahli gives his hand a tug and thankfully snaps him out if it.

"Thank you," he manages to say eventually. His gaze drifts past Malek to watch the activity in Meren's bedroom as they prepare him for the healers. "Can I stay while they heal him?"

Malek sighs and shakes his head. "No one is allowed in the room while they perform their rituals, not even me."

“You use magic?” Jerath asks, confused. He didn’t think there was any magic outside of the Forest Goddess’s domain.

“Yes.” Malek smiles indulgently. “You’re not the only people to benefit from the Goddess’s benevolence. She was very generous with my people when we agreed to leave her forest.”

Jerath remembers the story Meren told him the night before.

“She bestowed magical healing abilities on a select few of the village elders, and it has been passed down through the generations,” Malek continues, stepping forward. The door closes behind him and Jerath starts toward it, but both Mahli and Malek pull him gently away. “Come.” He gestures to the chairs set around a large wooden table. “We can wait here while they work.”

THEY sit around the table for what seems like hours. Malek tells them both stories of his village, when they used to be hunters in the forest of Eladir. Jerath and Mahli listen with rapt attention as Malek tells them his people and the shifters of the forest were once very close.

“The elders say that we have ties to the moon that are just as strong as yours. We still have certain rituals that are performed on the full moon.” He smiles ruefully at Jerath. “Which is why I’m not overly surprised that Meren bonded with a shifter. No one here ever held his eye for long.”

Jerath blushes and Mahli giggles behind her hand.

“Do you bear his mark?” Malek asks with a raised eyebrow.

“His what?”

Malek laughs softly and shakes his head. “You haven’t talked much about the customs of our people, then?”

“No… not really.” Jerath blushes again, because Malek will know very well what they’ve been doing with their time. He sees Mahli grinning out of the corner of his eye but refuses to look at her.

“We can’t shift like the people of your village, Jerath, but we each have an animal connection. Though not everyone chooses to find it.” He moves in his seat and spares a glance over at the closed door of Meren’s bedroom before he carries on speaking. “When two people are joined, the union is blessed on the full moon by one of the village elders. After that night, each will bear the other's mark—an image of their animal."

"But we haven't been blessed," Jerath says quietly. He suddenly feels as though they've done something wrong. They've ignored the customs and rituals of both villages in their rush to be together. Jerath's heart sinks and his gaze drops to his lap.

Malek stretches across the table and grips Jerath's forearm. "The next full moon is in three weeks' time."

He doesn't say anything else, just lets the idea sit between them, and Jerath wonders just how much Malek's aware of. Whether he knows that although Jerath and Meren have bonded, they've made no plans beyond that. Jerath absently rubs at the dull ache in his chest. The thought of leaving Meren and never seeing him again makes everything hurt, and he's not so sure he'll be physically capable of doing it when the time comes.

The door to Meren's bedroom creaks open and the healers appear, motioning for Malek to come closer. He gestures for Mahli and Jerath to remain seated and walks over to the women. They point over at Jerath as they whisper, and he's desperate to know what they're talking about. He wants to know if Meren's okay, and it's only Mahli's hand on his that stops him from marching over there.

"Give them a few moments," she whispers.

Jerath figures he'll give them one, and then he's going to go look for himself. He respects that Malek is the chief of the village and also Meren's father, but *he's* Meren's *mate* and he needs to be with him.

Eventually Jerath can't take it any longer. The pull of their bond is too strong to ignore, and he stands up and pushes his chair back.

"Jerath." Malek's voice stops him before he can even take one step.

"How is he?" Jerath looks toward the door. "I need to see him… *please*." He walks over to them and one of the women smiles and catches his hand when he gets close enough.

"You are his mate, yes?"

Jerath nods.

"We have done our best, but—"

His breath catches in his throat, and he starts to panic until the surprisingly firm grip on his hand pulls him out of it.

"Calm yourself, child." She strokes her thumb over the back of his hand in soothing circles. "The boy lives… but he needs his mate."

Jerath almost collapses with relief. Only the sudden appearance of Mahli's strong arms around his waist keep him upright.

"We've healed the wound," she continues. "His body is still too weak, though. He needs your strength and your blood."

Jerath reaches for the door, not bothering to stop and check whether he's allowed in yet or not. The healer said Meren needs him and he's not waiting a moment longer. He tugs on the handle and rushes inside.

Meren's bedroom is much larger than his back home, Jerath notices as he spares a cursory glance around the room. It's sparsely furnished. A chest of drawers and a table by the bed are the only other pieces of furniture. Jerath approaches the bed slowly and trails his fingers over the top of the fur blankets. Meren is unnaturally still beneath them, and Jerath strains to listen for his heartbeat to reassure himself that Meren's still alive.

It's not as easy to focus on a single heartbeat as it is to pick out emotions. The bond is more a connection of the mind, not the physical body. But if Jerath pours all his concentration into listening for the steady beat, he can just about pick it out. It's slow but regular, and Jerath lets out a deep breath before he climbs up onto the bed beside Meren.

His face is still pale, but not as bad as before. Jerath gently sweeps Meren's hair away from his eyes and strokes his fingers down the soft stubble covering his jaw. Meren doesn't react to the touch, and Jerath tries hard not to read anything into it. He thinks of the healer's words again and pulls back his sleeve to expose his wrist. He bites deep into the flesh and then quickly positions his hand above Meren's face, tilting slightly so the blood drips down into his mouth.

Jerath tugs Meren's lips apart with his thumb and the blood falls onto Meren's tongue. Jerath watches as the taste registers, even with Meren unconscious, and breathes a sigh of relief as Meren starts to swallow it down. Jerath lowers his wrist until it brushes Meren's lips and Meren opens his mouth wider and starts to suck softly at the wounds.

Jerath closes his eyes—the feeling of Meren drawing his blood and taking strength from it fills him with warmth. He relaxes into the soft, rhythmic pulls and tries again to sense Meren's emotions. He's felt nothing for what seems like forever, and when the first wave of contentment washes over him, he nearly snatches his hand back in surprise.

Jerath's eyes snap open and Meren is looking up at him. His lids are heavy, barely open at all, but Meren is definitely awake. Jerath smiles, and his eyes tear up as the flood of emotion threatens to overwhelm him. He blinks rapidly, trying to stop them falling, but at least one escapes and slides down his cheek.

Meren's eyes track its progress down underneath Jerath's jaw, and his fingers twitch as though he wants to reach out and catch it. Jerath feels Meren's emotions change abruptly into worry and a touch of fear.

"Hey." He cups Meren's cheek with his free hand and gently removes his wrist from Meren's mouth. "There's no need to worry, Meren. I'm just happy to see you awake." He forces himself to relax, letting his relief and happiness flow through the bond. The effect is instant and Meren starts to calm again.

Meren drags his tongue across his bottom lip, catches the last traces of blood, and Jerath can't help himself. He leans over and kisses him, just the barest of touches, but Jerath's whole body hums with the contact. He rests his forehead against Meren's, breathing him in, and Jerath can finally allow himself to fully relax.

He's tired. The events of the day suddenly catch up to him, and it's all he can do to kick off his shoes and breeches and crawl under the covers. Meren's eyes have already fallen shut, his breathing evening out, and Jerath kisses him once more before taking his hand and slipping into unconsciousness.

WHEN Jerath wakes, the sun is shining through the large window in Meren's bedroom. He must have slept through the night. Meren is curled into Jerath's side, with one hand slung lazily over Jerath's belly. Jerath smiles and pulls him in a little tighter. He's warm and pliant and feels perfect tucked under Jerath's arm.

Jerath's stomach grumbles loudly, causing Meren's eyes to flutter open.

"Hungry?" Meren's voice is scratchy, but his eyes are clear and bright.

"Yeah." Jerath laughs as it growls again. "It's been a while since I ate." He rubs his hand over his belly and knows he needs to get up. "How about you?"

Meren licks his lips and grimaces slightly. "Am I imagining it, or did I drink your blood last night?"

"Um… yeah?" Jerath says, a little confused.

Meren willingly drank his blood to seal their bond, and it hadn't occurred to Jerath that he might not want to do it again. He looks away, not wanting Meren to see the flash of hurt in his eyes. Jerath's a shifter, and the offering and drinking of blood is part of many sacred rituals. He was thrilled when Caleb said his blood would help heal Meren. The sharing of blood is an honor, and Jerath thought that because of their bond, Meren would feel the same.

"Hey, Jerath?" Strong, slender fingers grip Jerath's jaw and force him to meet Meren's eyes. "Whatever you're thinking right now… you're wrong." Meren's hand slides up and cups Jerath's cheek.

"I'm not thinking anything."

Meren raises an accusing eyebrow. "Don't lie to me, Jerath. I can feel you, remember?"

Jerath closes his eyes and sighs. "I liked giving you my blood, Meren. It was…." He struggles to find the right words. "It made me feel closer to you, more connected." Jerath meets Meren's gaze again. "I kind of hoped, because you're my mate now, that you'd feel the same. But—"

Meren puts his fingers over Jerath's mouth to shush him. "I do feel the same."

"But I thought—"

"You thought wrong, Jerath. It's just I… I wish I could remember it better," Meren replies, shaking his head. "That's all."

"Really?" Jerath's well aware how needy he sounds, but everything's still so new between them and he's desperate for the reassurance.

"Yes, really."

Jerath manages a tentative smile and leans down for a kiss. "Good."

There's a knock on the door, and Jerath jumps out of bed and hurriedly pulls his breeches back on before opening it. Mahli's on the other side. She smirks and carries in a tray with two bowls of soup and two chunks of bread on it. "I thought you two might be hungry." She winks at Jerath as though they've been up to no good, and he just glares at her.

"Thanks."

He takes the tray from her and she disappears back out the door with a quick wave at Meren. "Hey, Mahli?"

She stops midstep and turns back to face him. "Yes?"

"Is Serim still with Ghaneth? How is he?" Jerath realizes he hasn't seen Serim since they arrived back at Chastil and he wants to make sure she's okay.

"Yes, she hasn't moved from his side." Mahli smiles fondly as she talks. "She was fast asleep when I went to see her this morning, so I haven't had a chance to speak to her. But Ghaneth seems to be doing much better."

"That's great. What about the others?"

"Everyone's looking a lot healthier after some food and rest."

Jerath relaxes a little at that, relieved his people are doing so well.

"Well, I'd better get back. I'll see you later, Jerath." She gives him one last smile and then leaves.

"Okay." Jerath puts the tray down and helps Meren to sit up a little. "Let's eat."

MEREN is still extremely weak, even with Jerath's blood helping him heal, so Jerath keeps his visits to a minimum during the day to let him rest. But he spends his nights wrapped around Meren, keeping him safe and strengthening their bond.

It's been three days since they rescued the prisoners from the raiders' village, and Jerath senses the restlessness in the makeshift camp where they're all staying. It's a little crowded with all the extra men, but Jerath knows it's more than that.

He grabs a plate of food and finds a seat over by Mahli and Serim.

"Hey." Serim greets him with a warm smile and a hug. "How's Meren?"

Jerath hasn't seen much of her these past few days, and it feels good to have her close. He buries his face in her hair and holds her tight.

"He's doing much better." He sits back and takes a bite of the meat and moans at how good it tastes. "Still gets tired easily, though. Ryla, the healer who's been working with him, says it'll be another two weeks until he's fully recovered."

Serim glances over at Mahli with a worried expression and Jerath sighs. He puts his plate on the ground, his appetite gone all of a sudden, and turns to face both of them. "It's time to leave, isn't it?"

Serim nods and Jerath's heart sinks into his stomach.

"We need to get back home, Jerath. There are worried families waiting, and there's also the Choosing to prepare for. Some of the men only have one more full moon to perform it."

He knew this was coming, knew they'd have to leave eventually, but now that the time has come Jerath doesn't think he can do it. He doesn't want to. "When?"

Mahli nudges Serim until she takes hold of Jerath's hand and holds it tight. "Tomorrow."

Jerath gasps and almost chokes out the word. "Tomorrow?"

"Yes." Serim squeezes his fingers. "Ghaneth is almost fully healed, as are the other shifters. And we need…." She swallows thickly and Mahli takes over.

"We need to take the bodies back to their families, Jerath. We can't wait any longer."

"Of course." It's not that Jerath has forgotten about the three shifters who lost their lives, but he's been so busy with caring for Meren he hasn't stopped to think about it. He feels the guilt wash through him.

Mahli gets up to leave but Serim waves her off when she asks if she's coming too. "I'll be there in a minute."

That obviously means she wants to talk to Jerath alone, and he has a good idea why. She wastes no time in coming straight to the point. "You don't want to leave, do you?"

Jerath meets her steady gaze and answers without any hesitation. "No."

"Oh, Jerath." Serim sighs and shakes her head. "How does Meren feel about it?"

"I don't exactly know," he mutters, and Serim raises an incredulous eyebrow at him. "What? It's not something we've discussed."

"Jerath!" Serim lowers her voice and hisses the words at him. "The two of you bonded. He is your mate. How is it possible that you haven't talked about this?"

Jerath knows she's right, they should have had this conversation already, but Meren hasn't exactly been awake long enough for a serious talk. And Jerath has been putting it off—afraid Meren might not feel the same way. "There hasn't really been time since he was injured." He takes a deep breath. "And… I was scared."

"What of?"

He sighs heavily and knows he has no choice except to tell her everything, lay out all his fears and insecurities and just hope she doesn't think he's ridiculous. "Meren didn't want to be bonded in the first place, Serim. He told me he'd never leave his village and that he wouldn't ask me to leave mine."

"But I don't understand, Jerath. You said he changed his mind." She looks confused now. "You knew what would happen if you bonded, didn't you explain this to him?"

Jerath knows how foolish it seems now, to have made such a decision on the spur of the moment, but he can't bring himself to regret it. "We said we'd work something out after the rescue."

"Well, Jerath, that time has come and you need to work out what that *something* is." Her tone is verging on angry, and Jerath bristles.

"What do you suggest?" he hisses back. "He won't leave here, and he won't ask me to leave Eladir!" He throws his hands in the air and glares at her, but she just eyes him curiously.

"What do you want, Jerath?"

It's such a simple question, and Jerath smiles ruefully as he realizes that the answer is just as simple. "I want to be wherever he is."

"Then you have your *something*." Serim smiles at him, and Jerath catches the look of sadness that passes over her face before she pulls him into a hug. "It'll be okay, Jerath."

She kisses him good night and heads back to the tent she shares with Mahli, leaving Jerath to sit and think about what he needs to do. He knows it's the right thing, but it's still going to hurt.

CHAPTER 15

MEREN'S still asleep when Jerath enters his bedroom and quietly closes the door behind him. The color has returned to Meren's cheeks now and he looks so much healthier already, but he still has a long way to go.

Jerath sits down on the edge of the bed and looks at his mate. He runs his hand through the bright blond hair that frames Meren's face and smiles when Meren frowns in his sleep. He uses his fingers to trace the shape of Meren's eyebrows, his nose, and the slight bow of his full lips. Meren stirs and opens his eyes, and Jerath grins at him before he leans down for a kiss.

"I didn't expect to see you just yet. I thought you were going to see Serim?" Meren smiles back and reaches out, slotting his fingers with Jerath's on top of the covers.

"I did see her… Mahli too." Jerath pauses and takes a deep breath. This is it. This is the point that will shape the rest of his life, and he's so full of nervous excitement he can hardly get the words out. "Meren, the rest of the shifters… they're getting ready to leave. It's time to go home."

The smile disappears from Meren's face and he looks up at Jerath with wide eyes. "Are you going with them?" he asks, voice so soft Jerath has to lean forward to hear it.

"Yes, I have to."

Hurt flashes in Meren's eyes. He pulls his hand back and tucks it away under the covers. "I see." Pain and desperation flares across the bond, making Jerath flinch. He carefully grips Meren's shoulders and holds him in place.

"No, Meren, I don't think you do. I ne—"

"I understand, Jerath." Meren sighs and closes his eyes in resignation. "You need to go home, to your family and friends. We knew this was going to happen… I just… I thought…." He scrubs a hand over his face before meeting Jerath's gaze, and this time he smiles softly and the bond is flooded with warmth and longing. "Letting you go will be the hardest thing I've ever done, Jerath. But I understand why you need to leave."

Meren's eyes shine in the late afternoon light, and Jerath shakes his head as he struggles to find the right words. This is not how it's supposed to go. He's doing it wrong, not explaining himself well at all, and he needs to sort this mess out before things get any worse.

"I'm coming back, Meren."

"What do you mean?"

Jerath feels the spark of hope in Meren's chest and he smiles big and wide. "If it's okay, if you want me… I'm coming back here"—he slides his hands up to cup Meren's face—"to be with you."

Meren stares at him for a moment or two before the words finally sink in, and then he reaches up and drags Jerath down until they're kissing. Harsh, desperate kisses full of relief and joy, and Jerath is overwhelmed by the surge of emotion that flows over him.

"Fuck! Jerath." Meren's eyes are bright and his smile is huge when he eventually pulls back and lets them both breathe. "Are you trying to kill me?" he asks, but he's laughing and Jerath has never seen him so happy. "I thought you were leaving for good, and that I'd never see you again. *Fuck!*"

He kisses Jerath again, but he's smiling too much to do it properly. Jerath laughs and gently pushes him back onto the pillows. "So, does this mean you're okay with the idea?"

Meren rolls his eyes, but holds Jerath's hand again. "Of course I'm okay with it." He strokes Jerath's skin with the pad of his thumb. "So much more than okay."

They sit in silence, drinking each other in with the new realization that this is for keeps. Jerath struggles to wrap his head around the idea that he has a mate now, and he can live his life without hiding a part of himself because others see it as unacceptable. It's a heady feeling and almost too good to be true, but there are still some things he needs to take care of.

Meren seems to read his thoughts. "What about your mother? And your friends?" He looks worried again and Jerath's quick to put him at ease.

"They'll understand, Meren. I love my mother, and Serim, and Mahli very much, but I…." Jerath hesitates. They've never said the words before. It's all happened so quickly between them that Jerath hasn't dared to trust his feelings. But the magic of the bond is true, and he feels the love flowing between them both. He swallows down his fear and meets Meren's eyes.

"I love you." Jerath's heart swells at the sight of Meren's wide smile. "I want to be with you, and as much as I'll miss my mother and my friends… I can't live without *you*."

"Come here." Meren licks over his bottom lip and tugs on Jerath's hand. He can't sit up without help yet, so Jerath stretches out beside him on the bed.

Meren slips a hand around Jerath's neck and into his hair. He drags him closer until their lips are almost touching but not quite. "I love you too."

It's just a whisper of words, but Jerath feels them all the way down to his bones. He edges that bit closer and captures Meren's lips in a soft, lazy kiss. There's no need to hurry now, so Jerath takes his time to lick into Meren's mouth and savor every moment. They lie there on the bed, wrapped up in each other, and trade gentle touches until the sun starts to set.

THE morning light filters in through the windows in Meren's room, signaling the start of the day. Jerath watches Meren sleep, all tucked up under the thick fur blankets. He looks so peaceful and Jerath doesn't want to wake him, but his people are waiting for him. It's time for them all to leave and return to Eladir.

Jerath rests his hand on Meren's shoulder, leans down and kisses his forehead. "Meren." He gives him a gentle shake. "Meren."

Meren wakes up slowly, smiling as he focuses on Jerath. "Hey, you're up early."

"Yeah."

Meren's smile falters and fades as he takes in Jerath's expression. "Is it time, already?"

Jerath nods. "They're waiting for me."

The silence sits heavily between them. Neither one wants to be the first to say good-bye. It makes Jerath huff out a laugh and he reaches out to grasp Meren's hand. "I won't be gone long."

"Long enough." Meren sighs and squeezes Jerath's hand. "How will it react, being so far away from each other?" He rubs both their hands across his chest. "The bond, I mean."

"You'll feel an ache in your heart that'll get deeper the longer I'm gone, and it won't stop until I return." Jerath smiles softly and raises their hands so he can kiss Meren's fingers. "But I will return, Meren." He's not sure how long it'll take to get to Eladir from Chastil—he and Serim didn't take the direct route here. They have to cross the vast grasslands before reaching the edge of the forest of Arradil, but Jerath is determined to be back with Meren as soon as he possibly can.

There's a knock on the door, and Serim pokes her head in. "Are you ready, Jerath?"

She grins at Meren and comes in to hug him good-bye. "Thank you, Meren. For everything."

She leans down and whispers something in Meren's ear, making him laugh, and Jerath makes a mental note to ask her about that later.

Serim disappears back out the door with a pointed look at Jerath.

"I have to go."

Meren pulls him down toward the bed and buries his face in the crook of Jerath's neck. "Be careful, Jerath," he whispers. "I'll miss you." He draws back to look Jerath in the eye. "But don't come back until you've done everything you need to. I know how hard this is going to be for you, and everyone else."

Jerath curls his hand around the back of Meren's neck and kisses him hard. He pours everything into it—all the love and hope and desperation he's feeling—and prays it'll be enough to last them both. "Love you."

"I love you too. Now go, before they march in here looking for you."

Jerath already feels the ache in his chest as he turns and walks out the door.

EVERYONE'S waiting in the camp. Jerath sees Serim talking to Malek and Torek, and he walks over to join them.

"Finally!" Torek claps him on the back. "I thought we might have to send someone in to get you."

"Sorry." Jerath blushes a little and glares at Serim when she laughs.

Torek grins at him and excuses himself to go get everyone ready to leave.

"Torek and nine of my men will escort you home." Malek gestures behind him and Jerath sees the men and wagons loaded up with supplies. A few of the men are busy saying good-bye to their women. There are tight hugs and kisses, and Jerath knows just how they feel.

Serim slips her hand into Jerath's and he smiles, thankful for her silent support. "We can't thank you enough for all your help," Jerath says, offering his hand for Malek to shake.

Malek grips it firmly in both of his and nods. "Our two villages will always help each other, Jerath." He glances over his shoulder in the direction of Meren's house. "Even more so now."

The men are all ready to leave and Malek ushers Serim and Jerath over toward Torek. "I understand you'll be coming back to stay with us, Jerath?"

"Yes."

"I look forward to officially welcoming you into the family, then." Malek claps him on the back and says his farewells to Torek and the others before standing to watch as they start their journey to Eladir.

THEY'VE been walking for several hours when Kyr sidles alongside Jerath and falls into step with him and Serim. Ghaneth and Caleb are walking a little in front of them and off to the side, telling Torek all about life as a shifter. Caleb watches Kyr approach Jerath with a curious look, but doesn't pause in his conversation.

Jerath has managed to avoid Kyr since the rescue, but now it's only the shifters and a handful of Malek's men, it's harder to stay out of his way.

"So…." Kyr looks over at him and smirks. "I see your fangs came in after all, and now you can shift." Jerath's hackles rise as Kyr casts a sly glance over at Serim and Ghaneth. "Wonder how that happened?"

Serim glares at Kyr and slips her hand into Jerath's. "I'm not ashamed, Kyr, nor do I regret it." Kyr cocks an eyebrow, as though he doesn't believe her. "I love Jerath, and I am honored to have helped him through his Choosing."

"What about Ghaneth?" Kyr waves his hand in Ghaneth's direction. "I'm sure he's not very happy about the whole thing."

Kyr is obviously still smarting from being rejected by Serim. It's common knowledge that Ghaneth has asked her to be his partner for his Choosing ceremony, and that she's accepted. Jerath explained everything that happened between him and Serim, and Ghaneth understands. The fact that Jerath is now bonded to Meren probably helps.

"I can speak for myself, Kyr." Ghaneth steps back a little, tugging Serim under his arm, and Jerath grins at the scowl on Kyr's face. "I have no problem with it."

Torek turns back to look at them and raises an eyebrow at Jerath. He nods in Kyr's direction and Jerath just shrugs, not sure he can even explain why Kyr acts the way he does. Torek and Caleb slow their pace so that they fall in line next to Jerath and force Kyr out to the side. Kyr grumbles under his breath, but grudgingly moves over.

“Meren seems to be doing much better now,” Torek says. He nudges Jerath with his shoulder and Jerath grins back at him. He misses Meren already, the ache in his chest a constant reminder of the distance between them, but it’s good to have Torek along for the journey. Someone he can to talk to about Meren.

“Yes, the healers say he should be fully recovered in less than two weeks from now.” Jerath can’t wait. He hates seeing Meren in pain and unable to move around properly.

“I imagine having his mate with him will help with that.” Torek smiles and reaches out and grips Jerath’s shoulder. “I’m glad the two of you worked things out. You’re good for him, Jerath.” Someone shouts Torek’s name from up ahead, so he makes his apologies and leaves to go see what the problem is.

Jerath is still smiling to himself when Kyr calls his name. Serim has just asked Caleb a question, and Caleb shoots Jerath a look of apology as he ducks around him to talk to her, leaving Jerath next to Kyr. There’s no ignoring him now, so Jerath sighs and turns to face him. “What?”

“It’s true, then?” He edges closer, and Jerath sees the smirk on his lips. “I thought it was just a rumor, but you really have mated with a man. I always knew there was something wrong with you.”

Jerath tenses, his hands clenching into fists at his side. But Kyr is on a roll.

“Clearly Serim wasn’t enough to keep you interested in gi—” It’s as far as he gets before Jerath has heard enough. He draws back his fist and drives it home, connecting perfectly with the side of Kyr’s jaw and knocking him on his ass.

Jerath leans over him and hisses through clenched teeth, barely keeping his anger in check. “There’s nothing wrong with *me*, Kyr. Meren is my mate, and I love him.” He stands up straight and tries to calm down. “And what Serim and I shared was a sacred and beautiful rite in the eyes of the Goddess. Do you really dare speak of it like that?”

Kyr is about to open his mouth, but Ghaneth and Caleb are there, gently pushing Jerath over toward Serim. “We’ve got this.” Caleb grins and ushers Jerath away, while he and Ghaneth haul Kyr up and manhandle him a few feet away. Jerath sees them both whispering to him for several minutes before letting him go and walking back over to him and Serim.

“What did you say to him?” Jerath looks between the two of them as they smirk at each other.

“We just explained to him that if he wasn’t careful, we’d make sure none of the girls in Eladir or either of the other villages would agree to be his partner for the Choosing. And no one wants the elders to have to choose for them.”

Serim laughs and mutters something about pitying the poor girl who ends up getting that dubious honor, because in the end someone will have to do it, whether Kyr is Unchosen or not. Jerath just smiles his thanks and rubs at his sore knuckles.

Kyr has nothing more to say after that and falls into a sullen silence. Jerath had hoped this whole experience might have changed him for the better. When they first got back to Meren’s village, Kyr had been quiet and kept to himself, but the closer they get to Eladir, the more the old Kyr seems to surface. Jerath isn’t the least bit surprised none of the girls present will agree to be Kyr’s partner for the Choosing.

It takes them four days to get back home. Jerath and Serim seize the opportunity to ask about the raid on their village.

“Why did they take you?” Serim asks. She looks up at Ghaneth as he sighs heavily.

“They wanted to sell us.” He shudders a little and Serim hugs him tighter. “They knew to look for tattoos, and only took the older boys who didn’t have them.”

“So they thought those who hadn’t changed yet were easy targets?” Jerath says, and Ghaneth shrugs.

“Yeah, I guess. But they didn’t know about the Choosing ritual. They thought that shifters would get the ability to change forms when they came of age. They knew it had something to do with the full moon, and kept those with fangs under heavy guard during it. They planned to sell us each separately before the next one."

"Who to?" Serim asks.

"I'm not sure exactly, but apparently, shifter slaves would fetch a nice price further south. They have special collars to prevent the shift and only allow it for their entertainment. The raiders were very forthcoming with that bit of information."

Jerath shudders. He doesn't really know anything about the villages south of Kalesaan. Before Ghaneth mentioned it, he hadn't known they even existed.

"Thank the Goddess we got to you before they found out the truth." Serim sighs in relief, and Jerath knows just how she feels.

Everyone falls silent for a few moments. Jerath can imagine what would have happened. If the raiders discovered that their prisoners would never be able to shift and were therefore useless to them, they would probably have killed them all.

"When they attacked the village, why didn't the shifters change form and attack?" Jerath asks. It has been bothering him the whole journey. If everyone had shifted into their animal forms, surely they could have overpowered them?

It's Ghaneth who answers again. "They took everyone by surprise, Jerath." He looks a little guilty. "They grabbed seven of the children before anyone even noticed them and they threatened to kill them if we didn't go quietly." Jerath feels a little sick at the thought. "There was nothing we could do."

Jerath nods and doesn't comment further. Children are precious. No one in his village would do anything to put their lives in danger. He thinks about the raiders who died during the rescue and doesn't feel an ounce of remorse.

THERE are shouts and cries of disbelief from the people of Jerath's village as they finally break through the forest and reach Eladir. Word spreads fast, and soon the travel-weary group is surrounded by family and friends, all frantically searching for their loved ones. Torek and his men tactfully move off to one side and watch the reunions with soft smiles.

Jerath sees the families of the few who lost their lives. He feels their desperation and sorrow when they discover they have a body to claim and bury, instead of the warm hug they were hoping for. There are thankfully only three who died, but it's three too many, and Jerath sends a prayer to the Goddess asking her to take good care of them.

"Jerath! Oh, my boy!" Helan's voice is loud and clear as she barrels toward him and wraps him up in a fierce hug. "I can't believe you're back!" She sobs into his chest, so Jerath pulls her tightly against him and kisses the top of her head. He closes his eyes and breathes in her scent, lets it wash over him and soothe his tiredness away.

The trek back to Eladir seemed to take forever. Everyone had been eager to get home, and each time they stopped to eat or camp for the night, Jerath felt the restlessness getting worse. But they're here now, and Jerath holds his mother until her tears finally subside. His heart aches with the knowledge that he's going to leave her again soon, but he already misses Meren desperately and he knows without a shadow of a doubt that he can't stay.

"I'm okay," he says when she takes a shuddering breath. "I promise." He pushes thoughts of leaving to the side for now and instead smiles at her when she looks up.

"You have fangs!" she gasps, and her fingers flutter around his mouth as though she wants to touch them and check that they're real. "When did this happen?" She sniffles again and Jerath reaches out and wipes a stray tear from her eye.

"Come on, let me introduce you to a friend of mine and I'll tell you all about it."

Jerath takes his mother by the hand and leads her over to where Torek is talking quietly with his men. "Torek, this is my mother, Helan."

Torek smiles over Helan's shoulder when she wraps her arms around him and thanks him for bringing her son back to her. Jerath rolls his eyes and laughs, but he loves the way his mother so readily accepts Torek. She immediately invites him back to their house for something to eat and drink, and Torek tells her he would be honored. The rest of

Torek's men are being well taken care of by the village elders, so Helan leads the way back to their home.

Jerath slumps down into one of the kitchen chairs almost as soon as they get through the door. He's so tired and lets out a long sigh as he stretches out his legs under the table. Torek sits opposite him and does the same. Helan quickly rustles up a selection of meat, cheese, and fruit and laughs softly as both Jerath and Torek tuck in straightaway.

"Food was limited on the journey here," Jerath mumbles by way of explanation.

Helan allows them to eat their fill, then settles her elbows on the table and rests her chin on her hands. "Now, Jerath." She reaches up to ruffle his hair and he ducks away, blushing slightly. "Now that you're fed and watered, I want you to tell me everything."

So Jerath does. He starts at the beginning with his and Serim's fishing trip, which seems a lifetime ago now. He explains what happened when his fangs came in, how he and Serim found the perfect place to perform the ritual. He skims over the details, blushing profusely, and aims a kick at Torek under the table when he grins at him.

"You were right about everything, though," Jerath says as Helan wipes away more tears. "It was perfect, nothing to worry about."

She smiles at him and grasps his hand tightly in hers. "I knew it would be. Serim was the perfect choice for you." Jerath blushes again.

"Can I see it?" she asks. Jerath nods, then stands up and pulls off his shirt.

"Oh, Jerath!"

He glances back over his shoulder to see his mother looking at his tattoo with wide eyes.

"It's beautiful." She's smiling hugely now and Jerath grins back at her. "I know it'll be difficult to find your match here in Eladir, but there are some very nice boys over in Westril who have jaguars as their animal, and their elders aren't quite as rigid in their beliefs as ours. If you want to…." She falls silent as Torek coughs.

Jerath shrugs his shirt back on and turns to face her.

"What is it, Jerath?"

He catches hold of her hand again and gently sits her back down at the table. “I’ve met my mate,” he says, and just the very mention of it makes Jerath’s chest hurt. He rubs at it absently with the palm of his hand and sighs.

“Who?” Helan looks accusingly at Torek as she asks the question.

“No, it’s not Torek.” His mother relaxes, and Jerath knows she’s relieved because now she thinks it’s someone from their village. “His name is Meren. He’s the son of the chief.”

Jerath watches her face fall again.

“Are you sure about this, Jerath?” She clutches his hand tightly. “Once the bond is complete, one of you will have to leave their village. You do understand this?”

Jerath looks down at the table, suddenly unable to meet her eyes. Torek takes the lull in conversation as an opportunity to make his excuses and leave. He thanks Helan for her generous hospitality but tells her he needs to go and check on his men. He shoots an encouraging look over at Jerath and then disappears quietly through the door.

“Jerath?”

He’s been dreading this moment the most. There’s just no easy way to tell his mother he’ll be leaving again soon. For good this time.

“You’ve already bonded, haven’t you? And you’re going to live in Kalesaan.”

Jerath’s head snaps up to finally meet his mother’s gaze. He fully expects to see her eyes brimming with hurt and disappointment, but she’s smiling at him. There are tears steadily falling down her cheeks, but she’s still smiling.

“I’m sorry.” He can’t think of anything else to say.

“Sorry?” Helan says, and looks a little confused. “Why on earth would you be sorry?”

“Because you’ve only just got me back, and now I’m going to leave again.”

She pulls him into a hug and shushes him. “You have nothing to be sorry for, do you hear me?” She nudges him until he nods against her shoulder. “I’m going to miss you so, so much, Jerath. But you’ve found your mate, and Kalesaan is not like here. You can live freely there in a way that you never would've been able to here." She takes a deep breath and holds him even tighter. Her tears wet the front of his shirt, but her voice is full of love when she speaks again. "You're my son, Jerath, and I love you dearly. All I want for you is to be happy, even if that means you have to leave."

Jerath doesn't try to stop his own tears. He lets them fall and holds onto his mother for just a little while longer. "You'll come and visit, though. Won't you?" Jerath finally lets her go and sits back in his chair.

"Of course!" Helan wipes at her eyes and laughs at the mess they're in. "I need to meet this man of yours."

She gets up to make them both a hot drink, and Jerath takes a moment to get himself together. He feels wrung out and exhausted but so much better now his mother knows everything and she's happy for him. He should have expected nothing less.

"Now, Jerath." She sets the two steaming mugs down on the table and settles back in her seat. "Tell me all about Meren."

THEY'VE been back in Eladir for two days now. Preparations are well underway for the upcoming full moon and the two Choosing rituals that will be taking place. Ghaneth and Serim are virtually inseparable, much to the annoyance of the elders. There's no guarantee Ghaneth's animal will be a match for Serim's, but neither of them seem to care. Jerath prays Ghaneth's tattoo takes the form of a sleek black panther, just like Serim's. They both deserve this after everything they've been through.

Kyr will also be taking part in the ritual. Jerath finds it amazing that some of the girls in their village aren't put off by his arrogance and general meanness.

He watches the people as they go about their daily chores. It's something he won't be part of anymore, and the feeling is bittersweet. He needs to get back to Meren. It gets harder each day to be without him, but Eladir has been Jerath's home for eighteen years. He's going to miss it.

“Are you ready, Jerath?” Torek appears silently at his side. “My men are all packed and waiting at the far end of the village.”

“Yes.” Jerath has one last look around and takes a deep breath. “I just need to say my good-byes.”

Torek smiles. “Join us when you’re done.” He pats Jerath on the shoulder and leaves.

They’re all waiting for him outside his home, and he grins as Serim rushes up and jumps into his arms. “I’m going to miss you so much, Jerath!”

He swings her around and makes her squeal before setting her back down on the ground. “I expect to see you all soon. It’s only four days’ travel, and Serim knows the way now.”

“We’ll come and see you after the Choosing,” she replies, and steps back to let Mahli come in for a hug.

“I’m so happy for you, Jerath.” He can hear the waver in her voice and he squeezes her tight. “Meren’s lucky to have you.” She lets him go and studiously stares at the ground while she wipes her eyes. Next it’s Serim’s mother, Kinis, and then finally Helan.

“I’m so very proud of you, Jerath.” She cups his cheek and catches his tears with her thumb. “I know your father would have been too.”

Jerath pulls her into his arms and buries his head in her hair. “I love you.” He feels her breath hitch, and she whispers that she loves him too and that he’d better take care of himself or she’ll be having words with the chief.

Jerath laughs through his tears and steps back enough to lay a soft kiss on her forehead.

“They’re waiting for me.” He gestures behind him in the general direction of Torek and the others. He gives the girls one last hug, nearly having to peel Serim and Mahli off him, then turns to leave Eladir for good this time.

He waves until he can’t see them anymore.

Torek greets him with a small smile but doesn’t speak and Jerath’s grateful for the silence. He doesn’t feel like talking yet.

They walk out into the surrounding forest, and Jerath falters as he feels a surge of love through the bond. Meren will have sensed his pain and no doubt realizes that Jerath is leaving today. He rubs at his chest as the warmth spreads through him and he can finally breathe more easily. Jerath feels the weight lift from his shoulders. He's going back to his mate, and despite all the hurt of leaving everyone behind, he knows with all his heart that this is *right*.

He looks up to see Torek is waiting for him while the others move on ahead. Jerath walks up beside him and offers a small smile. "Come on," he says, and gives Torek a gentle nudge with his shoulder. "Let's go home."

EPILOGUE

JERATH rolls over in their bed to face a sleeping Meren. It's been six weeks since he left Eladir and he still finds it hard to believe that this beautiful man is his. *His mate.* Meren's warm, lazy contentment flows through the bond between them. It washes over Jerath, and his whole body relaxes in the soft furs. He doesn't want to move from this spot. He wants to stay here all day and just be with Meren, but they have guests arriving soon and they both need to get ready.

Meren stirs next to him, and Jerath smiles as thick eyelashes flutter open to reveal striking blue eyes. They focus on Jerath's face, and Meren's answering smile is full of love and happiness and Jerath is helpless to do anything but pull him in closer for a soft kiss.

"Hi." Jerath runs his hand under the covers and along Meren's bare hip. His skin is soft and smooth under Jerath's fingers.

Meren raises an eyebrow when Jerath gets teasingly close to his morning erection. "We don't have time for that."

"I know." Jerath just grins and wraps his fingers around the hard length resting along Meren's belly. He loves the feel of Meren's cock. It's hot and heavy in his hand, and he strokes slowly up and down, tightening his grip as it grows that little bit harder.

"Jerath… *oh*…." Meren closes his eyes and drops his head back onto the pillow. "We're… going to be…." He bites his lip when Jerath disappears under the blankets and takes Meren in his mouth to finish him off. "Late… *fuck*."

Jerath sucks hard and uses his tongue until Meren's cursing above him, with his hands fisted tight in Jerath's hair. Meren comes with a soft moan and Jerath swallows it all down before wiping at his mouth with the back of his hand.

He knows they're going to be late now, so it really makes no difference if he sits up and straddles Meren's hips. He watches as Meren's long fingers stroke him to completion, and they collapse together in a tangled, sticky mess.

By the time they're washed and dressed, their guests have arrived and everyone is waiting for them. Tonight, the elders of Meren's village are going to bless their union and Jerath will finally bear Meren's mark. He can't wait.

"LET me see it, then." Jerath gestures for Ghaneth to lift his shirt and laughs when he makes a face. "You can blame your mate." Jerath looks over at Serim, who just shrugs. "She's been going on about it nonstop since you got here."

Serim and Ghaneth have made the journey south to Chastil along with Helan, Kinis, and Mahli. They're all here to witness Jerath and Meren's blessing, but Serim and Ghaneth have brought good news of their own, and Jerath is so happy for them he can't keep the smile off his face.

Ghaneth slowly peels his shirt off and turns around to show Jerath his back. It takes Jerath a few moments to say anything, because the tattoo is breathtaking.

"See, I told you." Serim positively glows with pride and she walks over to Ghaneth and trails her fingers over the sleek, black panther that covers his skin.

Jerath smiles at the two of them, and his hand automatically goes to rub over his heart through his shirt. He can feel the warmth of the bond humming just underneath his skin and wonders how Meren's getting on over at Torek's house.

Traditionally, a mated pair only live together after the blessing takes place, but Jerath has been staying with Meren from the moment he arrived back. They've only separated now because Malek insisted that at least some traditions should be kept. Torek is helping Meren to prepare, while Jerath has Serim and, by default, Ghaneth too.

"Okay!" Serim claps, making both Jerath and Ghaneth jump in surprise. "We need to get a move on. You don't want to keep Meren waiting." She pinches Jerath's side and he sticks his tongue out at her, but can't resist pulling her in for a hug. He's missed her so much.

He's missed the others too, but he and Serim have an even deeper bond after going through his Choosing and he feels her absence the most. "Missed you," he whispers into her hair.

"I missed you too, Jerath." She squeezes him tight, then steps back. "Now get dressed, before we're late."

THE blessing ritual takes place in a large, circular clearing in the center of the village. There's a huge fire burning brightly over to the right and at least four large roasts being cooked over it for the feast later.

Serim and Ghaneth left Jerath a little while ago and now Jerath walks into the clearing alone, dressed in the traditional white flowing breeches and with his chest bare. His tattoo is on full display and he hears some of the gasps behind him as he walks past the villagers present for the ritual. He feels the magic pulse through his veins and he knows the jaguar on his back will look vibrant and alive.

He sees Meren waiting for him, and everything else fades into background noise. Meren stands in front of one of the elder healers and watches Jerath walk toward him. His gaze rakes over Jerath's body, and Jerath can almost taste the want and hunger coming off him.

The healer directs them both to kneel and face each other and she comes to stand beside them.

She makes a small cut on each of their chests, just above their hearts.

"Let these two be joined in the eyes of the Goddess." She instructs them to reach out and run a finger through the other's blood and then taste it. "Let their bloods mix together and form the mark of their union." She raises her hands to the sky and closes her eyes.

Jerath and Meren stare at each other. Jerath's body begins to tingle as the magic curls around them and slides beneath his skin. Meren couldn't tell him where or what the mark would be, because he said he didn't know. Meren has yet to discover his animal connection.

Jerath sucks in a breath as the cut above his heart starts to heal. The skin on either side of it starts to knit back together, and Jerath winces as it pulls slightly. He glances over at Meren and sees his is healing as well. He's about to ask if that's supposed to happen, when the area around Meren's cut begins to shimmer.

Jerath watches, transfixed, as a tiny, perfect replica of his own jaguar tattoo slowly appears on Meren's skin. Jerath leans forward to get a closer look. It's identical, the pattern of the coat, the eyes… everything. Jerath wants to touch it, but he's not sure if he's allowed yet. Seeing his own tattoo on Meren, marking him as Jerath's, makes something raw and primal unfurl deep in his belly.

Jerath looks up and tries to catch Meren's eye, but his gaze is focused on Jerath's chest. When Meren eventually looks up, his eyes are dark, almost black. Jerath knows that look far too well.

"Jerath… look." Meren slides his hand down Jerath's chest until his fingertips trace over where the cut used to be. "We match." Meren's voice is full of reverence and wonder as he looks at his own mark, now etched into Jerath's chest.

Jerath immediately looks down and gently pushes Meren's fingers away so he can see for himself. The cut has disappeared completely, and in its place is the sleek, familiar form of a jaguar. It's not like the tattoo on Jerath's back, though. This jaguar is crouched down low, its muscles coiled tight and ready to spring into action at any second. As if it's hunting. The bright-green eyes seem to glow in the candlelight, and Jerath can't tear his eyes away from it.

The healer is talking to the rest of the gathered villagers. Jerath vaguely registers that she's telling them all that the Goddess has blessed the union, and the marks have been made. A huge cheer echoes around the clearing and then their family and friends all come forward to offer their congratulations. But Jerath can't really focus. He nods and smiles, but his mind is still reeling at the discovery of Meren's animal connection.

It's a jaguar, like Jerath's. They match.

Meren is laughing with his father and Torek, and Jerath watches, his fingers still running back and forth over his new tattoo. He doesn't notice the healer come up to stand beside him until she puts a hand on his shoulder and leans in to whisper in his ear.

"Why do you think the bond took so quickly and is so strong between the two of you, hmm?"

"Because we're a match?" Jerath asks as he turns to face her.

She smiles up at him and rests her hand on his arm. "Yes. A hunter of the old forest and a shifter—a perfect match." She closes her eyes and smiles. "Yes, the Goddess is very pleased with this union."

Jerath has no idea what to say to that, but the healer is gone before he has a chance to even try.

"Hey." Meren walks over to stand in front of him and slides a hand over the mark on Jerath's chest. "You okay?" He rubs his thumb back and forth over the tattoo and smiles. "I love this. I love seeing my mark on you." Meren steps closer and Jerath feels the warmth radiating off his body. "I love you." He leans a little closer and catches Jerath's lips with a fleeting kiss.

It's enough to stir the desire in Jerath's belly, desire he'd just about managed to push down and out of sight. "Meren…." He growls it out in warning, but Meren just laughs and presses even closer. He's hard and ready and pushing into the curve of Jerath's hip. "We can't leave yet," Jerath says in protest, but his hands are already settled on Meren's waist to hold him in place.

"Why not?" Meren nuzzles at Jerath's neck.

His hot breath makes Jerath shiver and struggle to remember his train of thought. "Because…." Meren licks up the side of Jerath's neck and nips at the soft skin behind his ear. "Guests." It's not what he meant to say, but Meren's tongue is far too distracting and he can't focus on words.

Meren laughs softly against Jerath's skin. "They expect us to leave. The magic for the blessing is very potent, Jerath." Meren pulls back, looking him in the eye, and Jerath swallows thickly. "It means that we need to celebrate our union, just like you do for your Choosing."

"So we have to…."

"Yes." Meren rolls his hips so Jerath is left in no doubt. "I have to fuck you this time."

"Finally." Jerath drops his head onto Meren's shoulder and moans. It comes from deep in his chest and sounds more like a rumbling growl, but he doesn't care who hears him. "Let's go now." Jerath has been waiting for this moment. Meren persuaded him that they should hold off until after the ceremony and now he knows why.

Meren lifts Jerath's chin and kisses him softly on the lips. He rests his forehead against Jerath's for a moment or two before stepping away. "Wait here."

Jerath watches his every move as he marches over to Torek, leaning in and whispering something in his ear. Jerath fights the urge to blush when Torek looks over at him and winks. He claps Meren on the shoulder, and then Meren is hurrying back over to Jerath with a triumphant look on his face.

"Torek will explain our absence." He doesn't stop to say more, just grabs Jerath by the hand and pulls him away from the clearing and in the direction of their home.

Meren's walking so quickly Jerath stumbles a little in his efforts to keep up. "Slow down, Meren." Jerath tugs on his hand.

Meren turns and pushes Jerath against the side of the nearest building. Nearly everyone is still celebrating at the feast, and this part of the village is deserted. "I need to get you home, Jerath." He punctuates his words with gentle thrusts of his hips, and Jerath feels all of Meren's need as he presses against his stomach.

Jerath smiles and pushes back. He kisses Meren hard and fast before shoving off the wall and taking Meren with him. "Come on, then."

They half run, half stumble the rest of the way, stopping every few moments to kiss and rut against each other. Finally they reach their house and they fall through the doors and into the bedroom.

Jerath stops in the center of the room and slowly pushes his breeches down over his hips. They fall to the floor with a whisper. Meren stares and licks his lips, and Jerath's cock twitches as Meren's gaze lingers over him. "Your turn."

Meren smirks and obediently shrugs out of his own breeches. He steps out of them as they pool at his feet and leads Jerath over to the bed. Jerath wants this, wants it more than anything, but they haven't done this before and he feels a touch of nervousness start to creep in.

Meren turns to face Jerath and takes hold of his hands. "Don't worry." He pulls Jerath closer and whispers in his ear. "Trust me to take care of you."

Jerath nods and closes his eyes for just a moment. He takes a long, deep breath to steady himself, climbs onto the bed, and then scoots back until his head rests on the pillows. "Come here."

Meren follows him. He settles in between Jerath's open legs, and Jerath cups Meren's face and draws him in for a kiss. It's wet and filthy, and Jerath wraps his legs around Meren's waist as he sucks on his tongue. They kiss until they're both gasping for air. Then Meren trails a path of licks and nips down Jerath's throat to his chest.

Jerath closes his eyes and shivers as Meren licks over his new tattoo. His mouth is hot against Jerath's tender skin, and each swipe of Meren's tongue has him arching and moaning as the pleasure curls and contracts at the base of his spine.

Meren comes back up and claims Jerath's lips, rubbing his hardness against the length of Jerath's cock. They're both sticky and wet with precome and they move together in a delicious slide of warm, soft skin.

"I can't wait," Meren whispers against Jerath's lips, already reaching over to the table beside the bed.

Jerath spreads his legs farther apart in silent invitation. He bites his bottom lip as he watches Meren spread the oil over his fingers and his cock. They haven't had full sex since before Meren was injured, and the anticipation is almost too much. Nervous excitement floods Jerath's body and he tenses when Meren's fingers slide over his entrance.

"Breathe," Meren whispers.

Jerath takes a deep, shuddering breath and wills himself to relax. He looks up at Meren and smiles softly. "I'm okay."

Meren leans in and kisses him, licking along Jerath's bottom lip as he gradually works his fingers inside. He takes his time, keeping Jerath occupied with his mouth as he slowly stretches him open.

"Ready?" Meren stills his fingers. Just his thumb moves as he traces it around the edge of Jerath's entrance.

"Yeah."

Meren slowly withdraws his hand and asks Jerath to turn onto his belly with a gentle tug on his hips. Jerath knows why as soon as he feels Meren's hands on his back. Smooth fingertips trace over his jaguar tattoo, and Jerath hisses at the slight sting when Meren starts to push his cock inside him.

Jerath growls, deep and feral, as Meren keeps pressing forward until he's all the way in. Jerath breathes heavily, his fangs extend, and he can feel his claws digging into the furs beneath him. Meren's hands soothe up and down his spine and urge him to relax.

Jerath senses Meren's concern and worry through the bond, feels it in the soft touches of his hands. He knows Meren's trying to be gentle with him and he loves him for it, but it's not what Jerath needs. The magic from the blessing is hot under his skin, igniting his animal instincts and all the raw, primal desire that comes along with them.

He needs Meren to claim him, take him as his mate, and he doesn't want him to hold anything back. He tries to convey his feelings through the bond, pushes back against Meren and growls out a warning for him to hurry up and just *move*.

Meren must pick up on what Jerath needs because one of his hands immediately clasps Jerath's hip while the other grips his shoulder, and Meren slides nearly all the way out before slamming back in. Hard. Jerath roars and braces himself on his elbows as Meren fucks into him, holding him tight and gasping his name over and over.

The air crackles, the magic of the bond and the blessing merging and wrapping around them. It seeps into Jerath's skin, setting his nerves on fire, and he knows Meren feels it too.

Jerath's claws sink deep into the furs as his body tightens with pleasure. It draws up all the way from his toes, licking up his spine and out to the tips of his fingers. He throws his head back and cries out his release as it crashes over him.

"Oh *fuck*…." Meren's pace falters and he digs his fingers into Jerath's skin, clinging to him as he tenses and comes deep inside him.

The room is quiet except for their ragged breathing. Jerath aches all over, wants to collapse under Meren's weight, but he feels so alive with magic that he laughs.

Meren grunts and slowly pulls out before he collapses beside him. "Something funny?" he asks, and when Jerath looks over at him, he has his eyes closed, but there's a smile on his face.

"No." But Jerath can't stop the grin that takes over. "It's just…." He arranges himself so he's facing Meren and avoiding the mess he just made of their bed. "I'm so tired, I feel like I could sleep for days, but at the same time I've never felt so alive and connected to everything. It's a very strange feeling."

Meren opens his eyes and grins too. "I know." He reaches out and lays a hand on Jerath's waist, tugs him closer, and places a soft, chaste kiss on his lips.

Jerath basks in the love and warmth surrounding them, and his eyes flutter closed.

"Do you think it will always be like this?" Meren asks quietly.

Jerath opens his eyes, but Meren's are closed again, so he takes a moment to really look at his mate in the faint light of their room. Meren's bright, blond, sex-mussed hair stands out against the dark furs. His skin is flushed, lips bruised, and in Jerath's eyes he's never looked more beautiful.

Meren sighs, shuffling around until his head rests in the crook of Jerath's neck. It's so easy between them, and Jerath's chest aches as he thinks again how lucky he is to have him.

"Yes," he finally whispers, not sure if Meren is still awake. "I think it will always be like this."

ANNABELLE JACOBS lives in the South West of England with her husband, three rowdy children, and two cats.

An avid reader of fantasy herself for many years, Annabelle now spends her days writing her own stories. They're usually either fantasy or paranormal fiction, because she loves building worlds filled with magical creatures, and creating stories full of action and adventure. Her characters may have a tough time of it—fighting enemies and adversity—but they always find love in the end.

You can contact Annabelle via Twitter:
https://twitter.com/AJacobs_fiction, her website:
http://www.annabellejacobs.com, or e-mail:
ajacobsfiction@gmail.com.

Also from DREAMSPINNER PRESS

CPSIA information can be obtained at www.ICGtesting.com
Printed in the USA
LVOW10s1328211013

357846LV00004B/107/P

9 781627 981903